Dance Am

DANCE AMONGST THORNS

MAUREEN STEPHENSON

2Sp 14/9

COSMAX COMPANY WARWICKSHIRE

Dance Amongst Thorns

© Maureen Stephenson 1996
first published in Great Britain 1996

ISBN 0 9527051 0 9

Cosmax Company
Ansley Mill
Ansley
Warwickshire CV10 0QT

Typeset, printed and bound by
ABC Commercial Services Limited,
Eversholt, Bedfordshire,England.

Chapter 1

Crossing the Liffey by the O'Connell Bridge, Liane proceeded up O'Connell Street, Dublin's main thoroughfare, a cold easterly wind bringing colour to her cheeks.

She had been waiting three months for the phone call, but at last it had come, not from an English film company as she had expected, but from the Priory Theatre, Dublin, who had set up a film production unit to make a series for television. Liane had been engaged to be in charge of continuity, a job she had been doing on a free lance basis for the past eight years. The relief was enormous to be back in the old job.

It was also a relief to get away from London and Conal, thought Liane as she approached the end of O'Connell Street. When she had discovered Conal was a cheat and a liar, the pain he had caused had been deep.

She had of course given him his ring back, and he had had the effrontery to tell her she was intolerant. He always had that way of making her feel it was her fault, whatever the circumstances.

As she approached the Priory Theatre Liane wondered if she would be able to get a few days off at the end of the first production to try to find Tavanomore, the farm in County Monaghan her father had so tragically lost. He had only ever told her the briefest details. His mother had died soon after he was born. He had been the only child, and instead of his father leaving him the farm, he had left it to a friend. It had left an empty ache in his heart. Two years ago he had died, a bitter, unhappy man.

The Priory was a small eighteenth century theatre a turning near O'Connell Street, maintained by the largesse of an Irish American millionaire. Liane entered the small marble foyer, which led into a crimson carpeted corridor, then through swing doors she found herself in the small gold gilt and crimson auditorium.

An elderly smiling grey haired man approached.

"Liane O'Neill? I'm Ian Stratton your director. Sorry there was no one to meet you. Found your hotel all right?"

Liane nodded smilingly.

Ian handed her a copy of the script. "Shooting starts in the morning at 8.30am." he continued. "Most of this production will be shot on location. Tomorrow we'll be at Greystones. You'll be picked up at 7.45am sharp. We've got a tight schedule," he warned.

Liane spent the next three weeks working with a happy unit. Ian Stratton turned out to be a fair minded man with a calm temperament which reflected on the crew. And even though she spent every evening until bedtime typing out the shots, she was a comparatively contented woman.

At the end of the day when she finally climbed into bed she was too tired to think of the faithless man she had loved, and during the day too busy checking the shots. Work, Liane decided, was the best antidote for an unhappy love affair.

At the end of the last day of shooting Ian Stratton came across to her.

"Hold take four in that last shot Liane. Print take five."

Liane wrote the instructions in her notebook.

"Well, that's our first one in the can," Ian continued, a look of satisfaction on his face. "Next production starts in two weeks. We have finally decided on the location. We thought we'd give our audiences a change from Dublin and its environs. We're going to Luxor in Upper Egypt."

Liane looked pleasantly surprised.

"Do you know it?"

"No, I've never been there, but my father's great friend, Father O'Brien is the priest there. They corresponded through the years; Dad even paid him a couple of visits."

"When the shooting's finished, you'll have to visit him. Now you'd better get your jabs," continued Ian in his practical manner. "You'll need some. And don't forget your anti-malarial tablets. I don't want the crew going sick on me.

Liane spent the following week script typing, and helping out generally in the office. On the Saturday she had the day off and after much deliberation, decided her top priority was to hire a car and set off for Carrickballyduff in County Monaghan in search of her grandfather's farm. She felt she owed it to her father, to at least visit the place, even though loyalty to a long lost farm was entirely a waste of time.

There was a light rain falling as Liane left the northern suburbs of Dublin and took the N.2. She was doing what her father would have wanted her to do.

A misty memory surfaced in her mind of a childhood visit to the farm. All she could remember was a curving, elegant staircase leading out of the entrance hall.

Two hours later she entered the quiet sleepy town of Carrickballyduff, the main street wide enough for stalls on market day. Her mother's memories too were vague regarding the whereabouts of the farm, and she had advised her to contact the local priest. He would know everything there was to know about everyone and anything in the locality.

She found the priest's house next to the church with little difficulty and knocked on the door. The housekeeper showed her into Father O'Shea's study. A few moments later the priest entered the room. He was very old, at least mid seventies, walking slowly with the help of a walking stick.

"The bishop says I must retire and let a younger man take over the duties of the parish, but I'm not ready for that yet. Now young lady, what can I do to help you?"

Liane introduced herself.

The old priest sat down, and motioned Liane to sit also. There was a puzzled look in his faded blue eyes.

"Would I be talking to the daughter of Patrick O'Neill who used to live at Tavanomore?"

Liane smiled. "You certainly are."

"Well, what a pleasure meeting you to be sure. I remember your father well. He was a choir boy here in this very church, and a good

7

one. How is he? I haven't seen him for a very long time."

"I'm afraid he died two years ago."

Father O'Shea made the sign of the cross and bowed his head.

"May his soul rest in peace, amen."

At that moment Father O'Shea's housekeeper entered the room with cups of tea and slices of griddle bread.

"I take it you'll be wanting to have a look at the old place?" Father asked as he offered Liane a slice of the griddle bread.

"I'd like that very much."

"Take the road to Cavan, and just about a mile out of the town you'll see it on the right hand side. As a matter of fact the late owner, Joseph McMahon died a few months ago and his son Brett is over from the States having a look over his inheritance. You might see him. I'm afraid he has no interest whatsoever in farming. Broke his father's heart it did when he went off to America. Now Liane, are you on holiday?"

"No Father. I'm working at the Priory Theatre in Dublin. They have set up a films division."

Father looked thoughtful for a moment.

"I hear Brett McMahon is a playwright and I do believe last year the Priory Theatre produced one of his plays. I was told it was very good. I'm too busy looking after my parishioners to go off gallivanting to Dublin theatres" he added with a smile. "How long will you be working in Dublin?"

"A few weeks," Liane replied. "Then we're off to Luxor in Upper Egypt to shoot the exteriors for the next production. It's a comedy..."

Father O'Shea wasn't listening, there was a faraway look in his eyes.

"When your father lived here, his best friend was James O'Brien. And for many years James has been the priest in charge at Luxor. He would be most upset if the daughter of his best friend did not visit him."

"Actually I have been thinking of calling on him. Have you got his address. I could phone my mother for it."

The old priest rose to his feet and walking slowly across to his desk took out a sheet of paper and wrote it down.

8

Dance Amongst Thorns

"Here you are Liane. Church of Our Lady of Sorrows. I'm sure anyone in Luxor would direct you to it. Father O'Brien is well known for his work for the poor."

After saying goodbye to Father and thanking him for his hospitality, Liane set off as directed and soon found the farmhouse. It was situated down a short tree lined drive.

She got out of the car and leaned against the five barred gate, staring at the old house. She was afraid she might have been disappointed, but there was no question of it as she gazed at the symmetry of eighteenth century architecture, with the long, oblong windows spaced evenly on each side of the impressive front door, and dormer windows in the roof. In a field to the left of the house, a flock of sheep were grazing.

It was a strange, sad feeling leaning over that gate staring at the house, the memories it evoked, the stories her father used to tell her of ceilidhs held in the large kitchen on Saturday nights.

All the young people would come, she remembered him telling her. And the not so young, dancing Irish jigs to the tunes of the local fiddler till the small hours. Then the following morning they would be up early feeding the animals before making their way to Mass.

Liane turned to look at the farmyard to the left of the house. A white Mercedes was parked between the stable block and the barn. Brett McMahon no doubt checking up on his inheritance. If Dad hadn't been cheated mused Liane sadly, this farm would have been her home, and as she was the only child, she would have inherited it. It made her angry thinking about it.

In the fields to the right of the house she watched a tractor spring ploughing, and she thought of the hard times they had had when she was young; Dad struggling to make a living, trying one thing and then another. Dad wanted to have his own business, but lack of capital had always frustrated him.

By chance he had entered the film industry in London starting off as an assistant in the buying department, and ending up a set dresser. That was why she had entered the film industry. Dad always taking her to the studios when she was a small child, and getting permission to take her on the set.

She turned and looked back at the house remembering Dad had lived there until he was twenty. This was where he had been happy, where he had wanted to end his days. Tears rose to her eyes.

A man came out of one of the barns. He was tall, broad shoulders with black curly hair, wearing a pale grey anorak. Hastily Liane brushed away her tears.

"Hi! Can I help?" he called. The accent was distinctly East Coast American. Then he started walking quickly across the farmyard and down the short drive.

"No thanks." Liane called back.

The man was now at the gate gazing at her in a coolly, appraising manner. His eyes were deep blue, fringed by long black lashes, his mouth was very firm, his jaw strong. He projected a strong masculine image.

"I've just put the farm on the market." His tone was authoritative. "Interested?"

Buying the property that was rightfully hers. Liane shook her head and gazed at him coldly.

"Then why were you looking at the house a moment ago with such rapt attention?" His look now turned to one of curiosity.

Liane gave him a mocking smile. "That's my business."

Brett McMahon pursed his mouth, giving her a sizing up look. "On holiday?" he continued.

"I'm working here."

"In Carrickballyduff?" He looked puzzled.

"No, Dublin."

"You're English," he commented slowly, "With the slightest trace of an Irish accent."

"That must be because my father was Irish."

"Was he from County Monaghan?"

Liane looked firmly at the farmhouse. "He certainly was. Look, Mr McMahon..."

He smiled and raised his eyebrows. "So you know my name."

"Word has got around you are in the vicinity."

He gave her an amused smile. "Been to see Father O'Shea?"

Liane looked away. The least she said to this man the better.

"I'd rather you called me Brett. He gave her a smug look. "You intrigue me. You are obviously interested in Tavanomore even though you deny it. I saw your car parked outside Father O'Shea's house a couple of hours ago and you are still lingering in the area."

He gave her a hard inquisitive look.

"My name is O'Neill," Liane replied looking past him at the stableyard.

There was silence for a moment, then Brett said. "I see."

"You don't see at all," she replied in an icy voice. "You haven't the faintest idea..."

Brett placed his hand on her arm.

"Bury the hatchet."

Liane shook his hand angrily from her arm. "Today for the first time since I was a small child I saw my father's old home. Of course I can't expect you to be interested in my father or the hard life he had in England. My grandfather and father did have their differences, most families do, but to influence a man to cut his only son out of his will..."

"If you have a complaint," cut in Brett, his blue eyes cold as steel. "Why don't you go to a lawyer?"

"I may very well do that" Liane replied heatedly.

She always felt upset whenever she talked or thought about the injustice her father had suffered at the hands of the McMahons. As for going to a lawyer her father had done that and run out of money.

Liane turned away and moved towards her car.

"By the way," Brett called from the gate. "For some unknown reason I seem to be implicated in this matter. When it all happened I was at Harvard. I had nothing to do with it whatsoever. When I got my degree I decided to stay on. I've lived there ever since. One day you will forgive me."

"Forgive you for what?"

"For being a McMahon. May I ask what you do in Dublin?"

"I work at the Priory Theatre," she said in an cold voice.

"Ian Stratton is a friend of mine."

Liane looked up feigning surprise.

"What do you do at the Priory? Act?"

"No. I'm a technician with the films division."

"We may meet again. Ian says he has some work lined up for me. Pity, because you and I can never be friends. Goodbye."

And with that Brett McMahon turned and started walking back to the house, and as he did so it started to rain, a heavy downpour sweeping the drive. Liane quickly got into her car and drove off.

She was in a curious state of mind. There was something about Brett McMahon that had touched a chord. She disliked him, yet at the same time, felt a curious sense of deep sadness as if he made her conscious of the empty life she led.

CHAPTER 2

It was a dull, heavily overcast day when Liane and the rest of the unit and cast took off from London Airport.

Some five hours later they were flying in brilliant sunshine over the winding blue ribbon of the Nile, with green irrigated fields spread out on each side. Beyond lay the desert. Liane was filled with a sense of excited anticipation.

The only cloud on the horizon was Brett McMahon. Ian had told her he would be joining the unit at the end of the week, to write some extra scenes. What had happened to the script writer who had written the rest of the film?

They landed at Luxor in brilliant sunshine. It was hot, with the temperature in the nineties. The handsome customs officer who told her with an appreciative expression in his dark eyes that he liked her honey blonde hair was Liane's first encounter with Egyptian men.

Her second was with the owner of the perfume shop at the hotel. After she had purchased an elegant, gold gilt bottle containing lotus blossom perfume, he proposed marriage. Fay the unit hairdresser who was also blonde had the same problem.

The unit was given the evening to settle in, then shooting started the following morning. They had scenes to shoot in the souk, on a felucca, and in the Temples of Luxor and Karnak.

Checking the continuity of the film was an exacting job. It was Liane's responsibility to see that the dialogue was correct, and also the action, particularly entrances and exits, and where the director wanted to insert a closeup. She had to note every time the camera moved, time the shot, check the costumes were correct, also note the correct props were used in the shot.

At the end of the day, particularly on location when often it was not possible to type in the open, Liane spent her evenings in her hotel room typing the verbatim report on each shot, the daily progress report, the call sheet for the following morning.

This usually took up the entire evening, and when she had finished, it was too late, and she was too tired anyway, to do anything else but lie in a warm bath, and then fall into an exhausted sleep.

Her friends in London asked her why she did it. She would go on location to the most romantic places, work a fourteen hour day, and all she ever saw of the place, apart from the shooting locales, was the inside of her hotel bedroom.

It was hard to explain, all Liane could tell them was, first it gave her enormous satisfaction to help make a film, and secondly the money she earned gave her a feeling of security which she otherwise did not have.

It was on the Saturday afternoon when they were shooting in the Temple of Karnak that Liane suddenly remembered with a sinking heart Brett McMahon was due to arrive.

It had been a good week, not a single holdup. No one had been taken ill, there had been no temper tantrums from a certain nameless actress, and of course every day the weather had been perfect, the sun shining from a cloudless blue sky, no waiting for rain to stop which was common on an English or Irish location.

Now Brett McMahon's presence was going to spoil this otherwise enjoyable location. Liane couldn't really see why Ian wanted Brett McMahon to write extra scenes. Still he was the director. He made the decisions.

The light was starting to fade, making the colours of the temple deeper and richer. The cameras were set up in the Great Court. The electricians switched on the lights as Ian rehearsed the scene. This was the high point of the drama, when the private detective finally announces who has committed the murder.

The rehearsal finished and the make up man moved onto the set to touch up shiny noses and anything else he felt was amiss. Liane looked up from her script. Brett McMahon was standing on the other side of the second camera.

Liane felt her heart miss a beat. He looked what he was, a successful playwright, in his well cut tropical suit of palest beige, the gold watch flashing on his wrist. Hadn't he got enough thought Liane as she thought how little she had of the good things life had to offer.

Then he turned and looked at her and she felt a sudden inner tension that manifested itself in stomach butterflies. He walked round the camera and joined her.

There was no friendly greeting, no smile, no acknowledgment that they even knew each other. He could have been a stranger.

"I understand from Ian that tomorrow being Friday and the Muslim Sabbath and consequently the difficulty in getting the locals to work, he's decided to cut his losses and let the unit have the day off." His voice was sharp, and suddenly there were lines of tension in his face.

"Good opportunity to get the new scenes done," he continued in the same tone. "Come to my room in the morning at 10.30am. We should be finished by the middle of the afternoon."

Then without waiting for a reply he walked away.

"Going for a take?" called Charlie, the production assistant.

The shooting began. It was crucial the shot was in the can within the next fifteen minutes due to the fading light. The atmosphere was tense. Three takes and Ian was satisfied.

"Wrap up!" called Charlie. "That's it until Saturday."

Liane made a final note then closed her script. She felt annoyed. Brett McMahon hadn't even asked if she would mind working when the rest of the unit had the day off.

Then she turned to see Brett standing a few yards away. He was staring at her; a look she failed to interpret. Pity he was such an attractive male, she thought with a certain amount of irony.

Not in the photogenic way, it was more a strong sense of masculinity that he projected. His best point was his eyes, she decided, such an intense blue. Then she shrugged her shoulders. That's the way life goes, she thought sadly. It's never perfect. It's never the way you want it.

"Oh Mr McMahon. You didn't give me your room number."

"217." he replied, then he turned and walked away.

"I'll be there" Liane called after him in an expressionless, uninterested voice. She couldn't very well not be there. The production secretary had not come on the location, and she was the only person available.

And as Brett walked away Liane wondered at the look of self-satisfaction on his face. Why did he look pleased and smug with himself?

Liane, to say the least, was dreading the following day. How she wished fate had been kind to her, that when she had gone to Carrickballyduff, she had never met Brett McMahon. If only she had not succumbed to her curiosity, to see her father's birthplace, right now she would be scheduled to work the following day with a new scriptwriter. He would have dictated the shots, said goodbye and that would have been the end of that. She had worked with scriptwriters before and no one ever discussed their private lives, at least not in detail. She would never have known who he was.

In the minibus back to the hotel Fay the hairdresser sat next to Liane.

"Cheer up Liane. What you need is a break. You've been working much too hard. Well, we have the whole of tomorrow off to do exactly as we please. I've had an idea. In the morning, I suggest a swim in the hotel pool..."

"There's a very good reason why I'm not happy," Liane gave a big sigh. "I have to work tomorrow with the new script writer."

"So that's the dishy guy you were talking to. Some people get all the luck."

Liane pulled a face.

"It's going to be one of the worse days of my life."

Fay looked at her sharply. "I don't understand..."

"I know you don't."

"I take it you knew him before this location?"

"I certainly did," Liane replied with a certain amount of feeling.

"Like that is it!"

Fay smiled a teasing smile at Liane.

"Fay. It's not like that at all. There is, and never was, nor ever will be, any romance whatsoever in our relationship."

"Sounds very dull to me."

Next morning after breakfast Liane watched some of the unit strolling through the garden to the swimming pool for a morning swim, towels on their arms. Others with their sunglasses, their sun protection cream, were ready for a lazy day sun bathing. The more energetic were making their way down the drive to do a spot of temple gazing with cameras and binoculars.

Liane took the lift up to the second floor and knocked on room number 217. It was opened by Brett. He was in his shirt sleeves, unsmiling, an anxious expression on his face.

"Come in." he said curtly.

Liane entered Brett's room relieved to see Ian Stratton seated in a lounging chair on the balcony.

"Good morning Liane," he called. "Sorry you have to sacrifice your day off, but we have a dead line to meet. Brett has to leave for Cairo in the morning."

Liane placed her typewriter on the dressing table and plugged in.

"Can you take dictation straight onto the typewriter?" asked Brett looking through his handwritten notes.

"Certainly." Liane replied. What did he think she was? A complete novice?

She'd been working with scriptwriters for years.

"How many copies?" she asked, directing her question at Ian.

"Can you make it five."

Liane threaded four sheets of carbon paper between five sheets of paper, rolled them into the machine and the work began. Of course it would have been easier with a word processor, but that sort of luxury was unfortunately not available. Brett read from his notes, and as he did so he paced the room. Backwards and forwards he went, never still for a moment.

Liane couldn't help getting the impression Brett had a great deal of nervous energy to dissipate. It was like working with a caged tiger. Sometimes Ian would stop him to raise a query, the disagreement would be settled, and the dictation continued.

So the day progressed. At one o'clock a waiter brought in sandwiches and coffee, and whilst they paused to eat, Ian and Brett discussed the scenes. Rarely did Brett look in her direction, and when he did, his glance was totally impersonal. It was as if they had never met.

It was just after lunch when the phone rang. Brett answered it.

"You want to speak to Liane O'Neill. Yes, she's here."

He handed the phone to her, his eyes cold as steel. Liane took the phone anxiously. Who could be ringing her in Egypt? Perhaps her mother had been taken ill.

"Hello. Liane O'Neill speaking."

"Hello Liane," a male voice purred down the phone. "Guess who this is?"

It was Conal. The man she never wanted to see again. The man who had double crossed her, and she had been too naive to see it, until he had actually had to tell her there was someone else and all future wedding plans were off.

"What do you want?" she asked brusquely, her voice sharp.

"What do I want honey? I want you," came the smooth reply. "That's why I'm phoning all these thousands of miles just to hear your voice. I miss you. I'm lonely."

"That's unusual coming from you, but I'm sure you can rectify the situation."

"When you get back to London, let's meet. Phone me as soon as you arrive. We'll have dinner at the Ritz. I want to talk to you."

"I'm sorry," Liane replied in a stiff voice. "You seem to have misunderstood. It won't be possible for us to meet. I'm fully committed."

And with that she rang off, and returned to the typewriter, seething at the sheer arrogance of Conal McSharry and conscious of Brett's curious eyes upon her.

"Sorry for that interruption."

"Got a problem?" Brett asked.

Liane shook her head, "Not at all."

The work continued.

At three o'clock the work was completed. Liane took the last page out of the typewriter and sorted the work into five piles.

"Keep a copy for yourself." Brett told her as she handed the work to him.

Ian left the room. He had phone calls to make to Dublin. Brett turned to Liane as she placed the lid on her typewriter.

"You've done a good job Liane," he complimented her as he

flicked through the pages. Liane looked at him in suspicious astonishment.

"Like to have dinner with me tonight?" he asked suddenly.

Liane's astonishment increased.

"For the last four and a half hours you have ignored me. I received the impression I was nothing more than a nameless typist. Why the sudden interest?"

"You're being too hard on me. I just wanted to make up for you sacrificing your day off. Nothing more." His tone was light and easy. "What about the Winter Palace Hotel. We could dine there if you like. Quite an interesting place. Used to be one of the palaces owned by King Farouk."

"I'm sorry I can't come."

Brett looked surprised, then puzzled.

"The phone call you received this afternoon; you told the guy you are fully committed. Who is he? Someone on the unit?"

"There is no one on the unit. It was a white lie to let someone down gently. I'm built that way."

Brett gave her a relaxed smile. "In that case, there is nothing to stop you. I'll phone to book a table."

Liane shook her head. "I still can't go."

Brett now looked annoyed. "Stop this ridiculous nonsense. We probably won't meet again. And I want to have a long talk with you."

"Can't we talk now?" asked Liane, her voice cold but firm.

"Meaning you'll talk to a McMahon, but you won't eat with one."

"Take it any way you want." Liane turned away. She had had enough. Brett hadn't travelled out with the unit because he had had business matters to attend to in Ireland, so Ian had said. She knew exactly what that business was.

"For goodness sake, what's the matter with you?" Brett raised his voice. He was now exceedingly annoyed.

"Sold the farm? Or are you finding it difficult?" she asked, unashamedly sarcastic.

"I'm not finding it difficult at all," he said smoothly, his face unmoved, his eyes fixed on her.

Lying comes easy to a McMahon she thought as she picked up her

19

typewriter, her copy of the new scenes and left.

Liane went down to the pool and swam for an hour until her calm had returned. Half way through her swim, she saw Brett hurrying down the hotel drive, and hailing a taxi at the entrance.

For the rest of the day Liane felt strangely restless.

The next day shooting continued. In the lunchbreak Fay took Liane to one side.

"Was yesterday one of the worse days of your life?" she asked handing her a cup of coffee.

"It certainly was."

"What's it all about Liane?"

"My grandfather's will."

"I don't understand."

"Then I'll tell you all about it."

Liane told her the whole story, and when she had finished, Fay thought she was mad.

"Brett McMahon asked you out to dinner at the Winter Palace and you refused? He's got a play on Broadway. He writes for the Priory Theatre. And he's sexy into the bargain. Forget family problems. Life's got to go on."

Yes thought Liane, life has to go on. But I've got my principles, my standards, and they do not include fraternising with the son of the man who swindled my father.

At the end of the following week shooting the location scenes was completed. On the morning of departure the unit were busy packing, and bringing their luggage down to the hotel foyer ready for transportation to the airport in the late afternoon.

There was an air of excitement as people discussed last minute shopping expeditions in the souk, a final stroll along the embankment road to gaze at the Nile. The location had been of short duration but everyone as usual was glad to go home.

Suddenly Liane remembered she had promised to visit Father O'Brien whose church was somewhere in Luxor. She searched her bag and finally found the piece of paper on which was scribbled the address.

Liane found Fay in the hotel perfume shop.

"Hi Liane! I just had to buy some of this lotus blossom perfume. Did you know that Queen Nefertari was buried with loads of it, thousands of years ago."

Liane smiled and nodded. "I bought some the first day. Look Fay, I'm just off to see Father O'Brien. He's a priest in the Zamelak district, and an old friend of Dad's. I promised I'd go. I'll be back in an hour if anyone asks for me."

"Take care." Fay called, as Liane hurried out of the main entrance of the hotel, and down the palm lined drive.

Beyond the gates of the hotel, men in long flowing djellabahs beseiged her. They would be her guide, get her a taxi, sell her a damask table cloth.

She saw a taxi nosing its way through the crowd and stop before the gates of the hotel. The door opened and to Liane's surprise out stepped Brett McMahon.

"Liane!" he exclaimed. He seemed delighted to see her. "Where are you off to?"

"I have to pay a social call," she replied abruptly. "I'll take your taxi."

"Well, make sure you agree the price before you get in. Where do you want to go?"

Liane opened her bag and unfolded the slip of paper.

"Church of Our Lady of Sorrows," she read, "26th July Street, Zemelak."

Brett gave her an anxious look. "That's quite a way from here. I think it best if I come with you."

Liane gave him a suspicious look.

"Solicitous of my safety all of a sudden? Thank you all the same, but it won't be necessary."

As Liane turned to speak to the driver, Brett placed his hand on her arm.

"I'm coming with you," he said firmly. "Good chance to have a talk with you."

Then ignoring her protestations, he negotiated a price with the driver. There was really not much she could do, so Liane got into the taxi and Brett followed her.

21

They set off turning right into the crowded souk, then into streets less crowded, finally onto a wide road bordering the Nile. Here were private houses set in large gardens surrounded by high walls.

"And why may I ask are you going to church?1' asked Brett looking amused. "Got something on your conscience?"

Liane gave him a look of utter disdain.

"Father O'Brien was my father's life long friend." Then she turned to Brett, a puzzled look in her eyes. "I'm surprised to see you again in Luxor."

Brett gave her an enigmatic smile.

"I changed my plans. Liane, I would like you and I to stop fighting. Let's call a truce. What happened ten years ago between our parents has nothing whatsoever to do with us."

Liane took a deep breath. "It has everything to do with us. Your father should have refused the inheritance. He knew my father was still alive and living in London..."

Brett gave a hard laugh. "You don't know what you're talking about! It's obvious you are totally ignorant of the situation that existed between the McMahons and the O'Neills. Did your father never discuss it with you?"

"I don't know what you are talking about!"

"That is obvious."

The taxi had now stopped outside a small domed church.

"The christian church," said the driver turning round to face them. "I can wait?"

"You wait for us," Brett told him as they stepped out of the taxi. "Good idea. We are a bit off the beaten track."

Liane paused, Brett was right, it would be a good idea for the taxi to wait. She envisaged twenty minutes at the most. The priest would be a busy man. Brett negotiated a further price with the taxi driver, then she and Brett entered the church.

They walked in silence down the centre aisle of the building. On the south side near the altar a door led to the sacristy. Here they knocked. It was opened by an altar boy.

"We're looking for Father O'Brien," Liane told him.

The boy pointed down the nave to a corridor which led off about half way down. At the end of the corridor was a door. This led to the domestic abode of Father O'Brien. The housekeeper, an Egyptian woman in European clothes told them Father O'Brien was ill but insisted on taking them to his room.

Father O'Brien, an exhausted looking man in his late fifties, lay propped up on the pillows.

"I'm Liane O'Neill," Liane introduced herself, as she walked to the bed and took the priest's hand in hers. At the sound of her name, the old man's face creased into a gentle smile.

"I've been waiting for you Liane. Father O'Shea told me you were coming. Sorry about this, but I've got a touch of the old malaria. I'll get over it. I always do." Then he looked questioningly at Brett.

Liane introduced him, and they shook hands.

"Please sit down."

They sat down on cane chairs by the bedside and Father O'Brien turned to Liane, studying her face.

"At last we have met. I have heard so much about you through the years."

Liane smiled. "And I have heard a great deal about you Father."

"How is your mother?"

"She is very well, thank you."

"I was very sorry to hear about your parents. Always sad, a failed marriage." He gave Liane a gentle smile. "Well, I cannot believe I have finally met Patrick's daughter. You look like your father, got the same firm mouth, the same blue eyes."

He leaned back on the pillows. "Your father was a grand man, but I could beat him at running." He smiled nostagically, remembering. "Patrick used to say I should have been a professional athlete. But the call of the church was too strong. So I went to Rome and your father went to England, to look for the pot of gold," he added reflectively.

"He never found it," said Liane gently.

"I know. Now Liane, when are you returning to Dublin?"

"This evening," she replied. "And I'm so sorry I left it until the last day to come to see you, but as you probably know we have been busy making a film and every evening..."

23

"Liane, do not apologise. You are here with your young man, and that is all that matters."

Liane averted her gaze from the amused look in Brett's eyes.

"Now I want to give you a present. It is a painting your father always admired. I bought it at an auction in Italy many years ago, so it is my personal property.

There is nothing special about it, and I don't think it is valuable, but it is the one he particularly liked. I had bequeathed it to him in my will, and of course it never entered my head I would outlive him. So Liane, I give it to you, with of course my best wishes and I always remember your father in my prayers."

"Thank you Father. You are very generous."

"I wish I could give you more. Now the painting hangs between the 1st and 2nd Stations of the Cross. It's quite small, so you should not have trouble in putting it in your luggage. The frame unfortunately is in a fragile condition so handle it with care."

He rang a small bell on his bedside table. A moment later the housekeeper appeared.

"I am giving the painting of the Virgin and Child to Miss O'Neill. Will you show her where it is in the church?"

The housekeeper nodded her head in assent. Liane and Brett bid Father O'Brien goodbye, and wishing him a speedy recovery, followed the housekeeper from the room.

In the church she indicated where the painting was hanging. Liane and Brett said goodbye to her then walked across and Brett unhooked the painting from the wall. It was small as father had said, about two feet square, and the frame did look as though it was about to collapse.

He handed the painting to Liane who carefully placed it in her outsize cotton shoulder bag, then fastened the zip.

"I hope I get it home in one piece," she commented anxiously.

Two young Egyptian men in European clothes sitting in a pew on the far side of the nave, were watching her intently. Then as Brett and Liane turned and walked down the aisle towards the church exit, they rose quickly to their feet, and followed them from the church.

24

CHAPTER 3

The taxi was still waiting outside the church. Liane and Brett settled into the back seat.

"Take us back to the hotel," Brett told the driver as they moved off.

The two Egyptian men got into a Fiat parked nearby, moved out of the side street closely following behind the taxi.

"What a kind man," said Liane leaning back in the seat. "To give me the painting father always admired."

She unzipped her bag and partially withdrew it.

"I wonder who the artist is? There's a scrawl in the bottom corner. Can't make it out."

She pushed the painting back into her bag and zipped it up.

"I shall take very great care of it, although it will be difficult on the journey back. My luggage is a nylon zip bag."

"You could put it in my suitcase," suggested Brett, giving her a calculated look. "That is if you can trust me with it."

"I'll think about it," Liane gave him a wry smile. She was so happy she had been to see Father O'Brien. A link with her dear father.

"In other words, you don't."

"I don't want to quarrel, not just now."

Neither of them spoke for the next few minutes.

"As Father O'Brien and Dad were so close," said Liane, her voice quiet and thoughtful. "It is surprising Dad didn't decide to become a priest."

"He met your mother. Is she as beautiful as you?"

"Flattery has no effect on me," said Liane looking straight ahead.

Brett looked at his watch. "I haven't got the time to find out what does have an effect on you. I'm flying back with the unit by the way." Then he gave Liane a mischievous smile. "That is if you have no objection."

Liane gave a weary smile. "You can do exactly as you please. I say, did you notice those two Egyptian men who came out of the church behind us?"

"No, I did not," Brett replied in an uninterested voice.

Liane continued:

"One of them looked just like Omar Shariff. I saw one of his old films just before we left."

There was no reply from Brett.

"Are you coming back to Dublin with us?"

Brett had opened his diary and was fingering through the pages.

"When we get to Heathrow, we have to part company, you will be sorry to hear," he added sarcastically, "I have to fly on to New York."

She couldn't help wishing Brett wouldn't be travelling in the same aircraft even as far as Heathrow. His presence would always arouse unhappy memories, the unfairness of it all.

"I thought you wanted to talk to me," she began.

Brett glanced at the back of the taxi driver's head.

"I prefer to discuss the matter in private," he replied in a low voice. "Perhaps when we get back to the hotel."

At that moment the taxi overtook a horse and carriage. Liane turned her head and looked through the rear window to get a further glance at the leisurely mode of transport, and as she did so, she caught a glimpse of the car behind. It was the Fiat carrying the two Egyptians she had seen leaving the church.

"Omar Shariff is following us," she announced to Brett.

"He's not following me," he was quick to reply. "More likely you. No doubt you have noticed Egyptian men have a penchant for women with fair hair, particularly the Nordic blonde type. So you'd better watch out."

It was some five minutes later that Liane turned her head and again looked through the rear window. It was a mosque that had attracted her attention and she wanted to take another look. The two Egyptian men in the Fiat were still behind. She said nothing. It would only provoke a further comment about blondes and Egyptian men.

A few minutes later the taxi entered the souk, the crowds milling around the vehicle so that gradually the taxi came to a halt. Liane looked round and noticed the Fiat had also come to a halt, a distance about twenty yards behind.

Then it all happened so quickly. The men got out of the Fiat, and to Liane's horror one of them was carrying a gun. They started pushing their way through the crowd in the direction of the taxi.

Liane grabbed Brett's arm, fear chilling her body like a cold shower. She pointed through the rear window.

"The men who were in the Fiat, they're coming towards us. One of them has a gun!"

A pulse was beating in her head. It was like a bad dream.

"I have a horrible feeling they're out to get us. What have we done?"

"There's no time to work that out," said Brett. "Let's get out of here!"

Brett pushed a few notes into the taxi driver's hand, opened the taxi door, Liane picked up her shoulder bag, and they dived into the crowd, pushing their way through as best they could.

"They must be a couple of mad men," shouted Liane.

"Save your breath," called back Brett. "Here take my hand I don't want to lose you."

Brett turned into a short side street where there were fewer people and no stalls. They started running, and as they did so a shot rang out, the bullet skimming over their heads.

"They're trying to kill us," cried Liane.

A second later they were in the broad street running alongside the Nile. Opposite them a cruiseboat was moored at the quayside. The gangway was down and passengers were boarding.

Liane and Brett looked around them desperately, like cornered animals.

"What do we do?" asked Liane, terror in her face.

The two Egyptian men were now running down the side street towards them, shouting something in Arabic. Another shot rang out. This too missed them.

"Get on the cruise boat," ordered Brett.

They ran across the road and joined the last of the passengers boarding the boat. And as they did so they turned and looked back.

27

The two would-be assassins had been stopped by a traffic holdup.

Liane and Brett were the last passengers to board the Queen of the Nile. The moment they stepped onto the deck, two sailors quickly drew up the gangway, and closed the deck door. A few moments later the engines revved up, and the boat moved slowly out into midstream.

"What are we going to do? Our plane takes off in three hours."

Liane gave Brett a desperate look. They were standing in the crowded reception area of the boat. Passengers were crowding round the desk to receive their cabin keys.

"I think we have no alternative but to stay on this boat and get off at the next stop," announced Brett, watching Luxor disappearing from view.

"When will that be?" asked Liane in dismay.

"I really don't know. Could be worse," he added as he surveyed the mahogany panelling, the soft carpet underfoot, the Louis Quatorze style armchairs, and the crystal wall lights that sparkled in the late afternoon sun.

"Brett, we're going to miss our plane."

"There's nothing we can do about it."

"And those Egyptians tried to kill us."

"I know. When we get back to Luxor we'll inform the police. Did you make a note of their registration number?"

"No. Did you?"

Brett shook his head.

"Excuse me sir," called the male reception clerk. "Do you have a reservation?"

"I'm afraid not," said Brett walking up to the desk, and Liane followed. "But we'd like to make one. Have you two vacant cabins?"

"Yes sir," smiled the young man. "Cabins 101, and 102. Next to each other. A last minute cancellation."

A price was agreed. Brett wrote out a cheque and showed his bank card. The receptionist handed him two keys.

"Thank you sir. If you have any problems, or complaints, please do not hesitate to tell me."

Brett joined Liane, and handed her key 102.

"That was a lot of money to go to the next stop," Liane couldn't help commenting as they moved away down a corridor.

"I've paid to Aswan," said Brett.

Liane stopped, surprised. "Why on earth did you do that? What do we want to go to Aswan for?"

"We've missed the plane anyway, so what the hell. Let's go to Aswan." Brett shrugged his shoulders. The matter was finished.

"Look, Brett, you never even asked my opinion. You certainly take a lot for granted."

"I like you calling me by my first name. Makes the relationship kind of closer..."

"Don't read anything into it. And I go fifty fifty on the money. I'm no scrounger. Anyway, I'm getting off at the next stop."

"You get off at the next stop, if you so wish. I wouldn't dream of stopping you. Personally, I want to see a bit more of Upper Egypt. And as for the money, forget it."

Liane couldn't help smiling. As a McMahon he owed her a lot more than the fare on a Nile cruiseboat. Still, she must be fair.

"I insist on paying my way."

"I said forget it. Well, here we are, cabin 101 and yours next door."

He inserted the key into the lock and opened the door. They entered a medium size cabin, all colours in varying shades of green, twin beds, fitted mahogany wardrobe and cupboards, with a small dressing table. On the walls were framed papyrus prints of pharoahs and their gods.

A door led off to a marble and gold gilt bathroom. A vase containing red carnations had been placed before a large mirror.

"I like it," said Brett as he walked a tour of inspection. "Let's have a look at your cabin."

Liane's was exactly the same as Brett's. She put hershoulder bag down on the bed and unzipped it. First she took the painting out and laid it on one of the beds, then from the bottom of the bag she took out her make up bag and hairbrush and laid them on the dressing table.

"Do you think it's the painting they were after?" she asked, a puzzled expression in her eyes as she replaced the painting in the bag and zipped it up.

"Possibly. But Father O'Brien said it wasn't valuable. Anyway,

29

stop worrying about it. We've shaken them off. Changing the subject, I understand we could catch a bus from Aswan back to Luxor. Might be a long journey. Or we could take a train or plane. Are you still getting off at the next stop?" he added with a mischievous twinkle in his eyes.

"Definitely," replied Liane.

"Pity about that." His eyes gave her a half closed look that said a lot. "You're going to leave me alone in such a romantic setting. What a shame you're such a hard female with no romance in your soul. You and I could have had a wonderful time."

"There's plenty of romance in my soul but not where a McMahon is concerned."

The moment she had said it she was sorry. A hurt look came in Brett's eyes and he turned away.

"I'm going on a tour of inspection. You can accompany me if you wish." He spoke without looking at her, his voice cold and distant. "Dinner isn't until seven thirty."

She put her cotton bag into the wardrobe and followed him out of the cabin.

On the deck above they found the restaurant, a hairdressing salon, a jeweller's shop. On the deck above that they found a sun bathing area in the bows of the ship where blue leather sunbeds were laid in rows, cupboards holding soft white towels, and near the rails a few dainty tables and chairs for afternoon tea. Double glass doors led into an elegant mahogany panelled lounge, a white baby grand piano, and a bar. At the rear of this deck was the swimming pool.

Liane and Brett sat in lounging chairs by the pool.

"So you are the child of a broken home," Brett began, his voice hard and unfeeling.

"And what are you trying to say?"

"I am endeavouring to say that it explains a lot."

"Now look, when my parents' marriage broke up, I was heart broken. I loved them both. Of course it had an effect on me."

"When did it happen?"

"A couple of years before Dad had his heart attack and died."

"Which parent did you live with?"

"Dad of course, at Islington. I had to go on living in the London area because of my job. Mum went to live with her sister in Northumberland."

"What kind of a woman is your mother?"

"My mother is a wonderful woman," replied Liane defensively. "And Dad was a charismatic person. Everyone loved him, but he was difficult to live with. Money was the big problem. To Dad it was for spending. When he was working he spent every penny he earned and more. When he was out of work between productions, we were broke. They used to have the most terrible rows about money."

Brett decided to have a swim, whilst Liane passed the time chatting to a pleasant antique dealer and his wife who introduced themselves as George and Frances.

At seven thirty Liane and Brett went in to dinner and found themselves sat at a long table with a boisterous party of Italians. In fact, apart from the antique dealer and his wife, most of the passengers were either Italian or German.

"Like to have a drink?" asked Brett.

She could tell from the cold look on his face he still hadn't forgiven her. She must apologise. Forget pride and all the rest, but somehow the opportunity never seemed to arise.

"I think it best to avoid Egyptian wine," he said, looking at the wine list. "I recommend a German white."

"I'm quite happy with German white," Liane told him, her mind on more important matters.

Brett poured Liane a glass of wine.

"I take it you now live alone in the Islington apartment?"

Liane nodded. "And responsible for the mortgage repayments." Liane spoke in a weary tone.

Sitting opposite her in his pale tropical suit enhancing the darkness of his hair, his suntan, Liane noticed one or two of the Italian women were interested in Brett. Whenever they thought he wasn't looking, they would give him a sly glance.

Yes, wherever Brett went he would never be without a woman.

It appeared it was someone's birthday in the Italian group. They were drinking toasts amidst much laughter and merriment, then

31

suddenly they all rose to their feet and made for the dance floor, shuffling round in a crocodile formation to the latest Italian hit song.Someone grabbed at Liane and Brett. "Come. You dance," they said, and Liane and Brett found themselves joining the crocodile of dancers. The happy mood was contagious. Round and round they went. Then Liane and Brett returned to their table, laughing with the rest.

Someone held up a bottle of chianti, and poured a measure into Liane and Brett's glasses.

"You Americano?" asked one of the men.

"Brett smiled. "I am."

"My name is Alberto and I am from Roma. Which part of America are you from?"

"Cambridge, Massachusetts."

The man held up his hands. "My brother, he have a restaurant in Philadelphia. That is not far?"

More chianti was drunk. More dances were danced.

Around midnight Liane had difficulty in remembering why they were on the cruiseboat at all.

"Brett, I think it is time I went and had a good long sleep. It has been the most extraordinary day of my life."

Brett escorted her back to her cabin, and stopped before the door.

There was a thoughtful expression in his eyes. "God knows when we'll get back to Europe. No one seems to know anything about the bus service in Aswan. We could go to the railway station and just wait for the next train."

Liane was thinking about other matters.

"Brett, I'm sure you'll work something out." Then she hesitated feeling a little shy all of a sudden. "I-I want to thank you for your quick thinking today, and to say I am sorry for something I said when we first came on board."

"Save it honey," he replied in a sudden brusque tone, "Some other time."

Then turning he walked quickly away. He did not enter his cabin but walked to the end of the corridor then took the staircase to the deck above.

Liane entered her cabin and walking slowly across the room switched on the radio. There was a wail of Arab music. Her apology had been rejected. She had no one to blame but herself.

Why did she have to open her big mouth? Especially when she owed Brett so much. After a few minutes she switched the radio off and went into the bathroom. There she washed her hair, washed her tights, her 'blue cotton blouse, then lay down in one of the twin beds.

She was annoyed because he had rejected her apology. She turned on her side and tried to sleep. If only they had never encountered the gunmen she thought dejectedly. Now they were trapped on a Nile cruiseboat, in luxury she had to admit, but trapped all the same. Why oh why, couldn't it have been with a man who did not arouse such negative emotions. Who did not make her feel so angry and upset.

She gave a sigh and turned onto her back, staring at the ceiling, sleep far away. She had told Brett she would get off at the next stop, but if there was no public transport, what would she do?

Then her thoughts turned to the unit. Ian must be distraught with worry. His continuity girl and script writer had disappeared in Luxor. She wondered if he had notified the police.

In her wallet she had forty pounds in travellers' cheques. There had been no need for her to carry a large amount of money for all expenses when on location were paid for by the company.

Restlessly she turned again on her side to settle for sleep wondering if they would ever get back to Luxor. Then she wondered where Brett had gone. An assignation with one of those dark eyed signorinas perhaps? Angrily she switched that thought off. Brett McMahon could do whatever he pleased!

The following morning Liane awoke just after dawn to find the banks of the Nile gliding slowly past her cabin window. Tall papyrus reeds were growing at the river's edge.

She felt sleepy having slept badly, but a tingle of excitement started to creep through her as she lay there in that state of semi wakefulness. What would today bring, she thought!

She dozed off for an hour to be awakened by the phone ringing. For a brief moment she wondered if it was Brett, but it was an unfamiliar male voice.

"Good morning. This is your seven o'clock call. Breakfast is now being served. If you wish to view the Temple of Khnum, the ram god, please assemble in the main reception area at eight o'clock. Thank you."

Liane put down the receiver. The Temple of Khnum? Why not? After the visit she would enquire about transport back to Luxor.

She had a quick shower, dressed, and went up to the restaurant. It was a buffet style meal with a plentiful supply of orange juice, cereal and fresh milk, eggs cooked in a dozen different ways, bacon, sausages, freshly made toast and marmalade. She was pleasantly surprised.

Brett was already seated at one of the tables. Liane sat down opposite him. A waiter poured them both a cup of coffee.

"Good morning." he said in an impersonal voice. "Did you sleep well?"

"Yes thank you. Did you?"

He shrugged his shoulders. Liane thought he looked tired.

"You won't get far on that," he commented, looking at Liane's glass of orange juice and two slices of toast.

"I never eat a cooked breakfast," she replied coolly. "What time did you go to bed last night?"

"Twoish." he replied in a nonchalant voice.

"What was the attraction?"

"Must I tell?" he replied with a mischievous twinkle in his eyes.

"Do whatever you like," replied Liane, annoyed with herself for having brought up the subject.

"You sound jealous."

"Of the dark eyed signorinas you were chatting up last night. I have more important things on my mind."

Brett smiled into his cup of coffee, then looked up at her, the smile changing to a quizzical one.

"Tell me one of them."

"Gladly," replied Liane. "I wonder if we can phone Ian?"

"There is a radio phone on the boat but unfortunately it is for the captain's exclusive use. I made enquiries last night. I think I'll try to phone Ian when I get to Aswan. Now stop worrying. We got rid of

Omar Shariff and his companion. You're having a somewhat un-expected cruise up the Nile. Relax; what more do you want?"

Liane bristled at the mocking tone.

"I'm worried about my job."

"Ian has a high opinion of you. Stop worrying, and enjoy yourself."

"You're right. We've been very lucky. Could have been worse."

"Going to the Temple of Khnurn?" asked Brett casually, looking at her over his cup.

Liane nodded. "And you?"

"Sure," he replied. "I've got to catch up on my study of ancient Egypt."

Half an hour later Liane and Brett assembled in the reception area with those of the passengers who wished to view the temple. Malik, was their guide, an attractive young Cairo woman dressed smartly in European clothes.

"Where have you put the painting?" asked Brett.

"It's in my shoulder bag in the wardrobe."

"Good morning everyone," smiled Malik. Her accent sounded French.

"I hope you are enjoying your trip up the Nile. Come, we will now proceed to the Temple of Khnum, the ram god. It will be convenient if you do not get lost."

Malik stepped off the boat and onto the gangway. The rest of the party followed, scrambling up the rocky embankment, helped by the sailors. Liane was one of the last to leave the boat, Brett had gone on ahead. Slowly Liane climbed the steep, rocky slope. It was hot al-ready. As she neared the top, she paused and looked up.

She thought her heart had stop beating. There was a man standing on the top of the embankment looking down on her. He made her think of an animal who had caught its prey.

He was one of the men who had chased them through the Luxor souk, who had tried to kill them. The one she thought looked like Omar Shariff!

CHAPTER 4

"Liane!"

It was Brett calling her from the embankment road. It was like a voice from heaven.

"Are you coming or not?" An impatient note now creeping into his voice.

She scrambled up the last few feet of the rocky slope and ran swiftly across the road to him.

"I'm so glad to see you!" she panted, placing her hand on his arm. It was trembling.

"Well, that's a change," smiled Brett, then looking closer at her unhappy face added: "Are you feeling all right?"

"No. We can't talk here. Let's catch up with the rest of the group, safety in numbers."

Taking Brett by the arm she propelled him quickly to the comparative safety of the tail end of the tourists who had just entered the outskirts of a mud brick village dominated by the minaret tower of a small mosque.

Brett looked at Liane with bewilderment in his eyes.

"For goodness sake Liane, tell me what is going on?"

"You won't believe this, but I've just seen Omar Shariff. He was standing at the top of the embankment."

"You mean the guy who chased us at Luxor. His friend tried to kill us?"

Liane nodded. Her throat felt dry as they both looked back.

There was no one there.

"You imagined it," laughed Brett. "A touch of the sun."

She gave Brett a look of derision.

"And when you climbed up the embankment, I suppose there was no one there?"

"No there wasn't," Brett replied firmly.

"Well, I definitely saw him, and I'm worried."

"Liane, let's work this situation out logically. The boat's been travelling through part of the night so we're quite a distance from Luxor. If this guy is your Omar Shariff, how did he get here?"

Liane shrugged her shoulders.

"How do I know? Perhaps he travelled by car?"

"There's no car here."

"He's left his car on the other bank, and crossed by felucca."

Brett dismissed this suggestion. "You saw someone who looked like this guy," he insisted.

They were now in the main street of the village with open fronted shops on each side of the lane. Amongst the many items for sale were kaftans, fluttering in the slight morning breeze. The loosely fitting ankle length gowns decorated with brilliantly coloured stones, caught Liane's eye. You could wear one as an evening dress she thought, looking at them longingly.

An Egyptian boy thrust a pair of gold embossed leather slippers into her hands.

"Cheap!" he whispered. "Very cheap."

They had now reached the gates of the temple set in a high wall. Passing through they found themselves in a courtyard gazing at a great stone edifice, forty feet high or more.

Through the high square entrance they walked into cool chambers the walls of which were carved with gods, half human, half animal.

Malik, their guide, gathered the group around her.

"This temple was dedicated to the god Khnum, who created men and animals from the clay of the Nile. The Temple was built during the period of the New Kingdom, from 1,570 B.C..."

Liane found it hard to concentrate on Malik's lecture. She took a swift glance around her, feeling ill at ease, wondering what had happened to Omar Shariff, wondering if he had joined the tour. It was evident he had not.

Had she been mistaken as Brett had suggested? Was it someone who just looked like the man who had followed them from the church, then chased them through the streets of Luxor? She was certain it was him. And in that case, where was he now?

37

They moved to another building.

"...This temple," Malik's voice broke into her thoughts, "is Ptolemaic in origin, and from new evidence it appears that further work was done on the temple from about 180 B.C..."

Brett moved closer to her and touched her arm.

"I have a confession to make." he whispered.

Liane gave him a careful look.

"And what is that?"

"I know very little about ancient Egyptian history."

Liane smiled. "Me too. Now is our chance to learn."

They followed Malik into further chambers, the walls of all of them covered in carvings of ram gods, and numerous reenactments of festive rituals. There were even carvings expressing mockery of the Roman invaders. It was walking into another world, a fascinating world. For a brief period Liane forgot her worries.

An hour later they left the temple, returning through the souk, beseiged again by the little boy with the gold embossed slippers, who Liane again managed to evade, then along the embankment road to the cruiseboat.

There was no sign of Omar Shariff.

Liane stepped along the gangway with the rest of the tour party and onto the boat, looking about her warily.

"I don't know what you are worrying about," said Brett, following closely behind her.

"I think I have very good reason to worry. I am convinced I saw him. Look Brett, he might have come on board and booked for the rest of the trip. I've got to find out."

"How are you going to do that, when you don't know his name."

Liane smiled. "I've got my methods."

Walking up to the reception desk, Liane gave the desk clerk a confident smile.

"Your cabin key Madame?"

The clerk handed Liane her key.

"Thank you. Oh by the way, did a man come on board, a new passenger, whilst we were visiting the temple?" She tried to sound casual, but felt she hadn't succeeded.

"We - we feel we have met him beforeJ" Liane continued lamely. "Can't remember where it was. Might have been Luxor."

The desk clerk consulted his lists.

"Two new passengers have just joined us. Mr Ahmed Shawki and Mr Hassan Shawki."

The young man beamed happily at Liane and Brett. Liane looked at Brett, her heart sinking.

"Thank you," said Liane politely to the young man. They turned and walked away.

"What are we going to do?" she whispered to Brett as they paced the reception area. "They've both joined the cruise."

Brett gave Liane a sceptical look. "Liane. Ahmed Shawki and Hassan Shawki could be anyone. You're panicking. Now just take a firm hold of yourself."

"That is what I am trying to do, and I need your help. Let's look at it from the worse possible angle and Ahmed and Hassan Shawki are the men I think they are. Isn't it strange that they have to join the same boat as ourselves. We must have something that interests them very much. I can only think of the painting. Have you any suggestions?"

"Or one of them has fallen madly in love with you," suggested Brett sarcastically, "And can't bear you to be out of his sight."

"Don't talk nonsense," Liane scoffed at him. "Be serious, please."

"All right. I'll be serious. There is a possibility that these men may be interested in your painting. You say it is in your cabin?"

"Of course. Come and look."

They went down the corridor to Liane's cabin. Opening the wardrobe door she took out her cotton shoulder bag, put it on the bed and unzipped.

"Will you take the painting out of the bag?" asked Brett, sitting on her bed. "I'd like to have a good look at it. If what you say is true, what is so special about it, except your father liked it."

Liane took the painting from the cotton bag and handed it to him, then sat down on the bed next to him.

"The Virgin Mary holding the Infant Jesus," Brett murmured thoughtfully. "The Virgin's clothes are black and gold, Jesus is dressed in light brown and gold. Background is a mosaic design of gold, black, and a reddish brown. The mosaic makes me think of Arab influence."

He turned the picture over and examined the back.

"Painted on wood," he added thoughtfully, "It could be Spanish or Italian. I don't know. I wish I did. What do you think Liane?"

I'm the same as you. I don't know. I'm not an art expert. But I have a feeling that in spite of Father's opinion that it is not valuable, I think there is a possibility that it is ."

Brett handed Liane the picture and she returned it to the shoulder bag.

"It could be worth a couple of thousand," suggested Brett, "And if ever you wanted to sell it, I'd put it in a new frame."

"I'm not happy about leaving it in the cabin when we go out." Liane zipped up the bag. "Locking the door doesn't guarantee anything. The cabin boy will have a duplicate. Can you trust him?"

Brett shrugged his shoulders, then gave Liane a whimsically smile.

"There is the possibility that Ahmed and Hassan Shawki are respectable Egyptian gentlemen who have joined the cruise because they want to brush up on their ancient history."

"And there is the possibility that we are talking about two Egyptian crooks," retorted Liane impatiently, as she placed the painting underneath one of the beds. "I wonder if the ship has a safe?"

"No harm in asking," Brett replied.

They went back to the reception desk and asked if there was a safe available for passengers' valuables.

"Certainly," replied the clerk. "The manager has a safe in his office. Unfortunately it is only a small safe, ideal for travellers' cheques, cash, small items of jewellery."

They thanked the clerk and moved away.

"Lets have some lunch," suggested Brett, "And forget the painting for a while. I want to talk to you about something else."

They went up the curving staircase to the restaurant, and as they did so Liane took a quick glance at Brett. A certain tension had started in his face. It was the way he held his mouth, in a hard, firm line, and when he turned his head, there was a look of accusation in those steel blue eyes.

"I went with you to the Luxor church because I wanted to talk to you, not get mixed up with a painting, and someone who looks like a film star from the nineteen fifties, whose friend tried to kill us."

They had now reached the top of the stairs. Brett opened the glass swing doors and they entered the restaurant. Again it was a self help buffet style meal, beautifully set out in the centre of the room.

"You can't complain about the food," commented Liane as they made their selections. Brett did not answer, then they went and sat at a quiet corner table.

"You and I have a problem," Brett spoke in a sharp voice.

"We certainly do," Liane replied, a harshness in her voice as she turned to him.

"First I'll give you a few facts. My grandfather was a very difficult man. The two men quarrelled, which was inevitable, and Dad went off to England. They made it up, Dad loved his father, and grandfather promised he would leave the farm to Dad. I think your family..."

"Well, all I can say to you is express an opinion when you know the full facts, and you know nothing about my family."

"I do know about your family. I think they are the most grasping, greedy people I have ever come across," Liane flung at him.

"You have made accusations that are unjust."

"I've told the truth. And I cannot find sufficient words to express the depth of my feelings. Do you know the unhappiness your family caused my father..."

Brett rose to his feet, and picked up his plate.

"My motto is, where you're not wanted, get out..."

"Zayak!" Malik greeted them light heartedly as she walked towards their table and sat down in the empty chair next to Brett.

"Please do not go Mr McMahon. It would give me pleasure to eat with you. Please sit down."

Sheepishly Brett sat down. The atmosphere was tense to say the least.

"The salmon looks delicious, don't you think?" She looked at them both.

Liane and Brett agreed the salmon looked delicious.

"Did you enjoy the visit to the Temple of Khnum?"

Brett looked enquiringly at Liane. "I enjoyed it. Did you?" His voice was smooth as silk.

Liane gave him a faint smile.

"Yes. I enjoyed it," she replied in an even tone. How she longed to escape to her cabin, to peace and solitude, but with Malik there, it was difficult. She suddenly remembered she had forgotten to enquire about public transport back to Luxor when she came out of the temple.

"Malik, I've been wondering about public transport, taxis or buses..."

Malik wasn't listening. "Will you be coming this afternoon to the Valley of the Kings?" she asked, looking at them both.

"I'm not sure..." Liane began hesitantly.

"But you must," cut in Malik, insistance in her voice. "If you don't, you will regret it all the days of your life. Please."

She looked beseechingly at them both. Liane relented. She knew without enquiring there would be no means of getting back to Luxor, except under extreme difficulty. She had to face the fact whether she liked it or not, she was on this boat until Aswan.

Sorry," said Brett, "I can't make it this afternoon."

Malik looked upset. "I hope that I am not responsible for that decision." She spoke in a sorrowful voice. "But it is very difficult for me to try to give you five thousand years of history in four days. In fact it is an impossible task."

"I'm sure it is," Brett agreed with her. "But don't worry, you have nothing to do with my decision."

Brett gave Liane a withering glance across the table, and in return Liane glared at him.

Brett continued: "Actually I am eager to learn more about ancient Egypt. That part of my education was sadly neglected. The only ancient Egyptian I know of is Cleopatra."

Malik smiled.

"Cleopatra, Queen of Egypt, Daughter of the Sun, Sister of the Moon. She became famous as the mistress of Julius Caesar until he was assassinated. Then she became the mistress of Antony, until he was killed in battle. You know the rest of the story.

But she did not kill herself for love. We have a different story in Egypt. The truth is she could not bear the humiliation of being taken to Rome as prisoner of Augustus, for Augustus was one of her rejected lovers. How he would have triumphed over her tragedy! And in what terrible ways would he have taken his revenge. Now don't forget, we leave at three o'clock prompt, and don't forget your sunhat."

And with that, Malik rose from the table and left the restaurant.

Brett leaned forward and gave Liane a hard look. "Men have many ways of getting even with a woman, particularly those who have a bigoted outlook."

Liane gave him a big sigh. "Let's give it a break."

Brett stood up, his face relaxing in a smile.

"Let's have a coffee outside."

Liane followed Brett up the stairs to the sun bathing area in the bows of the boat. He was the second man she had ever met who could arouse such anger in her. Conal had been the first. Would she ever meet a man who could raise positive emotions in her?

A waiter took their order, returning a few minutes later with two cups of coffee. Liane took a sip of her coffee, then placed the cup in the saucer.

She had to keep her feelings under control. They were going to be together for the next few days. It would be wise to say as little as possible, for if she did not exercise tact, within the confines of the small cruiseboat, all the passengers would soon learn of their family feud. It would be embarrassing. She had to make the best of a difficult situation. She could start off with an apology.

"Brett, I would like to say I am sorry..."

"...for the insulting remarks you have just hurled at a member of the McMahon family. You don't mean a word you are saying."

He gave her a derisory smile.

"But I do, really I do," Liane persisted.

"Are you telling me you want to bury the hatchet?"

Liane hesitated. "Well, while we're on the boat."

"You beat them all."

Brett took off his jacket, rolled up his shirt sleeves, and lay down on a sun bed. Liane unbuttoned the top buttons of her blouse, then she too lay down on a sunbed next to Brett, and closed her eyes.

"I mustn't lie here too long," she murmured to Brett, "I don't tan, just go an awful red. Anyway, it isn't healthy."

She fell into a drowsy state, the sun making her feel sleepy, enjoying the luxuriating feeling, at least for a short time, of its hot rays on her body. Some five minutes must have elapsed when suddenly Liane heard someone call her.

"Madame, madame, I must speak to you."

Slowly Liane opened her eyes. Omar Shariff was sitting in the chair next to her! He was looking at her with a look that could only be described as lascivious, his eyes lingering on her half revealed breasts.

She sat up immediately, shocked and astonished, as she quickly buttoned her blouse, her heart beating wildly.

Thank God for Brett, lying on the sunbed next to her.

"What do you want?" she demanded.

"I am sorry for waking you madame," his voice purred with a slight French intonation, "But I would very much like to speak to you." "You and your friend tried to kill us."

At that moment Brett opened his eyes and rolled over on his side.

"What's going on?" he muttered sleepily. Then recognition dawned as he looked at the man seated next to Liane.He gave him a slow smile.

"You were right Liane. Our friend from Luxor. I understand you have just checked in, having taken a sudden interest in a Nile cruise."

Now that Brett had joined in the conversation he turned to him, giving a dazzling smile. He was a handsome man with jet black hair brushed back from his forehead, brown eyes, regular features and beautiful white teeth.

"You have been checking up on me?" he asked politely.

"I'll say we have," Brett replied, a sharp tone in his voice. "And where's your companion? The one with the killer instinct."

The man raised his hands. "I am here to apologise for my brother Hassan. He is a crazy man." He pointed to his head with his forefinger, then lowering his voice added: "He is in his cabin. He is not feeling well. I have taken the gun from him, and he will never use it again. I cannot apologise enough. He could have killed you!"

"I'll say he could!"

Brett looked at Ahmed, a puzzled expression marring his brow. "Why have you just joined the cruise? To apologise to us? I don't understand. You don't even know us. What are you up to Ahmed? What is your game?"

Ahmed gave them both a slow, calculating look. "My game is, we could do a deal."

CHAPTER 5

Brett swung his legs round and stood up, his face dark with suspicion as he stared at Ahmed.

"We could do a deal!" he exploded, "A deal about what for God's sake?"

"The painting of course," replied Ahmed, not batting an eyelid, his voice easy and smooth. "What else could I be talking about? I saw you take it from the church."

"It is a gift from Father O'Brien." Liane protested vehemently.

Ahmed stopped smiling. "He gave it to you? I don't understand."

"My father was his friend, and the gift is a memento of that long friendship."

Ahmed's handsome face broke into a wide grin. "That is clever and original."

"It is not clever and original," exclaimed Liane, now feeling extremely annoyed. "We're telling the truth, and it is most offensive to be accused of stealing."

There was now a look of contempt on Ahmed's face. "A Gorregiani, and you are asking me to believe that this christian priest gives it to you as a memento of a friendship?"

"Yes, because my father has died," said Liane quietly.

"I am sorry your father had died." From the look on Ahmed's face he looked anything but sorry. "We are talking about a Gorregiani. Come now, you must think me a simpleton, a peasant."

Liane looked at Brett.

"Are Gorregianis valuable?"

Brett shrugged his shoulders. "I don't follow the art market."

"Gorregianis valuable?" Ahmed repeated, amazed they did not know. "I could sell the work of that sixteenth century Italian for fifty thousand dollars. I am an honest art dealer."

"Fifty thousand!" repeated Liane. She looked at Brett, bewilderment in her face.

"Liane is not selling," retorted Brett. "To receive a gift which is a memento of a lifetime's friendship, then to rush off immediately and sell it." He turned to Liane, "That would be unforgiveable."

It was as if Brett had not spoken.

"I have a good contact in New York," Ahmed continued, pride in his voice. "If Gorregianis continue to hold their price, and the way the market is going, they could even increase, my contact would of course have to have his commission, - which means you should make at least twenty thousand dollars, if we split fifty fifty."

A look of anger swept across Brett's face.

"How many times do I have to tell you? The painting is not for sale. It doesn't matter how valuable it is. Now, will you stop pestering Liane or I'll be forced to report you to the boat manager."

"Mr Shawki, please leave us in peace," Liane joined in. "I will never sell the picture. The sentimental value is far too precious for me to ever do such a thing."

Ahmed looked at Liane. "I do not understand what you are talking about."

Then he turned to Brett, anger in his face. "If you report me to the boat manager I will tell him you have a stolen painting in your possession. I will tell him I saw you steal it from the christian church in Luxor. He will believe me. And I know what he will do. He will inform the captain who will inform the police, and they will be waiting for you at Aswan."

"A bit of old fashioned blackmail eh?" Brett spoke to Ahmed in a low, tight voice. "Well, it won't work."

Ahmed gave him a greasy smile, shrugging his shoulders. "I am an honest art dealer from Cairo. And I am not used to being treated in this manner."

"You are disreputable and dishonest," Brett told him in no uncertain manner. "You came on board this boat to buy what you thought was a stolen painting."

Ahmed smiled, and shrugged his shoulders. "I spend my life buying second hand paintings. Some are the property of the genuine owners, some are not. It is part of life. Good day my friends."

And with that he rose to his feet, his dark eyes full of mischievous venom, and left the sundeck.

"He still doesn't believe us," said Liane watching his departure with deep apprehension. "And is he telling the truth about the fifty thousand dollars?" she added turning to Brett.

Brett sat down on the seat vacated by Ahmed.

"I don't know. It isn't possible to check." Brett pursed his lips thoughtfully. "But whatever the value, there is no deal. Agreed?"

Liane nodded. "Agreed."

Brett frowned. "The problem is, what do we do now? We've got this guy on our backs to Aswan, and maybe back to Luxor. Now, we've got to make a plan for the next few days. By the way where did he say the mad guy is?"

Liane shrugged her shoulders.

"Ahmed says he is in his cabin. Brett, I think you should have taken an easier line," Liane reproached him. "Play it casual. We'll just make it harder for ourselves antagonising him. I don't want him to get nasty again. Remember, he's got Hassan's gun."

"Liane, I don't understand you. You want me to play it cool. Yes, I know he has the gun. You are not by any chance suggesting we do a deal with him?" he added sarcastically.

"Calm down, of course not," smiled Liane. "I just want to make the cruise as pleasant as possible. There is no question of selling the painting. I feel it's father's property and it is in my safekeeping for my lifetime. To sell it would be so, - unethical."

"In the past being unethical never worried the O'Neills." Brett's face creased into a derisory grin.

Liane gave him a look of pure hatred.

"I don't know what you are talking about, and let's discuss our private problems some other time, if you don't mind, then you can insult the O'Neills to your heart's content."

Brett walked across to the rail and leaned against it.

"Right now, we've got to work out a plan of action." He gave her a firm look. "As we won't do a deal with Ahmed, and lost him the chance of making twenty thousand dollars, he's going to be upset. I think it wise to take the painting this afternoon to the Valley of the

Kings."

Liane looked alarmed.

"Why - what do you think he's going to do? Try and steal it?"

"I wouldn't put it past him," Brett was quick to reply. "Remember he told us twice he was honest. That makes me suspicious straight away. Beware of the man who is always telling you he's honest."

Liane nodded in agreement. "And now that I know how valuable it is, I don't trust anyone, not even the cabin boy, and he has the face of an angel. Isn't that sad? I trusted everyone before, but then I never had anything that was worth stealing."

"You're learning fast. Now, I'm going to change my plans," added Brett, giving her a thoughtful look. "I will accompany you this afternoon as protector of the painting, that is if you have no objection."

Liane smiled. "My! That is gallant of you. No, I have no objection."

They left the sun deck, walked across the lounge, then down two flights of steps to their cabins.

"Do you think Ahmed might join the tour?" asked Liane as she opened her cabin door.

"He's capable of anything," smiled Brett. "Chances are he's had enough of Egyptian history. It's only foreigners that are interested."

The journey to the Valley of the Kings took them through the arid Theban Hills, the hillsides steep and bare, fissured by searing heat and wind.

The Nile cruise was now becoming bizarre, thought Liane as the bus turned off the unmade road onto a narrow track. It was bad enough being forced into the company of a man she despised, now she had to add a dubious Egyptian art dealer and his brother Hassan, wnom she must avoid at all costs. How she was going to do that, remained to be seen, for the Queen of the Nile was a comparatively small boat.

The bus had now stopped in a hot valley. Malik led the party into a long narrow tunnel dug into the hillside lit by electricity. There was no sign of Ahmed, for which Liane could only feel intense relief.

On the walls were astonishing paintings of pharoahs and a goddess.

49

"The goddess looks so modern," observed Liane to Brett as they walked the tunnel, "She looks as though she's wearing a tight evening dress with thin shoulder straps. I like her wide lacy looking necklace, and that's a strange looking crown on her head."

Malik caught her puzzled glance and started to explain.

"The goddess you see here is the goddess Isis, Queen of Heaven, Earth and the Underworld. She was the greatest goddess in the ancient world. She is wearing the double crowns of Upper and Lower Egypt..."

Her large shoulder bag containing the painting was proving cumbersome. She changed it to the other shoulder. Was she going paranoic about the painting? Was she going to carry it everywhere she went? It was understandable. She had never owned anything of value in her entire life.

Twenty thousand dollars! It was a lot of money. If a time ever came when she couldn't pay the mortgage on the apartment she might, heaven protect her, be forced to sell the painting, no matter what Brett said. It was all very well having lofty ideals, but when you came down to the practicalities of life, these things had to be done.

Then it occurred to her if she sold it independently without any middle men she could make fifty thousand dollars.

It was hot in the tunnel, and she could feel beads of perspiration on her brow. Suddenly to her horror she saw Ahmed. He was standing about twenty feet away, staring at her with his dark enigmatic eyes. And as he moved towards her through the crowd, her heart started to quicken.

"Miss O'Neill, may I carry your bag for you?" Ahmed stretched out his hand. "It is hot in the tunnel."

"No thank you," she replied, her voice brusque.

Ahmed placed his hand on the straps of her shoulder bag.

"I want to carry your bag," he persisted, a firm note in his voice.

"Thank you but it is not heavy," she replied trying to remove his hand from the bag.

Ahmed's hand remained firmly on the bag strap.

"Please. I can carry it."

Liane was now starting to feel desperate. Would this man not take no for an answer? Her eyes searched the crowd for Brett.

"What is the matter? You do not trust me?" There was a hurt look in his eyes as he removed his hand. "I only want to carry your bag."

Now she started to feel annoyed.

"I would like to ask a personal question," he continued. "Are you going to marry your friend?"

"Brett? Oh no, he's just a colleague."

Ahmed looked puzzled. "What is colleague?"

"I worked for him, and the work is now finished."

The moment she had spoken, Liane realised her mistake. There was an unmistakable gleam in Ahmed's eyes.

"So then he has no claim on you?"

At that moment Brett joined them. "And what is so important that you have ceased to view the wall paintings?"

Ahmed smiled. "I have discovered that Liane is not your affianced."

"What's that to you?" Brett's tone was aggressive.

"It is only idle curiosity on my part." And with a mischievous smile on his lips Ahmed moved away, much to Liane's relief.

"Keep away from that guy," Brett warned her tersely. "He means trouble."

"Don't worry I will. He was pestering me to carry my bag. Do you think he knew..."

"I'd say yes."

Malik and the tour party started to exit from the tunnel.

"Brett, look! Ahmed's waiting for us at the entrance. He's determined to carry my bag. What shall I do?"

"Let's look at these paintings, and he'll get tired of waiting for us," suggested Brett.

They had been admiring the wall paintings several minutes when suddenly the iron gate at the end of the long passage closed with a resounding clang, and the old keeper was turning the key in the lock. Ahmed was no where in sight.

Liane and Brett started to run shouting for him to wait. But the old man was either deaf or preferred not to hear. As they reached the gate he had disappeared from sight. The last of their tour party were boarding the bus about two hundred yards away. Malik was last in the queue.

"Malik!" they both shouted. "We're locked in!"

She obviously did not hear their shouts for she mounted the steps of the bus.

"Malik! Malik!" they shouted again in unison.

As the bus started to move off Liane in desperation took the pink scarf from around her hair and waved it through the bars of the gate. Someone saw it for the bus suddenly stopped, and Malik descended the steps and waved.

She ran the short distance to them.

"This is most unfortunate," she spoke to them through the bars of the gate. "Do not worry, I will find the keeper."

The minutes ticked by and there was no sign of Malik or the tomb keeper.

"I'm glad you're with me," said Liane in a quiet voice, a pulse beating in her head.

Brett gave her a long hard look.

"My, the O'Neills are softening."

Liane gave him a wry smile. "Only momentarily."

After what seemed an eternity, Malik appeared with the old man who opened the gate.

"I am always afraid of this happening," she told them as they boarded the bus amidst joking remarks from the rest of the tour.

"Ahmed must be on the other bus," Liane observed looking around as the bus set off, and they settled into the back seat.

If she hadn't waved her scarf and attracted the attention of the passengers on the bus she would have had to spend the night with Brett. They would have fought all night. She turned and looked at him. She had a feeling he knew what she was thinking. There was a mischievous smile on his lips.

"That was a merciful release."

When they reached the cruiseboat they went straight to Liane's cabin.

"I can't go on like this," she said with a great deal of emotion as soon as she had closed the door. "Until we leave the boat at Aswan

I'm going to be worrying about the painting every minute of the time. It is worth a lot of money, fifty thousand dollars. Brett, if I wanted to sell it, and of course at the moment I don't, surely I go straight to reputable auctioneers like Sothebys."

"Of course," replied Brett promptly. "You don't do deals with crooked Egyptians like Ahmed."

Then Brett smiled happily at Liane. "Look, I can solve your problems. I will take the painting and store it in my cabin."

"Thanks for the offer, but its passing my responsibility."

Liane had a sudden thought.

"I know. Under the mattress of the other bed. The cabin boy never touches it."

"I have this feeling Ahmed Shawki could get real nasty if he doesn't get his own way," said Brett pacing the cabin. "I think he still thinks you stole the painting, and if he could somehow get me into the background he could do a deal with you and make twenty thousand into the bargain."

"Don't worry Brett. He would never get me to change my mind. Anyway I do suggest a softer approach. I really feel we will gain from being more friendly."

"I'm sure you would," he replied an acid tone in his voice. "Let's go up to the lounge, after you have hidden the masterpiece."

Liane pulled back the bedspread of the second bed in the cabin, lifted up the mattress, and placed the painting under it.

"If you can think of a better place, let me know."

They went up to the lounge and sat in a quiet corner.

"Ahmed must be resting in his cabin," said Liane glancing round the room.

"And working out some devious plot no doubt to seduce you and steal the painting."

"Don't be ridiculous!" retorted Liane. "Why on earth should seduction enter into it?"

"I can see you are ignorant of the ways of the Arab. Seduction always comes into it."

He gave Liane a curious, almost accusing look, that made her feel angry - of what, she wasn't sure.

53

"Hello!"

It was George and Frances, the antique dealer and his wife that Liane had met the previous day. They sat down with Liane and Brett, and Brett ordered four zibeebs.

"What is a zibeeb?" asked Frances, when the drinks arrived.

"A sort of aniseed drink," Brett told her. "Drunk on the rocks."

Gingerly Frances took a sip and smiled hesitantly. "Not bad."

"Did you enjoy the Valley of the Kings this afternoon?" asked George affably.

Brett gave them a brief resume of the incident. "Well it wasn't life threatening, we would have been released in the morning." He gave Liane a curious smile, then directing his conversation to George continued: "I presume electricity has only recently been introduced to the tombs. I wonder how it will affect the murals."

Then followed a long discourse on the effects of light on ancient paintings.

"Are you going to the fancy dress party tonight?" Frances asked suddenly, directing her conversation to Liane. "It's on the notice board."

"I haven't read the notice board," Liane had to confess.

"Well, are you going to dress up? You can hire a costume at the hairdressers. They are all Arab style by the way. The ladies will be members of the harem, and the men will be dressed up like sheiks. Why don't you Liane? You need a bit of fun after your experience."

Liane laughed looking in Brett's direction. "You're absolutely right."

"In that case you should get your costume now," urged Frances. "It's already half past six."

Liane looked enquiring at Brett.

Brett shook his head. "No, I do not want to be a sheik for the evening."

"Spoil sport," laughed Frances.

Liane left Brett talking to Frances and George, and went to the hairdressers on the deck below. She chose a flimsy blue kaftan decorated with glittering silver sequins, and a blue head veil similarly decorated.

She went straight to her cabin and slipped into the kaftan, then arranged the blue head veil so that the silver sequins were draped across her forehead.

On viewing herself in the mirror Liane decided the only thing that spoiled the Egyptian look was her honey blonde hair.

The restaurant that evening was crowded, and there was a buzz of excited conversation at every table. Everyone it seemed, except Brett, was in traditional Egyptian costume. They were sharing a table with George and Frances, and the Italians they had met the previous evening.

The meal that night was traditional Egyptian food. A choice of minced lamb balls or pigeon, fried with spices served with rice, onions and parsley. This was followed by the most delectable cakes, very sweet and covered in honey, others were made of flaky pastry, paper thin, covered in marzipan, served with grapes.

Alberto directed his conversation to Brett, whilst Liane noticed his beautiful, sultry eyed daughter could not take her eyes off Brett.

"We are going to America in the autumn," Alberto proudly announced. "To see my brother after all these years. It would be so nice if we could meet. You say you live in Cambridge, Massachusetts?"

"Actually I spend most of my time in New York City," Brett told him. "I've got an apartment on East 74th."

Alberto beamed and raised his hands. "You give me your telephone number and we meet. I take you to lunch."

Then he reached the point of the conversation.

"Last night you told me you are playwright. My daughter Maria," He waved his hand in the direction of his beautiful daughter who sat looking at Brett with a Mona Lisa smile on her lovely face. "Maria, she want to be an actress. She has been to the School of Drama in Roma, but she cannot get a job."

Brett was trapped and bitterly regretting he had ever disclosed his occupation. He knew what would happen, Maria would haunt him until the boat reached Aswan.

Liane looked around the restaurant. She was looking for Ahmed, and praying she would not see him. And then to her dismay she noticed he was sitting at the next table, and as if conscious of her gaze he turned his head and their eyes met.

At that precise moment the music started, couples moved onto the floor, and to Liane's horror Ahmed rose from his seat, dressed in his sheik's outfit and walked across to her.

"It will be an honour if you would consent to dance with me."

Liane hesitated, embarrassed, and looked in Brett's direction. But Brett was too busy talking to Maria. Perhaps she could excuse herself by pleading tiredness.

"Ahmed..."

"Please," he cut in, "I have something to say to you."

She had better hear it, considering he had accused her of thieving.

She got up reluctantly and moved slowly to the dance floor. Ahmed was a good dancer, a good sense of rhythm, and held her a respectful distance from him, smiling all the while. The music was traditional Egyptian adapted to Western style, supplied by drums, tambourine and an oriental type of guitar.

"You like our music," he asked when they had danced around the floor once.

"Yes I like it. Ahmed..."

"Please, I have something important to say to you. A misunderstanding has arisen between us." Ahmed was looking intently into her eyes, searching for a reaction. Liane kept silent, her face expressionless. She was waiting to hear the rest.

"First I accused you of stealing, which I now realise was very wrong of me. You see I had been to the Luxor church many times, asking the priest if he would sell the painting to me. Always he refused. I was angry, and frustrated.

Then I go to the church for the last time. I ask to see the priest and the housekeeper says he cannot see anyone he is ill. So I went and sat in the church, wondering what to do. Then I see you and your friend. It was an easy mistake to make."

"Of course it was. Forget it."

"You are most generous lady. I have decided if you do not wish to take up my offer, that is your affair, and I accept it graciously."

Liane smiled. "Thank you Ahmed."

"Now that is settled," Ahmed gave her a look of triumph, "We can

56

be friends."

Liane relaxed. What a storm in a teacup she thought as the dance ended, and she returned to her table. Maria's mother and Frances were busy exchanging recipes, and Brett appeared to be fixing an auditon for Maria in New York.

"Remember the director casts the play. He may ask me for my opinion..."

The music started and Ahmed approached asking Liane to dance again. Liane consented. His whole personality had changed, or so it seemed to Liane. Gone was the predator, now he was just a charming man.

"You look very beautiful in your harem costume. If I was a sultan I would make you my favourite."

Liane smiled. "Would you indeed."

"I have had another thought about the painting," he gave her another charming smile. "Now that I know it is not a stolen painting we can do a fresh deal."

There was an expression in Ahmed's eyes that made Liane realised he was taking the conversation seriously.

"Look Ahmed. I'm not sure. I'll think about it, and let you know."

He shrugged his shoulders. "Take as long as you want."

He drew her closer to him. "You could bring the painting to my Cairo shop." He drew her even closer. "We could have a good time in Cairo my 'gameel'. I take you to the best night clubs, see the best belly dancing in the whole of Egypt. What do you say, just you and me."

She knew it would be more than visiting the best night clubs. It would be sliding the slippery slope.

She tried to move away from him, but each time she did, he only tightened his grip around her waist.

"It won't be possible for me to go to Cairo. I have to return to Ireland as quickly as possible. My job is at stake."

"At stake"? What does that mean?"

"I don't want to lose it."

Why didn't she have the sense to tell him Brett was her boyfriend, and a jealous one at that. At least the lie would have given her a little

57

less harassment.

How much longer could she endure it she thought as Ahmed swirled her round the dance floor. Two more days until they reached Aswan, then she would say goodbye to him forever. She would return to Luxor, and go straight to the airport, catching the first available plane to London, en route for Dublin. If she ever sold the painting it would not be to Ahmed Shawki.

It was a relief when the dance ended and she returned to her table. The next time Ahmed asked her to dance she politely refused.

Around midnight Liane started to feel tired. George and Frances had retired to their cabins Brett was still in earnest conversation with the Italians. Once or twice he appeared to remember Liane was with him, and would look enquiringly in her direction.

Liane touched Brett on the shoulder.

"I'm going to my cabin now. See you tomorrow."

As Liane reached the glass swing doors to her surprise Ahmed was waiting for her.

"I would like to say again, it would give me much pleasure to meet you in Cairo. Please think about it. I would give you very good time."

His hot hand grasped her hand and held it, his dark eyes staring lustfully at her well shaped breasts.

"I'm so sorry, but it will not be possible," she said firmly, extracting her hand from his perspiring grasp.

She watched him walk away with a sense of relief. Then opening the swing doors, she walked down the stairs to her cabin. Never in a million years would she go to Cairo to have a 'very good time' with Ahmed Shawki. She was not offended, just amused.

As Liane climbed into bed she was feeling comparatively contented. The trauma of the last couple of days appeared to have ended. She had learnt the modest painting Father O'Brien had given to her was worth fifty thousand dollars. To some people that wouldn't be much, but to Liane it was a fortune, and gave her a warm feeling of security she had never had before.

There was a knock at the door. She had a sudden thought, it might be Ahmed trying his luck. If it was, she would deal with him in a very firm manner.

"Who is it?" she called, suspicion in her voice.

"It's me, Brett."

Relieved it was Brett, Liane quickly put on her skirt and blouse, and opened the door, only to find Brett gazing at her with a thunderous expression on his face.

"Done a deal with the viper?"

"Of course I haven't!" Liane was quick to reply.

"You two did a lot of talking tonight."

Liane nodded. "He said that now he knows the painting was not stolen we do a fresh deal."

"You're more naive than I thought. Don't you understand you can never trust that type."

"I only said I'd think about it. And I do agree with you, I could never trust him."

"My God!" he continued, in the same angry tone. "It was sickening tonight watching you. You were throwing yourself at him. Haven't you any self-respect?"

"I wasn't throwing myself at Ahmed," Liane protested. "I only danced with him a couple of times. What is wrong with that?"

Now she was feeling as angry as Brett, and sorry she had ever opened her cabin door.

"Did you have to let him hold you so close? You were making yourself cheap. You were behaving like a..."

"How dare you..."

Liane raised her hand to slap his face but before she could do so Brett suddenly grasped both her hands, then kissed her with such fierce intensity on the mouth, she was left stunned and shaking as he walked away down the corridor.

CHAPTER 6

Liane closed her cabin door. Never had she felt so angry! How dare Brett say she had been making herself cheap! How dare he kiss her! If it had been a casual social kiss, that would have been different, but he had been aggressively sexual. It had been a violation!

She fell asleep, tossing and turning her mind filtering troubled dreams. About three a.m. the ship's engines suddenly throbbed into life as the boat started the move upriver to the next temple.

It was impossible to sleep. The noise and vibration were so bad Liane felt her cabin must be located right over the ship's engines.

Somehow she gradually fell into a light sleep, to be awakened about three hours later by the phone ringing, piercing a blessed silence, for the boat was now stationary.

"Good morning," came the polite male voice. "This is your seven o'clock call. We have now arrived at Edfu. Passengers who wish to visit the Temple of Horus please assemble in reception at eight o'clock. Breakfast is now being served."

Liane got out of bed, her head aching, and had a shower. She would visit the Temple of Horus; tomorrow they would reach Aswan, and soon this nightmare cruise would end.

Four days from now she calculated as she switched off the shower, with a bit of luck, she would be back in Dublin and life would return to normal. She shrugged her shoulders with an air of weary resignation. If life was difficult right now, she would just have to make the best of it. It was fate, her kismet.

She got dressed and went upstairs to the restaurant. The fancy dress party last night seemed to have taken its toll, there were few passengers taking breakfast. Brett wasn't there. Nor Ahmed. She breathed a sight of relief.

Liane went to the buffet table and helped herself to the usual orange juice and toast and sat down. The agony of being in Brett's company would only last a little longer, at least until they reached Heathrow in a few days time. And as for Ahmed it could be goodbye tomorrow.

A few minutes later a sleepy looking Brett entered the restaurant, tieless and his jacket looking extremely crumpled. He made his selection and sat down opposite her. He gave her a weak smile.

"Sorry about last night. I must have had too much to drink."

"Forget it," said Liane as the waiter filled their cups with coffee. "I have."

She had to look away; she wasn't good at lying. During the night when she couldn't sleep when the engines had started, she had recalled the pressure, the sensation of Brett's mouth upon hers, the strange excitement it had evoked. It was that, more than the engine noise that had taken her such a long time to return to sleep.

"What else did that bastard say last night?"He asked as he stirred his coffee.

"Why so interested?"

"Look Liane, I'm concerned about your personal safety, and the painting."

Liane made an exasperated sound. "I don't take any notice of Ahmed. He wants to meet me in Cairo."

"Are you going?" asked Brett, looking up watching her closely.

"Of course I'm not going," exclaimed Liane heatedly. "Do you think I am a complete idiot, without a brain in my head? Anyway, stop worrying about him."

"Stop worrying?" exclaimed Brett. "What do you think he's on the boat for? A holiday? I'd say the meeting he suggests in Cairo is a new approach to his problem. Get the girl and the painting in a hotel room. Seduce the girl..."

Liane looked at Brett coolly, dispassionately. "You seem to be very interested in seduction."

"Men usually are." Brett's eyes were laughing into hers.

"Brett, do you mind not talking about sex. It's a bit early in the day for me."

"It's never too early for me," Brett murmured softly, looking at her over his coffee cup, laughter in his eyes.

Liane decided to ignore this banter. It was the peacock showing off.

She looked away, and as she did so a man entered the restaurant and walked across to the buffet table. As Liane recognised him, she felt she had suddenly been dowsed in a cold shower. She gave an involuntary shiver.

"Brett," Liane lowered her voice to a whisper. "The man who has just entered the restaurant is the man who tried to kill us at Luxor."

Brett looked round. The man's back was now towards them.

Liane nodded. "I'm certain it's Hassan."

The man had now seated himself at a table on the far side of the restaurant. Brett stole a quick glance at him.

"You're right Liane," he whispered.

"Oh Brett, what are we going to do? That man is dangerous."

"Just keep out of his way."

The man suddenly looked up and glanced in their direction. The look was sullen and suspicious. Liane felt a nerve tighten in her stomach.

Brett gave a slight shrug of his shoulders.

"Forget him. Going to the Temple of Horus this morning?" he asked, changing the subject.

"Yes," Liane replied. "There's nothing else to do. And you, are you going?"

Brett gave her a faint smile. "As you say, there is nothing else to do." He glanced at his watch. "Time to go."

At eight o'clock prompt Liane and Brett, together with the rest of the tour party left the boat, accompanied by Malik. George and Frances were in the party, and Ahmed and his brother, much to Liane's consternation.

"At least we can keep an eye on them," Brett told Liane.

There was something about the two men that made Liane cringe. They made her think of a couple of snakes lying in the grass waiting to pounce.

They scrambled up the steep rocky embankment the sailors as usual helping the women in the party. At the top of the embankment they were greeted by a sign reading: "WELCOME TO THE TOWN OF ENJOYABLE MEETING."

They were standing on the outskirts of a village of flat roofed houses, all colour washed, with shutters at the tiny windows. Freshly washed blankets and carpets were hanging over balconies to dry in the hot sun.

The main street of the village was crowded and noisy. Men pedalling bicycles, their djellabahs flying in the breeze, weaved recklessly in and out of the crowd comprised mainly of women in black gowns and head veils on their way to the souk. Liane cautiously looked around. Ahmed and his brother were engaged in conversation with the Italians.

The situation was now doubly worse with the appearance of Ahmed's brother. And as she walked along Liane suddenly realised how glad she was that she was in Brett's company. He gave her a feeling of security. Strange how he had suddenly become a knight in shining armour.

Malik joined Liane and Brett in the crowded street.

"You look puzzled when you look at the Arab women in black." She directed her remark to Liane.

Liane nodded. "I have never understood why they wear black."

"Only married women wear black," Malik informed her with a gentle smile. "For after a woman has married, there is no need to attract the attention of other men by wearing beautiful colours."

"Not a bad idea," smiled Brett teasingly.

They had now reached the souk, the stalls by the roadside piled high with oranges, tomatoes, grapes, and as always, the eternal kaftans covered in glittering coloured stones. Liane was tempted. After all she had a painting in her possession worth fifty thousand dollars.

She paused to admire a kaftan made of stiff white cotton with imitation rubies and sapphires sprinkled across the front, and was immediately beseiged by half a dozen Egyptian men.

"Buy it," whispered Frances, walking up to her, coming to her rescue. "I speak Arabic. I'll do the bartering for you. George and I used to live in Cairo many years ago."

Frances expertly took over.

"There you are," she said smilingly a few minutes later. "Two English pounds. The cotton is top quality, and the coloured stones are artistically set into the material."

"Thanks Frances," said Liane gratefully. "That was very kind of you."

"Come on, we'll have to hurry to catch up with the others."

Brett and Malik had walked on with the rest of the party, and Liane and Frances walking quickly soon caught up with them. They met at the entrance to the temple, and as they entered through the gates, Ahmed and his brother joined them.

"May I introduce my brother Hassan."

Liane looked at the man. He was standing a few feet from her. He had small eyes and they were cold and dark. There was no emotion in them. Liane saw him for what he was, a man with a killer instinct. A psychopath. He could kill and it would have no effect on him whatsoever, like a normal person killing a fly.

Brett was speaking to him; Liane had to look away. She could not bear to look at the man. He made her feel sick. She could never forget he had tried to kill them.

Hassan moved away and Ahmed started talking to Brett. Brett was frowning.

"Come, follow me," came Malik's voice.

They were now standing in the Temple of Horus built around an inner courtyard surrounded by a colonnade. They followed Malik into a bare room of stone walls leading off the courtyard.

Gathering the party around her, she began:

"This room was a chapel dedicated to Osiris. He was a god-king, and married to Isis. She bore him a son, Horus, to whom this temple is dedicated..."

Liane turned her head to look at a carving on the walls and instead met the eyes of Ahmed, dark and flirtatious, his face creasing into a big smile. He moved across to her, and standing close whispered:

"Do not worry about Hassan. I have told you I have taken the gun from him. He cannot do any harm."

"I find that hard to believe,'t' Liane retorted quickly, looking across at the lone figure of Hassan standing on the edge of the group. Just looking at him made her blood run cold.

Ahmed smiled at her. "Let us talk about something more interesting. I saw you buy the kaftan. You are going to be beautiful

Egyptian woman when you come to Cairo!"

"Ahmed, let's get this straight. I am not going to Cairo," said Liane firmly, giving him a cold, steady gaze, moving a pace away from him.

Why did he have to stand so close? Why did he have to look into her eyes with such intimacy? She had neither done nor said anything to encourage such behaviour. He would not behave like this with an Egyptian girl.

She knew the answer. Western women have a reputation for being sexually promiscuous. Particularly if they travel alone, and she had made the mistake of telling him Brett was not her husband or fiance. She looked around the group. Hassan seemed to have disappeared.

"Where is Hassan?"

Ahmed shrugged his shoulders. "I do not know or care. Let us talk about us. You will change your mind and come to Cairo," he said in a tone of utter confidence. "I am a wealthy man. I have big apartment in Cairo."

"What are you trying to do? Buy me?"

There was a mischievous smile playing about his lips as he turned and moved across to George.

Ahmed was rapidly becoming one of the most popular members of the tour party thought Liane with disdain. She decided that in future she was going to ignore this persistent, amorous Egyptian next time he spoke to her. She would choose not to hear him, and he could think what he liked. As for his brother Hassan, she would keep well away from him.

Two hours later, back on board the boat Liane and Brett, Ahmed and the Italian family gathered on the sundeck in the bows of the boat, ordered cool drinks, then happily chattered over the morning's events. Hassan had gone to his cabin, much to Liane's intense relief.

Ahmed was a charmer. Polite to the women, considerate in his opinions when talking to the men. Brett, Liane noticed, watched Ahmed with cautious eyes.

The ship's engines started and The Queen of the Nile moved graciously out into midstream, then slowly started moving upriver. The Nile was placid as a millpond. Donkeys and a few cows grazed on the river bank. There were scattered coconut palms, still in the windless air. Bare rocky mountains in the background. It was hot.

One by one the passengers drifted down to the restaurant until only Liane and Brett were left. Liane lay down upon a sunbed. Brett lay down on the adjoining one.

"Not going down for lunch?" asked Brett, turning to lie on his back.

"In a few minutes," Liane replied sleepily. "There's no hurry."

There was a wail of Arab music from the radio in the lounge. Brett sat up, took off his jacket, followed by his shirt, and now revealed a very masculine chest of black hair. There was no mistaking the fact, Brett was a very attractive male. And a passionate one from the way he kissed.

Liane closed her eyes for a few minutes, then opened them again. She couldn't help taking another furtive glance at that sleek, smooth, suntanned body. Then Brett turned and their eyes met. Liane looked away, suddenly selfconscious, guilty, as though she had been doing something that she shouldn't. What was the matter with her? Was it the heat?

Brett stood up and put on his shirt.

"I'm hungry. Let's go and have something to eat."

"Brett, I have to say it, although it is none of my business, but why don't you hand your shirt in to the laundry."

"For the simple reason it only operates during the day and I would have to be bare chested in the dining room. The boat manager asks for informal but smart appearance. That doesn't include a bare chest. Didn't you see the notice in reception?"

"I'll wash it for you tonight, hang it up in my shower room and tomorrow morning hand you a clean shirt."

"My, the O'Neills are getting friendly. Beware of Greeks bearing gifts."

"Oh shut up Brett. It's just that I don't like walking around with a man in a dirty shirt."

He gave her a hard look. "You like your men in clean shirts. Does the one who phoned you at the Luxor hotel always wear clean shirts?"

The thought of Conal made her feel depressed. "I have no interest in what he does," she retorted sharply. "And I would be obliged if you don't bring the subject up again."

She opened the swing doors and walked into the lounge. Brett followed. He gave her a smug smile.

"Like that, is it?" He looked pleased.

"Yes," Liane replied, her eyes flashing.

When they reached the restaurant George and Frances were still there. Liane and Brett joined them after having helped themselves to the appetising cold dishes set out in the centre of the room.

"This is one of the good parts of the holiday," said Frances. "A complete break from cooking, much as I love it."

Brett and George were talking about European art. They discussed the French Impressionists, and then Brett introduced the subject of the Italian Renaissance.

"Why did the Renaissance start in Italy?" he asked George.

"Because the situation in Italy in the fourteenth century was most favourable." George spoke with a certain amount of relish. It was obvious Brett had got him talking about one of his favourite subjects.

"The presence of rich merchants and bankers," he continued, "made patronage of men of genius possible. The Renaissance reached its height in the sixteenth century under the patronage of Julius II and Leo X with Leonardo da Vinci, Michelangelo, Titian, Raphael,..."

"...and Gorregiani," put in Brett.

He gave Liane a quick look. Liane remained impassive, waiting for George's comments.

George slowly nodded his head thoughtfully. "...and Gorregiani.

Interesting you should mention him. For centuries Gorregiani was a forgotten, unappreciated artist, languishing in the shade of Raphael and Titian. That is until about twenty years ago or so when an American millionaire bought one of his paintings and for the first time Gorregiani came into prominence. People suddenly started to notice him, and the price started to climb.

Very gradual at first, then in the last few years it has escalated. In fact I heard that one of his paintings was sold at auction in New York last month for half a million dollars!"

Liane looked at Brett in stunned silence. There was nothing to say, not there in front of George and Frances.

Suddenly Liane looked up. Ahmed had just entered the restaurant, and she felt herself tense up in sheer anger as he walked slowly towards their table, his dark eyes caressing her, a smile on his lips.

CHAPTER 7

"Ahmed!"

George indicated the empty chair next to him.

"We were just discussing Gorregiani," he continued, "a most sought after painter at the present time. Not many of his paintings about unfortunately, and those that are, are fetching a very high price indeed."

Ahmed sat down and appeared completely unconcerned, his face a mask of indifference. Liane stared unhappily at him. He had told her it was worth 50,000 dollars.

He was both a liar and a cheat.

"I was on the trail of a Gorregiani," he said in a light voice, "but unfortunately the sellers backed off."

Then he turned his head in Liane and Brett's direction, giving them a playful smile. Brett glowered at him, Liane gave him an angry look. Then shrugging his shoulders Ahmed continued: "That is my life. Sometimes I win the battle, sometimes I lose it. My fate is in the hands of Allah."

"Are you an art dealer?" asked Frances, giving him a curious stare.

Ahmed laughed. "For thousands of years my family were tomb robbers, then this century they became respectable and are now art dealers."

"What do you specialise in?" asked George.

"We have just started a line in Christian church art. I have recently been to Sicily negotiating a deal.

"I hope you offered them a fair price," said Brett, a harsh tone in his voice.

Ahmed's dark eyes gave Brett a steady look.

"Always I offer a fair price my friend."

There was an uncomfortable silence for a moment.

"Art dealing is a difficult occupation," said George. "When someone I don't know comes in to sell, I must always insist on proof of ownership. I remember once buying an item and found the police on my tail."

"Never had that experience Ahmed?" Brett couldn't help chipping in, an ironic smile on his lips.

"What is your occupation Mr McMahon?" asked Ahmed suddenly in a quiet voice.

"I'm a writer," Brett answered promptly.

"That occupation will have problems. You must be careful not to slander people's character either directly or by insinuation. You could be taken to court."

Frances tactfully changed the subject. "Coming to the Kom Ombo Temple this afternoon?" she asked looking round the table.

"Yes, we're coming," Liane answered. "I'm getting hooked on Egyptology. Never thought I would."

Frances stood up. "George, let's go up to the sun deck. Coming Liane?"

"I'll follow in a moment Frances."

Frances and George left the restaurant, Liane continued sitting uneasily between Brett and Ahmed. Never could she leave these two men alone, not whilst Brett remained in this aggressive mood.

"Until a few moments ago," said Brett, giving Ahmed a look of accusation, "We didn't know the true value of a Gorregiani."

"Yes, the market has taken an upward swing," came Ahmed's smooth, unruffled reply.

"I'll say it's taken an upward swing," came Brett's sharp retort. "No doubt you knew all about last month's auction in New York."

"I did not know about it," protested Ahmed. "Mr McMahon, I say you must believe me. I do not read American or European newspapers."

"I don't believe a word you are saying Ahmed. You knew the true value and you were out to cheat Liane."

The tension grew minute by minute. There was a new harshness in Brett's voice, combined with the clenching and unclenching of his fists. Any moment she felt a fight could break out. At length she could stand it no longer.

"Brett," Liane gave him a warning look. "Give it a break. What does it matter whether Ahmed was trying to cheat me or not. We would never do a deal. Let's go up on the sundeck. See how near we are to the next village."

Relieved she watched Brett rise to his feet.

"Coming Ahmed?" he asked. "We'll call a truce for the time being."

Ahmed shook his head. "No. I will remain here," he replied in a stiff injured tone.

Liane and Brett left the room.

"I don't think it wise to antagonise Ahmed," she told Brett the moment they were through the swing doors.

"That runt?" exploded Brett. "If he tried anything... Personally I think you should be worrying about the brother. Can you believe Ahmed when he said he has taken the gun from him? Where did he put it for safety?"

"Perhaps he threw it overboard. Look Brett, I don't know, but I know this for sure. We're all trapped together on this small boat. There's no escape, not even when we visit a temple.

So keep the tension to the minimum. If things get out of hand, I'm sure the mentally unstable brother would not be able to control himself. Someone might get hurt. I hate trouble."

Brett gave Liane a slow smile. "That's rich coming from you. I thought trouble was your speciality."

"Stop it Brett. We've got a serious situation on our hands." Then lowering her voice to a whisper continued: "I've got half a million dollars worth of painting under the mattress. How do you think I'm going to sleep tonight?"

"If you're nervous I could keep you company," said Brett, giving her a sly look, a smile playing about his lips.

The thought of Brett in the other twin bed, to her surprise gave her a rise in temperature.

"Brett, I want you to be serious."

"I am being serious."

They had now reached the sundeck, and selecting two sunbeds

Dance Amongst Thorns

close together in a shaded spot, they took two white towels from the deck cupboard, spread them over the sunbeds, then lay down upon them. From the radio in the lounge came the soft sound of a never ending Arab melody.

The long, hot afternoon stretched ahead, the peace of which was shattered whenever their ship past another, and each vessel sounded its klaxon. On the margins of the Nile coconut palms grew in thick clumps. After a while they ceased, and the land was taken over entirely by sugar plantations.

Looking at Brett still gave Liane that curious warm feeling. He had stripped to the waist revealing his musular sun tanned body. Donning a pair of sunglasses, he turned and looked at her. If circumstances had been different, thought Liane with a sigh, this would have been a cruise to remember.

"Liane."

"Yes Brett."

"I have been thinking about the painting. It was entrusted to you, so you make the final decision. But I advise you to return it to the priest at Luxor. It is obvious he hasn't the faintest idea of its value. He may wish to sell it and give the money to the poor, or whatever cause he thinks fit, and perhaps keep part of it for his retirement. I presume priests do retire. Anyway, I feel he should be given the opportunity to make the decision."

Liane paused a moment thoughtfully.

"I think that is a good idea. And I think Ahmed should be told our intentions. Who's going to do it, you or me?"

"I'll do it. You may overdo the friendly approach," he added giving Liane a wicked grin.

"Why, may I ask, are you so interested in my relationship with Ahmed?" She gave him a teasing look. "When we leave Egypt I doubt if you and I will ever meet again. Once you have sold Tavanomore, you will no doubt return to the States. As for myself, I will finish my contract at the Priory, and go back to London. After that I could work for years in the London area and never return to Ireland."

Brett got off his sunbed and stood at Liane's side, gazing down at

72

her.

"You'll be surprised how strange life works out. I, for example never thought I would meet an O'Neill, let alone be on a Nile cruise with one."

Liane stared back at him. "I don't think of myself doing a Nile cruise with you. Stage struck Maria gets a lot of your attention."

"Jealous?"

"How could I be jealous?"

Taking her by the hands he pulled her to her feet and held her close to him. "Yesterday I made an insulting remark. I wish to apologise."

Liane looked puzzled. "What insult?"

"I apologise for kissing you and said I must have had too much to drink. You're kissable anytime."

Liane could feel her face grow hot as Brett's lips hovered close to her own.

He gave her a thoughtful look then relinquished her hands.

"Wrong time, wrong place," he murmured, then walked across the deck and leaned against the rail.

Liane walked across and joined him. "You could say that."

Then there was a long silence between them.

"Brett," Liane leaned on the rail next to him. "Go ahead and tell Ahmed our plans, then he knows nobody is going to make any money out of the painting except of course Father O'Brien. If he has any sense of decency that should get him off our backs."

"I'll do it, but you're expecting a lot."

At that moment a dusty looking flat roofed town came into view round the bend of the river.

"Can you see the ruined temple on the promontory?" asked Brett as he gazed down the river.

"Yes I can," said Liane, shading her eyes with her hands. "Kom Ombo, the temple dedicated to the God of the Morning Sun and the Crocodile God. Crocodiles were worshipped and fed on the richest food."

Brett laughed. "I can see you've been reading your guide book. Pity they still haven't got the crocodiles. I'd like to give them a change of diet."

"That was a wicked thought!"

"If Ahmed goes to the temple," Brett continued, "And provided I can get him away from George and Frances for a moment. I'll speak to him there."

An hour later the boat docked, then they were scrambling up the embankment, negotiating their way through a mêlée of battered lorries and Arabs on donkeys.

Inside the ruined temple, Malik gathered the members of her tour party together.

"This temple was built in the Ptolemaic-Roman period," she told them, "And is dedicated to two divinities..."

Ten minutes later they were in another part of the temple. Malik waved her arms. "Here sacred crocodiles used to bask in the sun..."

Brett saw his opportunity and walked across to Ahmed. Ahmed was examining carvings on the walls.

"I always find it hard to believe," he said as Brett approached, "But here are modern looking medical instruments."

"Your brother not interested?"

Ahmed shook his head. "He is in his cabin."

"Ahmed," Brett spoke in a low voice. "Liane is going to return the painting to the priest at Luxor so nobody is going to make a fortune, except possibly the church."

"I understand," he replied, in a slow calm voice, much to Brett's astonishment. "You are Christians."

"I thought you would be displeased. You were very keen to buy."

Ahmed shrugged his shoulders. "Everything has changed. I have new plans."

"If you wish to see the mummmified crocodiles," came Malik's voice, "Please follow me."

"Interested?" Brett asked Ahmed as Liane joined them.

They both shook their heads.

"Let's start the trek back to the boat," Brett suggested. "And we'd like to hear about your new plans Ahmed. Where are you off to next?"

"The Yemen," Ahmed replied, as they walked along the unmade lane, beseiged at every turn by sellers of alabaster cats, gold embossed slippers, and necklaces made of green granite. "I am on to something big."

Brett and Liane exchanged looks of surprise.

"It is a Christian statue of Mary Magdalene; fourth century. And she is holding a baby in her arms. It is not widely known that Mary Magdalene had a baby."

Brett and Liane now exchanged looks of astonishment.

"Worth a lot?" asked Brett wryly.

"A king's ransom," was the reply. "I will take it to America and make my fortune. I must now say goodbye to you. I have relations in this town and they would be offended if I did not pay them a visit. If you see Hassan tell him where I have gone. I will see you later this evening."

"Watch the time. I wouldn't like to see you miss the boat," called Brett as Ahmed walked towards a small house set back from the lane.

"Thank you my friend."

Brett turned to Liane as they continued walking along the embankment lane. "You guessed of course I was lying."

"I sure did," smiled Liane.

When they reached The Queen of the Nile, they climbed down the stony embankment, onto the gangway, and stepped on board.

In a corner of the lounge a group of waiters were chanting an Arab song, and clapping their hands in rhythm to a drum beat.

The chanting was reaching a crescendo.

"Come down to my cabin and I'll wash your shirt," suggested Liane suddenly. "I'm not very keen on Arab music. I'll dry it in the sun and you'll be able to wear it this evening."

"Why so solicitous all of a sudden?" Brett asked, an amused look on his face as he followed Liane from the lounge.

"Take your shirt off," Liane instructed, as they entered her cabin and walked through to the shower room. Liane filled the washbasin with warm soapy water.

Brett took off his shirt and handed it to Liane. She plunged it into the water and commenced rubbing. Brett stood watching her.

"You'll make someone a good wife one day," his voice was soft, almost self conscious, as he watched her rubbing the soiled material.

"If I find the right man," she laughed, but the laugh was bitter and

75

she hadn't meant it to be. She could feel Brett staring at her, questioningly.

"What do you make of the statue Ahmed is after?" she asked quickly, changing the subject. "It sounds crazy to me. Mary Magdalene and a baby! I never heard such nonsense."

"Someone has been pulling Ahmed's leg. And I suggest you tell the Priory Films Division to avoid the Yemen for the next couple of years at least. I presume you don't wish to bump into our friend again or his brother."

At the mention of the film company Liane paused and a worried expression marred her face.

"Ian will have engaged another continuity girl by now. He has to do the interiors and the studio space was already booked. He can't hold up the shooting because I've disappeared."

"My agent in New York will be a worried man. I'm supposed to be there right now to sign a contract. Both our careers are on hold."

Liane shrugged her shoulders. "There's nothing we can do," she said sadly, as she rinsed Brett's shirt, and wrung it out.

"Do you know what I do when I'm waiting for a film job? "

Brett shook his head.

"Temping for a secretarial agency. I can't tell you the boredom of it and the poor pay."

Liane pulled a face, remembering.

Suddenly Brett placed his hand on her arm. "There is something we can do. There is a painting in this room worth around half a million dollars, and you're worrying about losing your job. With that money we could start our own film company. Or better still we could buy the Priory Theatre and films division. There's a rumour about financial problems."

Liane gave Brett an amused smile. "Did I hear 'we'?"

Brett gave a sheepish grin. "All right, slip of the tongue. You could buy the Priory, and engage me as your writer/director. Liane, I've always wanted to direct my own scripts. Look what happens. I write a script, hand it over, the director makes changes as he thinks fit and there is nothing I can do about it."

Liane considered this for a moment. "And what do I do, besides provide the money?"

"We could set up a business partnership."

Liane looked at him feeling slightly dazed. "A partnership, between you and me?"

"It's not such a bad idea," Brett replied enthusiastically. "And Liane, if you have your own company you can do anything you want."

"I would like to be a script writer. Actually a few months ago I wrote a screenplay and one of the top London agents liked it and is trying to find a producer."

"You could produce it yourself!"

Liane walked out of the shower room holding Brett's wet shirt. "Hold it! I like your ideas but you're going to fast for me. Haven't you forgotten we have agreed to give the painting back to Father O'Brien?"

"What about going equal on the money with the priest? I think that's fair."

"The most important thing right now," she paused and smiled, "Is getting your shirt dry otherwise you won't be allowed in the restaurant tonight. Let's get our priorities right. Sorry to be so practical. I think the sundeck is the best place,"she continued, "It will dry quicker up there."

Brett laughed. "I need someone like you around."

They left Liane's cabin and walked the few paces to the door of Brett's cabin.

"I think the boat manager is being unreasonable," pronounced Liane. "You can be half naked on the sundeck, but in the restaurant or lounge, smart informal is the order of the day.

"Brett smiled. "Whatever happens, you must be correctly dressed. It's a hangover from the British in India in the nineteenth century. I think I'll give the sundeck a miss if you don't mind Liane. I want to do some writing in my cabin."

"Stage or film?"

"Can be both."

"I'll let you know as soon as your shirt is dry."

Brett inserted the key in his door and gave a sigh.

"Tonight I have to finalise a meeting place with Maria. She's now coming to New York next month. How did I ever get into this?"

"Familiar situation?" she asked unsmilingly. "Stage struck beauties, beseiging you at every turn."

Liane went up to the sundeck. She spread the shirt out in the hot sun on a sunbed. It should be dry in about thirty minutes she thought as she lay down upon the sunbed next to it.

Maria, the Italian beauty was languishing on a sunbed not far away, and gave a limp wave, pouting her lovely crimson mouth, her ample bosom barely covered. Liane gave a faint smile in return.

As she closed her eyes in the sleepy heat Brett danced before her eyes. What a strange meeting she had just had with him. And what he had just suggested was a dream. It could never be anything more.

A business partnership between an O'Neill and a McMahon! It would make her father turn in his grave. But imagine buying the Priory Theatre and films division, she thought, a smile upon her lips. It was heady!

Then the guilt set in, hard and strong. Her father had taught her to hate the very name McMahon, the name that was synonymous with cheating.

Yet without Brett's protection, Ahmed's attraction towards the blonde Nordic type, would not have been kept under control. She had heard of women travelling alone in Arab countries and the stories they had told were of unbearable sexual harassment.

"Liane!" It was Frances' voice.

Liane opened her eyes. "Hi Frances. How did you like the stuffed crocodiles?"

"Horrible," she shuddered. "I've always disliked crocodiles. I just met Ahmed. He's giving a party when we get back to Luxor. I can't think why. It's no one's birthday. Still I suppose you can have a party for no reason at all."

Liane looked at her surprised. Ahmed did not strike her as the kind of person who gave parties for no reason at all.

"Who's invited?"

"You and Brett definitely," she replied eagerly. "I saw your names at the top of his list."

CHAPTER 8

The thought of socialising with Ahmed and Hassan, Liane presumed his brother would also be there, filled her with nothing but fear.

"I'm sorry Frances but I definitely can't go. When I get back to Luxor my top priority is going to be getting back to Dublin. As for Brett, I doubt if he will be able to come."

"I am disappointed," Frances gave her a soft smile, then glanced quickly at her watch. "I'll have to go, I've made an appointment at the hairdressers."

Frances left the sundeck and Liane, picking up Brett's shirt which was now completely dry, took it down to his cabin.

When Brett opened his cabin door he looked a worried man.

"Here's your shirt, clean and dry," said Liane, placing it on the bed. "I'm afraid the service does not include ironing. What are you writing?"

"I'm trying to get a plot for a play. Just tossing ideas around. I'm interested in Nefertiti, one of the most beautiful queens in ancient Egypt. You should see the sculpture of her in the Cairo Museum."

"I've seen a photograph of it," Liane replied, sitting on the other bed, "And she is one of the most beautiful women I have ever seen. You look worried. What's your problem?"

"She was the wife of Akhenaton. He was madly in love with her. Yet somewhere around his twelfth year as pharoah, Nefertiti packed up and left him. I'm having trouble trying to
work out why she went. The marriage seemed idyllic."

"Brett you can forget ancient Egypt, there's enough happening on this boat to write a couple of contemporary plays."

Brett gave a faint smile. "What's the latest?"

"Ahmed has invited us to the party he is going to give when we all get back to Luxor. I don't like it at all. I told Frances I couldn't go and doubtful about you."

Brett frowned and shook his head. "I'm not interested. I can't hang around Luxor for a party. I've got to get to New York."

He picked up his shirt and commenced to put it on.

"Thanks Liane. You've done a good job. You don't completely hate my guts?"

He gave her a quizzical smile, then as she turned away, he caught her by the waist, and drew her to him.

"You and I need to talk."

"We don't," replied Liane, eyeing him defiantly.

"I disagree."

Then suddenly his hands rnoved down to her thighs, she could feel them hot beneath her thin cotton skirt, and as he held her close, his lips gently caressed hers.

For a few seconds she allowed herself the pleasure of enjoying his lovemaking, then her brain still ruling her heart, she removed his hands and took a step back.

"Don't!" she said softly. Suddenly she felt near to tears.

"You're afraid of me." As he spoke his eyes caressed her anguished face.

Yes, she was afraid. She was afraid of falling in love, but more than that she was afraid of rejection. She couldn't go through that again, not in a thousand years.

"I suppose I am," she said softly looking away. "I had a hard time with someone in London. Put me off men I can tell you," she added bitterly.

"I thought your attitude towards me was in connection with my inheritance," he said, a note of relief in his voice.

"That as well."

His arms enveloped her, as he looked intently into her eyes.

"Liane," he said softly, his voice full of emotion. "Let's talk about it."

"Brett, don't you think we should be discussing more immediate problems."

Brett smiled. "Such as?"

"The painting. Ahmed has told us I have a Gorregiani, but after

80

that nonsense he gave us about Mary Magdalene, I feel I need an expert opinion."

"When did you last check it is still beneath the mattress?"

"Yesterday."

"Don't you think we should go and make sure?"

"If you insist."

They left Brett's cabin, and went next door to Liane's.

After firmly closing her door and locking it, Liane walked across to the other bed, pulled back the covers, and lifted the mattress.

It was still there!

"Brett, I've given this matter a great deal of thought, and I've decided I must show it to George. He's a reputable London antique dealer. He knows a fair amount about paintings. I'm sure I've seen his place in Albemarle Street. It is important to have an expert opinion."

"Why are you so concerned?"

"Well, we would look silly, if we return it to Father O'Brien, telling him it's worth a fortune, and actually it's just some unknown painter worth very little."

Brett shrugged his shoulders. "Go ahead. He's the only one on this boat I would trust."

Just then there was a knock at the door.

Liane opened it; George was standing there.

"George, just the person we want to see."

"Have you seen Frances?" he asked, frowning a little, as he entered the cabin. "Been looking for her everywhere. There's a trip to Abu Simbel. I want to know if she's interested."

"She's at the hairdressers," smiled Liane. "I expect she forgot to tell you. George, I wonder if you would do us a favour."

"You only have to ask," he beamed at them amiably.

"Well, an unusual situation has developed, and to cut a long story short, I have acquired a painting. I have been told it is a Gorregiani. Will you confirm it?"

Liane pulled back the mattress, brought out the picture, and handed it to George who scrutinized it carefully for several minutes, then examined the back.

"I'd say it is a Gorregiani" he said slowly, placing the painting on the bed. "I saw one in Italy a few years ago. All his madonnas have that same whimsical smile. Sometimes he signed his paintings, sometimes he did not. This is one he honoured with his signature. See that indecipherable swiggle in the corner?"

Liane smiled with relief. "I have been wondering what that was."

"Actually it's not really my line, so I advise you to get the opinion of an expert on sixteenth century Italian," he continued, "Having said that, I'm sure I am right. You develop a instinct about these things. How did you get hold of it by the way?" He turned to Liane, a puzzled look on his face.

"It was given to me by the priest at the church in Luxor..." Liane began, then Brett butted in:

"George," Brett looked anxious. "I would be pleased if you did not mention this matter to anyone."

"Of course, you can rely on me. Discretion is the keynote of my business. Well, I'll go and see if Frances is through at the hairdressers. I didn't even know there was one on the boat."

George left the cabin, and Liane returned the painting to its hiding place under the mattress.

"Hungry?" asked Brett.

"I'll say I am."

"I'm not sure you should have mentioned the painting," commented Brett as they entered the restaurant.

"He said he wouldn't tell anyone," returned Liane. "I'm sure it will be all right. Anyway, I'm satisfied it really is a Gorregiani."

Liane and Brett took their seats at their usual table.

"Actually now that I know it is a genuine Gorregiani, I'm more worried than ever."

George and Frances joined them a few moments later, Frances' hair now transformed by large sausage curls. She looked embarrassed.

"I had difficulty in explaining what I wanted," she told Liane as she sat down. "Still he was very nice and gave me a marvellous head massage."

"I hear we are going to be entertained by Nubian dancers after dinner," announced George as the Italian family joined them, greeting everyone profusely, especially Maria, pouting her full lips at Brett.

Liane was beginning to feel weary of Maria, and definitely did not like the idea of Brett meeting her in New York, even though it would be a business matter, and papa would be present. She knew Maria would use Brett mercilessly.

"Where's Ahmed?" asked Frances, looking around.

"He's visiting relations at Kom Ombo," Liane told her.

"It's so nice making friends with people of the country," Frances told everyone. "It's so common to go abroad and only meet other tourists."

Half way through dinner Ahmed arrived, with his brother Hassan, then to Liane's embarrassment, the two of them approached their table.

"May we have the honour of joining you?" Ahmed asked bowing in an obsequious manner.

"By all means," replied George waving his hand at them.

They sat down on the two empty chairs nearest Liane. Her heart sank. It was going to be a terrible meal.

Then Hassan turned and stared at her. There was a look in his eyes that made her blood run cold.

He was the aggressive male, menacing, waiting to pounce. She turned her head, averting his glance, and joined in a conversation with George and Frances.

A few minutes later Ahmed turned to Liane.

"I would like to tell you a story from our ancient history. May I?"

Liane smiled and shrugged her shoulders. "If you must."

"Long ago male and female were united in one person," began Ahmed, "Then one day a mischievous god separated them. Ever since men and women have wandered the earth looking for their other half. A charming story, don't you think?"

Liane smiled. "Have you found your other half?"

"Yes," said Ahmed giving her a besotted look.

Sorry she had spoken Liane looked across the table appealingly to Brett, but at that moment the Nubian dancers arrived, and suddenly all attention was on them.

There were three men and one girl, all black, and bare footed.
The drums beat out the rhythm as the dancers spun, stamped their feet, clapped their hands. The rhythm was hypnotic; it went on and on and on.

Suddenly Liane felt Ahmed grip her hand beneath the table cloth.

"Liane, will you marry me?" he whispered.

"I'm sorry Ahmed, the answer is no."

She removed her hand from his grip only for Ahmed to grasp it again. Now there was such intense emotion in nis eyes she had to look away.

"Liane, will you marry me?" he repeated. .

She looked back at him. Pain and anguish was in his face. Perhaps he did genuinely love her, but marriage, never. She removed her hand from his hot damp grip.

"I love you. I must possess you," he whispered. "You must marry me. I will continue asking until you say yes."

There was only one course of action. She had to leave the room.

"I'm sorry Ahmed. I cannot marry you, and that is final."

The Nubian dancers had now finished and were leaving. Liane followed them from the room.

She was just inserting the key into her cabin door when someone called her name. She turned, thank God it was Brett!

"What happened? Was it something I said?" he asked giving her a curious look as he walked up to her.

"Of course not," Liane replied, opening her door. "Ahmed asked me to marry him. I turned him down of course. I had to leave the room. He was getting upset.

A look of fury darkened Brett's eyes.

"That's a new angle. Marry the girl and get the painting. Clever.

"And as for his party in Luxor," Liane shuddered thinking of it. "Never!"

Brett followed her into .the cabin. "Afraid he might make you change your mind?"

"Never."

"Glad to hear it. I reckon Ahmed's harmless, except where women are concerned. He was talking to Maria when I left.

Cutting you out?

Brett grasped her roughly by the shoulders.

"I haven't the slightest interest in what Ahmed and Maria get up to. What do I want anyway with an underage Italian kid? My God, what do you think I am? The one I cannot tolerate is his brother. I wouldn't trust him as far as I could..."

"Do you believe Ahmed when he said he had taken the gun from him?" cut in Liane anxiously.

"Of course he has taken the gun from that maniac."

"Oh Brett, I can't help worrying."

Suddenly Liane stumbled and they both fell on the bed. Brett encircled her in his arms.

"This is the bed that is concealing the masterpiece,"

Liane told him as she struggled to get up. "We don't want to crush it."

They both stood up. Brett looked disappointed.

"Thought it was going to be my lucky night."

"Thought wrong, didn't you?"

Then Brett took her in his arms, and his mouth plunged onto hers with such ferocity Liane was left breathless. As they stood locked in each other's arms, she could feel his urgent need of her. Instantly her whole body started to tremble. She felt hot and light headed.

Suddenly she had a feeling of deja vu, of a summer night with Conal in London. The same intense feeling of passion, of wanting to be loved. Afterwards he had cruelly told her there was someone else.

She pulled away from Brett, her eyes filling with tears.

"No," she whispered. "No. You'd better go."

She moved away from him and went and sat at the dressing table.

"Liane..." he said softly, pleadingly. "If it's about Tavanomore..."

Liane shook her head miserably. "It's nothing to do with Tavanomore ."

"Well, what is it all about?"

Liane remained silent, her tears falling.

"If it isn't Tavanomore," said Brett savagely. "It must be me. You can't bear me to touch you."

Then giving her an angry look, Brett walked quickly from the cabin, slamming the door behind him. Liane flung herself on the bed and gave vent to a burst of sobbing.

She knew then what had happened to her.

She had fallen in love with Brett, the man whose father had cheated her father. The man she had sworn to hate. And suddenly the problems of the previous generation seemed to blur, to cease to be so vitally important. They were another time, another dimension.

She rose from the dressing table and started to undress. Another factor had now loomed in her mind, which seemed to override everything else. Would she ever have the confidence to have a relationship with a man again?

Liane fell into a troubled sleep. Tomorrow this nightmare journey would end and never again would she see Ahmed or Hassan. Later she would say goodbye to Brett. When she thought of Brett she felt her heart would break. Tonight she had hurt him so deeply, the one person who was the most precious to her, and all because he had misunderstood.

CHAPTER 9

The following morning Liane found that breakfast was being served on the swimming pool deck. As she sat down at one of the tables her spirits were low. She was thinking of Brett and the misunderstanding last night. He thought she didn't love him. The truth was the opposite.

A few moments later Brett arrived and sat down opposite her. He looked tired and strained as though he had a burden of problems he could not solve. He gave Liane an ill tempered look.

"You won't be getting any more trouble from Ahmed," he announced to her, a sharp tone in his voice.

Liane gave him a quick, anxious look. "What have you done?"

"I've told him a few facts that should keep him off."

"Thanks," she replied, giving him a puzzled look, wondering what the facts could be.

Then Brett gave Liane a hard look, his voice hostile. "I would like to know exactly what your relationship is with the man who phoned you at the Luxor Hotel."

For a moment Liane was taken aback by the suddenness of the attack, for aggressive was the only way to describe the way Brett had just spoken to her. He looked as though he hadn't slept all night, the lines deep around his eyes. She took a deep breath. Her relationship with Conal was something she never discussed, not even with her mother who could always be relied on to give sympathetic murmurs. But there was something about Brett that morning, a belligerence, an anger, that had to be soothed.

"We were going to get married, until he found someone else." She spoke in a quiet voice, not looking at him, the pain of discussing her humiliation almost unbearable.

"Conal is an actor and in love with himself." An acid tone creeping into her voice. "He is going to marry the daughter of a T.V. producer, and work will be more or less guaranteed, unless he does something stupid like leave her."

There was silence for a moment before Brett spoke.

"Why did he phone you?"

Liane looked up at him, there was suspicion in his eyes.

"Guilty conscience," she replied in a hard voice. "He asked if I was all right and liking my new job. He even invited me to dine with him at the Ritz." She gave a hard laugh. "What a fool I've been. He just used me."

Brett gave a faint sad smile. "You're not the only one."

"Can you talk about it?" she asked softly.

Brett shook his head. "Not now. One day I will."

He looked away, a morose expression on his face. Liane's spirits started to rise. One day he would tell her his past problems. Their relationship had a chance. There was silence for a few moments before Liane spoke.

"Brett, what do you think of the idea of us just buying the films division of the Priory and concentrate on film making. With your scripts and contacts, and the money from the sale of the painting, we couldn't go wrong."

"We could go wrong, but I'd make damn sure we didn't." He gave her a faint smile, then looked past her and waved to someone. Liane turned her head to see who had attracted his attention.

It was Ahmed, the last person she wanted to see. He made a selection at the buffet table then sat down next to Brett, a sheepish expression on his face as he looked across to Liane.

"Thank you for inviting us to your party," Liane spoke in a kindly tone, she now felt sorry for the man. "But I doubt if it will be possible for us to come. When we get back to Luxor we have to catch the first available plane for London."

"I am truly sorry to hear this," said Ahmed solemnly looking at them both.

"Where's your brother?" asked Brett looking around the deck.

Ahmed shrugged his shoulders. "I think my brother still sleeps."

Brett smiled. "Had a late night, did he?" Then changing the subject added, "I suppose you're getting ready for the Yemen?"

Ahmed nodded with a smile.

"I hope you find your statue," commented Liane, trying to sound as though it was the most natural thing in the world to go looking for a Mary Magdalene statue holding a baby in her arms. But immediately Liane had mentioned the statue there was a look of consternation in his eyes.

"I spoke to you in extreme confidence about that matter. Please do not discuss it with anyone."

"Of course," Liane was quick to reply.

"Hoping to make a quick fortune if you find it?" asked Brett, a lightness in his voice, an amused smile on his lips.

"Of course," replied Ahmed sternly. "I have a living to earn. My mother is a widow and I have five sisters to support." Then he relaxed and smiled. "I am always on the lookout for something unique and ancient."

"Anything particular in mind besides the Magdalene?" asked Brett.

Ahmed smiled. "I am interested in Hatshepsut."

"Wasn't she a queen of ancient Egypt?" asked Brett.

Ahmed smiled, proud of his knowledge. "Hatshepsut was one of the great queens of ancient Egypt. She was the daughter of a king and married her half brother Thutmose. He died a few years after the marriage.

Due to the fact that there were no sons from this marriage, and Hatshepsut being a very popular queen, the king of the gods, Amon-Re came forth from the temple one day..."

Ahmed talked for a full half hour on the subject of Hatshepsut until he finally reached the point of the story.

"Now if I could find Hatshepsut's tomb and she would have been buried with all her jewellery and personal possessions, she was an extremely wealthy woman..."

Ahmed stopped and a dreamy look spread across his face.

"You would indeed be a rich man," smiled Brett.

Ahmed raised his hands. "Enough my friend. It is only a dream, but if Allah is willing, one day it may be a reality."

He turned his head and looked across to the east bank of the Nile.

"I do believe we are very near Aswan. Let us go to the prow of the boat and there we will have an excellent view of the approach."

He rose to his feet, so did Brett and Liane, and they followed him through the swing doors, through the lounge, and onto the sundeck in the prow of the boat. It was crowded but they managed to find space at the rail.

"There's Aswan," called Brett, pointing ahead.

In the distance on the left bank a small modern town with blocks of apartments had appeared.

"I must leave you my friends," said Ahmed giving them a gracious half bow. "And awaken my brother."

Ahmed left the sundeck, and Liane and Brett lingered by the rail, watching Aswan draw near.

"What was it all about?" asked Liane, frowning heavily as the boat drew alongside the quay. "That lecture on Hatshepsut. It was all very interesting, but it went on for such a long time. Actually he knows more than Malik."

"It's not surprising," Brett replied, "Considering his ancestors. And perhaps his present day relations are tomb robbers still. When you're in the trade you get to know more than the archaeologists."

People were leaving the sundeck and going down to reception. Liane and Brett followed.

"What do you say to leaving for Luxor in the morning?" suggested Brett suddenly. "And having another day on the boat?"

Liane paused a moment. Suddenly every moment with Brett was precious. Dublin and the Priory Theatre were on another planet.

"Why not?" she smiled. "What's another twenty four hours in a lifetime?"

Brett gave her a soft smile, the skin crinkling round his eyes.

"That's what I like to hear!"

In reception Malik discussed the day's programme with them.

"...and if you are interested in taking a sail in a felucca, they leave this afternoon at two p.m. crossing to the west bank, where you can climb the hill and visit the mausoleum of the late Aga Khan. I do recommend it."

Liane turned to Brett. "I'd like to go. How do you feel about it?"

"Whatever you say," Brett replied amiably.

"Give me two minutes. I must go to my cabin and collect my sunhat."

The moment Liane opened her cabin door she knew something was wrong. The drawers of the dressing table had been pulled out, the wardrobe door was opened, the door leading into the shower room was open. She was certain she had closed them.

Lifting the mattress she checked the painting was still there. It was, her investment for the future, and Brett's.

They left the boat a few minutes later, having decided to spend the morning exploring Aswan. And as they walked along the road bordering the Nile, Liane could feel a new closeness developing between them.

It was the softness in Brett's voice when he spoke to her, the relaxed expression on his face. They were going to be business partners, but what of their personal relationship? Fear of rejection still lurked at the edge of her mind. The harm that Conal had done was still there.

In the early afternoon they stepped aboard a one sail felucca. They were the only passengers as they glided smoothly and silently across the Nile. There was hardly a breath of wind so that their progress was extremely slow. Sometimes Liane felt they were not moving at all.

When they finally arrived at the opposite bank they past stalls set out with the usual kaftans and a proliferation of alabaster cats, then started the climb up the steep hill to the mausoleum of the late Aga Khan where, removing their shoes, they stood bare footed on the marble floor before the tomb. A single red rose in a glass vase stood on the tomb.

"The Begum has instructed that a fresh red rose is placed in the vase each morning, for the rest of her life," said the Arab guide. "This expresses her undying love."

On the climb down the hillside Brett became unusually quiet. There was a sad expression in his eyes. At the bottom of the hill he paused before a stall selling jewellery.

"I'd like to buy you a necklace."

Brett spoke to the stall owner, who brought out a necklace which he laid out before them.

91

It looked very old and fragile. Made of bone painted black, and gold and ochre. The stall owner spread it out like a piece of lace.

"It's very beautiful~" said Liane, as the old man picked it up and handed it to Brett. Brett secured the necklace around her neck. "Like it?" Liane nodded happily. The bartering began.

It started at one hundred Egyptian pounds, and ended at sixty. The old man wrapped the necklace in a sheet of papyrus paper, Brett paid the old man and they left.

"You have been very generous Brett," said Liane as they approached the shore where the felucca was awaiting them. "I can't thank you enough. I really appreciate it. In fact it is the most beautiful necklace I have ever owned."

As they stepped into the felucca the light was starting to fade; the setting sun casting a wide blood red band at the horizon. They were the only passengers. Liane sat next to Brett, the precious necklace in her bag.

It had been the best day of the cruise, she thought as she felt Brett's arm around her shoulder. Buying her the necklace seemed to symbolise the new relationship between them, strengthening the bond.

Darkness fell, and the slight breeze that had propelled them across in the early part of the afternoon had now dropped completely.

The felucca was becalmed, and they were about half way across the Nile. The Egyptian boat owner sat squatting on his haunches in the stern, and appeared to be either asleep, or in a stupor. Liane and Brett exchanged glances and smiled.

"What do we do now?" asked Liane.

"Stranded in the middle of the Nile with a beautiful woman? We could stay here all night for all I care."

Suddenly she felt his warm lips brush against her own, and instantly she returned the kiss, her eyes closed, feeling Brett's hand tightening on her shoulder.

Suddenly they heard the sound of laughter and the rhythmic dip of oars. Liane opened her eyes to see a felucca looming in the misty darkness behind them. It was moving swiftly, heading on a collision course!

Immediately Brett jumped to his feet, seized hold of the right hand oar, plunged it into the river, and started to propel the boat out of the path of the oncoming felucca. Several minutes later the other boat passed within feet of them.

Disaster had been averted, and to have been plunged into the Nile, so Liane had been told, could mean death or serious illness, for the Nile is one of the most poisonous rivers in the world.

The shouts from the passengers on the other felucca awoke the boat owner, who with a cry sprang to his feet, grasped the other oar and the two men started rowing in unison, following in its wake.

Liane sat there in the prow, giving silent thanks to Brett. They were safe; she could breath once more. The physical danger had passed, and suddenly an extraordinary change took place in her. A strength seemed to be gathering within her. It was like emerging from a dark tunnel.

She wasn't afraid of rejection anymore! That was being afraid of life, of living, and she wanted to live it to the full.

She looked across at Brett, love soaring in her heart as she watched his strong, muscular arms pulling on the oars. It was a moment she knew she would always cherish. And as the twinkling lights of The Queen of the Nile emerged from the dark night, lighting their way ahead, she felt a new person, filled with a total sense of utter contentment. Half an hour later they boarded the cruise boat.

"Thank you Brett," Liane said simply.

"What are you thanking me for?" Brett gave her a playful smile.

"Preventing the felucca from capsizing."

"That is nothing compared with what I am prepared to do for you." He glanced at his watch. "We're late for dinner..."

At that moment Maria hurried past.

"You were such a long time returning in the felucca we wondered if anything had gone wrong?" she asked smilingly.

"On the contrary," said Brett, turning to Liane with a soft look of love in his eyes.

Did he feel the same, thought Liane wonderingly, that something had happened to them?

Suddenly she caught sight of her dishevelled self in a mirror.

"I'll see you in the restaurant. I must tidy up and comb my hair. I look terrible."

"Not to me you don't," smiled Brett.

Brett went up the stairs to the restaurant whilst Liane left the deserted reception area and hurried away down the corridor to her cabin. She was actually humming a tune as she inserted the key into the lock, turned the knob and entered the cabin, closing the door behind her. Then she stopped, horrified, frozen to the spot.

The room was in a state of total disarray, bedspreads and blankets on the floor, the contents of her makeup bag spread across the bed.

Hassan was standing between the beds pointing a gun at her.

CHAPTER 10

"Give me the painting!" demanded Hassan, shaking the gun. "If you do not, I will kill you."

"I haven't got it," Liane lied, her voice hoarse. This is what she had feared, but always when the hideous thought had surfaced she had pushed it away.

"I do not believe you. If you do not give me the painting I will kill you," he repeated.

Now his voice took on a sharp, angry tone. She was irritating him. Liane gazed like someone mesmorised into those small, cruel eyes, then at the barrel of the gun. She knew there would be no mercy.

He released the safety catch. There was a sharp click. She would die, in a foreign land. For what? Half a million dollars. It wasn't worth it.

"It's under the mattress."

She pointed to the bed.

Keeping the gun trained on her, with his left hand he lifted the mattress and pulled out the cotton bag containing the painting. She was choking with unsobbed tears.

Liane took a step forward.

"Do not move. I may still kill you yet. Give me your key."

It was still in her hand. Slowly Liane extended her trembling hand and gave it to him. She felt sick.

"I am going to lock you in this cabin. If you shout, no one will hear you. They are all in the restaurant."

And with that, he left the cabin, locking the door behind him. Immediately she rushed to it, and hammered on the door.

"Help! Help!" she cried repeatedly.

But no one came. Hassan was right, everyone was in the restaurant. If only she had asked Brett to wait for her in reception. He would have seen Hassan leaving her cabin with the painting in her cotton bag, heard her shouts.

She banged on the door until her arms ached, then wearily she went and sat on the bed. She had never felt so angry and frustrated.

The telephone! Why hadn't she thought of it before? Lifting the receiver she waited for the reception clerk to answer. There was no reply. He obviously was also at dinner. Then she dialled the boat manager's extension. After the phone rang for several minutes, he answered it.

"The manager speaking. May I help you?"

"I'm locked in my cabin," Liane stormed down the phone, "And Hassan Shawki has stolen a painting from me. He has a gun."

"What is your cabin number?"

"102," Liane replied.

"I will free you as quickly as possible madame."

Liane sat on the bed waiting, a feeling of hopelessness engulfing her. Her dreams and well as Brett's, had dissolved. It was almost as if they had never happened.

She was back to the beginning. Little money in the bank, penny pinching, and worrying about the mortgage on her apartment. Now there would be no business partnership, no working together. No money to give to Father O'Brien.

It was all finished. It was all so cruel, she thought dejectedly, as she heard someone inserting a key in the lock and the door opened.

It was the boat manager, accompanied by Brett. At the sight of him Liane rushed into his arms, tears were very near.

"Hassan had a gun. He said he would kill me. He took the painting."

Brett gently stroked her head.

"I had to give it to him."

"There was nothing else you could do," Brett told her. "I couldn't understand what was taking you so long. I was on my way here when I met the manager on the stairs. He told me what had happened."

"Was the painting valuable?" asked the manager.

Liane nodded. "Estimated value - half a million dollars."

There was a look of consternation on the manager's face.

"And you kept it in this cabin. That was a foolhardy thing to do," he rebuked.

"But I asked the reception clerk if you could take it. And he told me your safe would only take small items like jewellery."

"You should have come straight to me."

"It's too late now, telling me what I should have done. I suppose Ahmed and Hassan are on the bus or train back to Luxor now?"

"The police must be informed immediately," the manager continued, "Unfortunately the captain's radio phone has developed a fault, and will not be repaired until the morning."

"Then we'll go to the police by taxi," Brett moved towards the door. "Coming Liane?"

"I cannot tell you how sorry I am to hear of this trouble," said the manager with obvious sincerity. "All my crew, and particularly the cabin boys, are chosen for their high standard of honesty."

"I have no doubt of that, but every man has his price," Brett added cynically.

Brett, Liane, and the boat manager left the cabin and proceeded down the corridor to the reception area.

"All the passengers are still at dinner. I will go up to the restaurant and inform them what has happened. No one, either passengers or crew, will be allowed to leave the boat. We cannot take any risks."

Liane followed Brett along the gangway, then up the steep steps cut into the embankment, the lights of Aswan lighting up the night sky.

They got a taxi immediately.

"Police Headquarters," Brett told the driver.

Liane sat in the back huddled against Brett. She felt cold, bereaved, dazed, and slightly sick.

It was only a short drive and within minutes they were speaking to the Police Superintendent.

"Right now, Ahmed and Hassan Shawki must be on their way to Luxor or Cairo," Liane told him, "En route for America."

Liane and Brett returned to The Queen of the Nile in an escort of three police cars. A total of five police officers boarded the boat where they were greeted by the boat manager, surrounded by a crowd of anxious passengers.

"I have managed many cruise boats and never has such an incident occurred before." The poor man was distraught with worry. He was worrying about his job.

"I have informed everyone," he continued, "That their cabin is going to be searched."

The Superintendent turned to the boat manager. "How many cabins have you on this boat?"

"Fifty for the passengers. Then there are the quarters for the crew."

"That is ten cabins each, plus crew quarters," he said, turning to his police officers.

"This way," called the boat manager.

The search began. At the end of two hours, no painting had been found. After that, they searched the crew's quarters. No painting was found there either. The boat manager looked relieved.

"No painting has been found in either the passengers' cabins or the crew's." The boat manager made the announcement. Then looking across at the clock on the wall he continued: "I would like to remind you that the Nubian dancers will be starting their evening performance in five minutes. Will everyone go to the lounge."

The passengers started to disperse. George walked across to Liane, Brett and the Superintendent.

"You ought to be at Luxor or Cairo airport," he told them brusquely. "The thieves will be making for the States; there's a vast market there for renaissance European art. You should not have been wasting precious time searching this boat."

"Our next step sir, is to alert the airports," replied the Superintendent. Then he turned to Brett and Liane. "Now can you give me a full description of Ahmed and Hassan Shawki?"

Liane and Brett described Ahmed and Hassan as best they could.

When they had finished the Superintendent put his notebook away. "What are your future plans?" he asked.

"We are returning to Luxor in the morning," Brett promptly reply.

"When you arrive in Luxor I advise you to contact Police Headquarters to see if there are any new developments." He shrugged his shoulders. "We can only do our best. It may be too late."

The police left the boat and Brett and Liane went upstairs to the restaurant.

"I know now why Ahmed gave us a lecture on Hatshepsut." Liane spoke with a bitter smile on her lips as they sat down at a table in the corner.

"Keep me out of the cabin whilst brother Hassan picked the lock, or bribed the cabin boy for the key. He was obviously interrupted. Couple of innocents weren't we?"

Brett clenched his fists. "If I ever get my hands on those two again, I won't be accountable for my actions," he said fiercely.

"And to think I said we do the friendly approach," Liane continued. "I think everything Ahmed told us was lies, and the operation had been carefully planned. To think at this moment they are sat on a bus or train, with that precious painting. They must be laughing at us."

Liane felt a lump rise in her throat.

"What we planned to do with that painting." She gave a big sigh. " The money we were going to hand over to Father. It was just day dreaming. It wasn't to be."

"Don't upset yourself Liane."

"And there's no statue of the Mary Magdalene and her baby. We knew that when he told us."

"That was a red herring," said Brett.

"What about the party?"

"That was another one."

"The marriage proposal?"

Brett shook his head. "He just wanted the painting."

"Lambs to the slaughter."

From overhead came the strains of Arab music as the Nubian dancers performed their gyrations in the lounge.

"Brett, I've behaved like a idiot."

Brett's hand closed over hers.

"Me too."

"Why didn't I think of speaking to the boat manager about the painting?" she continued, "Or take up your offer to have it. What a crazy thing I did, hiding it in my cabin under the mattress. If it hadn't been stolen by Hassan, it could easily have been someone else."

Brett kissed her gently on the cheek.

"I'd like your moral support when I break the news to Father O'Brien," she continued, "That I have lost half a million dollars."

Liane looked into Brett's deep blue eyes. "As you have no doubt realised by now, I'm not a super woman."

Brett put his arm around her shoulder.

"Brett, what time is the Luxor bus in the morning?"

"There's one at eight o'clock."

"I think we ought to be on it."

"Like to see the Nubian dancers?"

Liane shook her head. "I think I'll have an early night."

They left the restaurant and went down the stairs.

"The chances are that Ahmed and Hassan caught the bus," said Brett. "Rather than the train. I noticed a bus stop for Luxor just by the quayside. The police will be waiting for them when they arrive at Luxor, just you see. Malik told me the journey Aswan to Luxor takes about four to five hours. The police here will have phoned the Luxor police and the moment they step off the bus, they will be handcuffed. We'll get our painting back."

They were now approaching Liane's cabin door.

"I love your optimistic outlook."

Liane stopped and smiled at him, and there was such warmth in her smile Brett couldn't resist putting his hands around her slim waist.

"I have a feeling you and I have a chance!" he whispered, his mouth close to her hair. "Even though the business partnership is off."

Liane could feel a weakness setting in, that she was close to crossing the Rubicon.

He drew her closer, and she laid her head on his chest. She could feel his heart thumping as fast as her own. It was a heady moment.

"Brett! Liane!"

It was Frances. She hurried towards them down the corridor .

"Sorry to intrude. I just wanted to have a word before I turn in. I take it you will be leaving early in the morning for Luxor."

"We are," said Liane, trying to look pleased to see her.

"I do hope the police catch them. What horrible men! I've just remembered something that might be of use to you. Ahmed told me his uncle keeps the leather shop in the souk at Luxor. They might go there until things die down."

"Thanks Frances. They may very well go there. Don't you think Brett?"

Brett shrugged his shoulders.

"Who knows what they may do. I think we'll call there anyway."

"I'm so sorry about this," Frances continued. "It must be very painful for you both. George and I are leaving early in the morning. We're flying to Abu Simbel, then onto Luxor. Why don't you come with us?"

"That's very kind of you Frances," Liane replied with a smile. "But we have to get back to Luxor as quickly as possible."

"We'll be at the Osiris Hotel. If you're still in Luxor tomorrow night, give me a ring."

Then Frances waved goodbye and hurried off.

"We could go to Abu Simbel if you wanted," said Brett.

Liane shook her head. "I'm not in the mood. Thanks for suggesting it all the same. Goodnight Brett."

"Sure you don't want to watch the Nubian Dancers?"

Liane shook her head. "I'm tired Brett. I need sleep."

The bus journey to Luxor the following day was hot and tiring. Half way they stopped at a shanty village where the focal point of the village was the cafe where men sat smoking hubble bubble pipes. They gazed sullenly at Liane and Brett.

"I suddenly feel very homesick," said Liane.

They returned to the bus and continued their journey, and by the time they reached Luxor, Brett had received a detailed rundown of the last twenty six years of Liane's life. She still knew very little about Brett's life, apart from the fact that he had been to Harvard and had had several plays produced on Broadway and the Priory Theatre.

They booked into the Osiris Hotel. The receptionist was fortunate enough to get them tickets on a flight to London the following day, then they phoned the Police Headquarters in Luxor to discover that there were no new developments in the case. Ahmed and Hassan had disappeared.

They sat down on one of the settees in the large foyer of the hotel. Liane's spirits were low, the efforts of the past week had come to nought. She had failed, and suddenly she felt angry.

"I have to do something," she told Brett, "And I'm not sure what. Got any advice apart from advertising for them in the Luxor Daily News?"

Brett thought for a moment.

"What about visiting the leather shop in the souk? It may be a waste of time, but worth a try."

The leather shop was small and dimly lit, with that strong pungent smell of leather pervading the atmosphere. It was filled with handbags, belts, slippers, jackets, coats, in fact, anything that was made of leather. An elderly man stepped out of the shadows.

"May I help you madame?"

Liane took a deep breath. "Are Hassan and Ahmed Shawki here? We'd like to speak to them." She could feel her knees shaking.

"No madame," the man replied firmly.

There was silence for a moment. Liane had an instinctive feeling that the man was not telling the truth.

"I have not seen them for a long time."

"Well, when you do," cut in Brett, "Will you tell those two crooks that Liane and Brett called. Here's our address for them to contact us."

Brett scribbled the address of the Priory Theatre on a piece of paper and handed it to the man.

The man took it in silence, staring at them, his face a mask.

"I do not understand."

"You speak to Ahmed and Hassan. They will understand."

Then Brett turned and marched out of the shop. Liane followed him.

Oh Brett," Liane spoke in a melancholy voice as they walked through the crowded souk. "That was a waste of time. I'm sorry we went. I feel so upset about the whole wretched business."

Brett slipped his arm around her. "You haven't eaten today, except for that dried up bit of toast at breakfast. When we get back to the hotel we are going to have a good dinner and then decide what we do next."

The meal made Liane feel more cheerful. As the waiter poured them coffee Liane looked across at Brett.

"Let's go to the priest. Tell him what's happened. We have to leave for the airport in the morning and there may not be time."

"You mean now?"

"Yes. It's only half past eight."

At the end of the hotel drive they found a taxi and some fifteen minutes later they were standing before the church. To the left lay the modest priest's house. Slowly they walked across and knocked at the door.

The dreaded moment had arrived when she must tell Father O'Brien that the painting he had given to her, had not only turned out to be extremely valuable, but had been stolen.

CHAPTER 11

The housekeeper showed Liane and Brett into Father O'Brien's study, a small room filled with furniture from the last century. Father certainly looked much better than on their previous visit and was seated writing at a small desk by the window.

As they entered he rose to greet them.

"Liane and Mr McMahon. What a pleasant surprise! Do sit down. Well, as you can see I am feeling very much better. The old malaria attacks once every few years; I always recover, thanks be to God. When we last met I understood you to say you were returning to Dublin that day."

Liane gave an embarrassed smile. "So we should have been, but for an unfortunate incident. Two Egyptians chased us, one fired a shot, we thought we were going to be killed, so we boarded a Nile cruise boat to escape them."

"What a terrible experience. So you have been on a cruise boat for the past week." Then Father O'Brien paused. "I heard on the radio this morning that a valuable painting had been stolen from a cruise boat. It wasn't..."

"It was," put in Brett. "The painting you gave to Liane, stolen at gunpoint from her cabin. Estimated value half a million dollars. We know the man who stole it, and the police are looking for him right now."

Father shook his head. "And I never thought it was the painting I gave to you Liane. What a terrible thing. I didn't know it was so valuable. I bought it in a small town in Northern Italy. It must be thirty years ago. You say half a million dollars. Are you sure?"

"The opinion of a London antique dealer who knew quite a bit about paintings."

"And to think it hung on the church wall for all those years." He paused, a worried expression marred his face.

"I've just remembered, a young Egyptian, well dressed, well spoken, came to see me a couple of times. He wanted to buy the painting, and I told him it wasn't for sale. Could it be the same man?"

"That sounds very much like Ahmed Shawki," said Liane in a hard voice. "It was his brother Hassan who actually stole it."

"And to think that I was putting you at risk. I had no idea..."

"We know you didn't realise how valuable it was," Liane told him. "And we had planned to return it to you."

"That was most generous of you, Liane." Then a faraway look came to his faded blue eyes. "I had a dream that one day I would open clinics to give free medical aid to the poor." He gave a sad smile, "My dreams are too ambitious. I suppose there is no chance of the police finding the painting?"

"They are doing their best," Brett told him as they rose to leave.

"God go with you."

In the taxi returning to the hotel, Brett slipped his arm around Liane.

"I feel the chances of the police recovering the painting are extremely slim. Sorry to be so gloomy."

Liane patted his hand. "I feel the same."

"I think it more likely those two villains are right now at some remote fishing village," Brett continued, "Booking a passage on a fishing vessel in order to leave the country. They couldn't leave through the normal channels, customs would seize the painting immediately."

The taxi had now reached the hotel. Brett paid the driver, they entered the foyer and walked across to the lift.

"Brett," said Liane as they stepped into a lift. "It is possible a miracle might occur and the police do catch Ahmed and Hassan, and of course the painting is recovered intact."

"I don't believe in miracles. Never have, and never will," exclaimed Brett. "By the way, have you got that necklace in your bag?"

"I certainly have. My most valuable possession."

They walked along the corridor and reached Brett's room.

"Come in a moment. I'd like to have a look at it."

Liane followed him into the room. Then Brett switched off the main light and switched on a bedside lamp which sent a soft glow across the room.

"I'm glad you're with me," said Liane watching Brett as he walked across to the refrigerator.

"That's the second time you've said that."

"This time I really mean it."

"I know you do." He turned with two empty glasses in his hands. "Like a drink?"

"Coca cola," Liane replied sitting on the edge of the bed. "It's been quite a day. When we stopped for the break between Aswan and Luxor, I was definitely not happy about those Arabs in the cafe. There was a tension and I felt the slightest incident could have triggered off a situation we might not have been able to cope with."

Brett sat down next to her and handed her a glass of coca cola.

"It didn't happen. My motto is 'worry about it when it does.'"

Then putting his arms around her, he kissed her forehead, her eyes, the tip of her nose, and finally her mouth. It was gentle and tender, and Liane closed her eyes as she felt a warm glow slowly and imperceptively gathering within her.

"I thought you wanted to look at the necklace," she reminded him as she opened her eyes and looked up into his face.

To her surprise there was such intense emotion in his eyes, Liane felt herself stiffen, catching the enormity of his feelings. She looked away. She knew then she should have got up and walked out of the room. But she couldn't move, she just sat there, like someone in a trance, devoid of willpower.

"Sure, and I want to show you something," he replied softly.

He got off the bed and went across to his bag, opened it and brought out a black silk kaftan with long flowing sleeves richly embroideried with gold thread.

"For you," he smiled. "Put it on."

Liane looked at it amazed. It was a costly gown, a far cry from the simple cotton kaftan she had bought.

"When did you buy it?"

"Second day on the boat. When we visited the Temple of Khnum. See, I had my sights on you then."

Flattered, Liane slipped the kaftan over her blouse and skirt, then went and stood before the mirror. She had been transformed. No longer was she Liane O'Neill from a modest apartment block in a London suburb. Now she was a strange glamorous creature.

Going to her bag, she took out the necklace, and Brett standing behind her secured it around her neck. She felt a shiver run through her as he carefully lifted her hair, and his lips touched her neck.

"You look like an Egyptian Queen," he whispered. " I love you Liane. I think I've loved you from the day I first saw you at Carrickballyduff. I know you don't love me." He gave her a teasing smile. "Well, I'm going to make you change your mind."

"But Brett..." she protested. "I - I..."

Brett wasn't listening. He turned her to face him, and his mouth moved slowly from her neck to her lips, kissing her so softly, so sensuously, she started to tremble. Then his mouth moved down to the hollow between her breasts and the pressure increased.

Liane could feel the blood pounding in her veins, her heart thumping rapidly as Brett switched off the light and they were two shadowy figures in the moonlight. Slowly he slipped the kaftan from her shoulders, then the blouse that lay beneath. Then gently he picked her up and laid her on the bed. She knew she should have stopped him, knew she should have said no, but all will power had gone. She looked down at his dark head.

"I do love you Brett, I do..."

Then Brett's mouth moved upwards to hers, his hands gripping her thighs. Then they were two celestial beings, in a celestial world, flying in the Egyptian moonlight.

Next morning Liane awoke early. She turned lazily and contentedly to gaze across at Brett still asleep in the other bed. Had she dreamed the events of last night? No, she had not. There on the floor still lay the black silk and gold kaftan Brett had given last night, and around her neck still lay the Egyptian necklace.

Last night Brett had given her the most exquisite experience of her life. The very thought of it sent a warm tingle rushing through her veins.

Liane got out of bed and opened the shutters. It was going to be another hot day she thought as she looked at a minaret glistening in the early morning sun through a cluster of tall palms.

She and Brett loved each other. Love is the greatest gift one human being can bestow upon another she thought as she went across to the shower room.

A moment later Brett joined her under the shower. An hour later they were in the restaurant.

"What's all the rush?" asked Brett as they sat down at one of the tables.

"I'm hungry~" smiled Liane.

A few minutes later hotel guests who had been passengers on the cruiseboat entered the restaurant. Amongst them were Maria and her parents. The usual conversation started about their forthcoming trip to New York. Brett was looking for conversational escape which he found when George and Frances arrived.

"How did you find Abu Simbel?" asked Brett to George.

"Unforgettable. You should have come..."

Liane found she could now smile happily at Maria.

Frances was sitting next to Liane.

"You've got stars in your eyes this morning," she commented, her eyes giving Liane a knowing look. "Has he asked you to marry him?" she added in a whisper.

Liane looked across at Brett. How she loved him.

"No." she whispered back. "Not yet."

"Well, you see that he does!" Frances continued. "Men want all the pleasures and none of the responsibilities.

They're slippery as eels when it comes to matrimony."

Brett had told her he loved her but had never mentioned marriage, thought Liane as she sipped her coffee. When they reached London this evening, they would say goodbye; Brett would catch a plan for New York whilst she would go on to Dublin.

They had never discussed their future. A small feeling of apprehension started to gather at the edge of her mind with the sudden realisation that there was so little time left. When they had finished breakfast Brett drew Liane to one side.

"I think we ought to phone Ian and tell him what has happened."

They went up to Brett's room and phoned Ian.

"Hello Ian, it's me, Brett. I'm in Luxor at the moment with Liane. Hope you haven't been too worried. We've had quite a time. First Liane acquired a painting worth a fortune. We were shot at by a couple of Egyptian thugs and ended up on a Nile cruiseboat.

Not a happy ending unfortunately, because the two thugs later turned up on the boat, and stole the painting from Liane at gunpoint. Sounds a better plot than the one we shot? I'll say. Tell you the details when we meet. I'm off to the States for a couple of weeks then I'll be back and will contact you. Like to speak to Liane?"

Liane spoke briefly to Ian who was glad to hear she was safe and well, but sorry to hear of her misfortunes.

"We've been very worried about you, even phoned the police," he told her. "Anyway, glad it's all over. Harriet the production secretary took over your job. She did her best; we only had to do one retake. I'll be glad to see you back.t

Liane put down the receiver. "That's a relief, my job's still safe. I was beginning to wonder."

Brett then dialled his estate agent.

"Any news about Tavanomore? That's great. Hold everything until I get back in a couple of weeks."

He put the phone down and turned to Liane with a happy smile on his face.

"That's good news. The agent has received a very good offer for Tavanomore," he said in a cheerful voice. "Now Liane, it's time to pack; don't leave anything behind. It's nearly time to go to the airport."

As Brett opened the wardrobe door to take out his jacket he was humming a tune. Liane picked up the kaftan and went to her room next door, and as she pushed her belongings into her bag she felt strangely cold inside.

It was an unpleasant feeling, the realisation that Brett had suddenly become a stranger, and the close bond that had developed between them in the last few days was slowly disintegrating.

Brett was a happy man! He had been made a good offer for Tavanomore!

And suddenly she knew. She had felt Tavanomore didn't mean

anything anymore. It wasn't true. It still meant a very great deal, deep inside. It was part of her, her rightful inheritance. And but for the fact that grandfather had gone off his head, which she was sure had happened, it would have been her home.

It just needed something to trigger it off, like the news that Brett was going to sell it, for the anger, the deep sense of injustice, to rise to the surface. But what hurt just as much, he hadn't even asked for her opinion. It was as if she counted for so little, discussion was unnecessary.

She spent a long time combing her hair. Combing her hair always soothed her. When she felt she had gained a certain amount of control, she picked up her bag and left the room.

Brett was waiting for her in the corridor. She could not look at him, her anger was so great.

"I thought you were never coming," he said breezily, as they walked down the corridor to the lift. "I've got a feeling you don't want to leave Egypt."

They went down in the crowded lift. She kept her eyes averted from Brett. How could he do it? She was obviously of no importance in his life, her opinion not to be considered. They crossed the hotel foyer and entered the waiting hotel minibus.

Maria and her parents, and Frances and George, were already there. She must speak to Brett, the moment they were alone, tell him how upset she felt, there was no point in bottling it up. But when was she going to get the chance?

At the tiny airport they had to sit an hour in the small departure lounge. On a television screen a video was showing a brief history of ancient Egypt. Brett was talking to George.

She tried to concentrate on 2,700 B.C. and think about life in the Old Kingdom, but unfortunately her new worry about Brett kept winning. At length she gave up and walked across to him.

"Excuse me George, but I must speak to Brett alone."

Brett looked puzzled and walked with her across the room.

"What is wrong?" he asked. "There's been a hostile look in those lovely eyes for the past couple of hours."

"There most certainly is something wrong," Liane replied, a

tightness in her voice she couldn't control. "You care nothing about me. You say you love me, but you have no regard for my feelings whatsoever. You only think of yourself."

Brett looked at her in amazement. "How can you say that?"

"If I have to explain why I'm upset, there is definitely something wrong with our relationship. And to be crude, I think last night was just..."

A voice over the intercom interrupted.

"Will passengers for Flight 355 to London, please board the aircraft."

"Come on, that's us," Brett took her by the arm and propelled her to the exit door for the tarmac. "We'll discuss this matter later."

In the plane George sat between them. Liane feeling emotional exhausted, fell into a light sleep for part of the five and half hour flight, and during the period when she was fully awake, tried to compose what she was going to say to Brett at Heathrow.

Each time she did this, she changed her mind. She loved Brett with all her heart, but now she was sure the love he could offer her would only be of a limited selfish kind. He would always put himself first.

She felt used, and it was an unpleasant feeling.

At Heathrow they left the aircraft, entered the arrival building and collected their luggage.

"Brett, we've got to talk."

Brett turned and looked into her serious, sad face. "You mean right now?"

"Yes. It's about our relationship."

"There's nothing wrong with our relationship," he protested.

Liane gave a wry smile. "I disagree."

"Look Liane, I have to go. I'm going to miss my flight. But when I get back I promise you we'll talk for as long as you want, all through the night if need be. Goodbye Liane."

Then kissing her hard on the mouth, he picked up his bag and walked briskly away. Liane felt her heart was going to break. He was the most insensitive man she had ever met, and that bore ill for the future.

Liane arrived in Dublin around midnight and took a taxi to the hotel near Grafton Street where she had stayed prior to her departure for Egypt.

The following morning she travelled to the studios just outside Dublin where the interior scenes were being shot. There she was welcomed by Ian and the rest of the crew, particularly Harriet, the production secretary.

"Am I glad to see you!" she exclaimed when she saw Liane walk onto the set. "Last week was horrendous. Did you enjoy your trip up the Nile?"

Strange how everyone thought she and Brett had decided to take a holiday. Some even joked it had been a honeymoon trip. Ian was the only one who knew the dangers they had been in.

They were behind schedule so it was a seven day week for the next couple of weeks. There was no letter or phone call from Brett.

Liane concentrated on her work. Work and time are the great healers, she kept telling herself when she had difficulty in getting to sleep, or awoke in the small hours with a deep seated sense of un-happiness.

Finally the day came when the film was completed and everyone departed for a month's break. Liane was in the production office saying goodbye to Harriet when the door opened and Ian hurried in.

"I'm so glad I've caught you Liane. I've had to cancel the script for the next film."He shook his head mournfully. "We won't go into that. It's too depressing for words. Brett's back and I've been talking to him on the phone. I want him to write a new script for me and it's got to be ready in four weeks. He wants you to be his co-writer. You never told me you write scripts."

Liane gave him a faint smile. She couldn't believe what she was hearing.

"You'll be working with Brett in Galway for a week," he continued. You fly there Monday. Where you go after that hasn't been decided. Brett likes to write where the action takes place."

CHAPTER 12

"A warm welcome to Galway!" the smiling stewardess told her passengers as the Aer Lingus Commuter came to a stop on the small runway at Galway Airport.

Liane stood up and took her bag from the overhead shelf. Why had Brett asked for her to be his co-writer? Was it his attempt to try to improve their relationship? He had never seen anything she had written.

Leaving the aircraft Liane walked across the tarmac in the warm sunshine. She had mixed feelings about the whole venture and a strong sense that the next few weeks would prove to be difficult.

As she entered the small airport building, Brett was talking to the man at the hire car desk. He turned and smiled, but it was a weak, indecisive smile, not welcoming at all.

"Hello Liane," He gave her a quick kiss on the cheek. "Good to see you again," he said mechanically.

He sounded weary and depressed, and Liane had the distinct impression his thoughts were far away from Galway.

They left the airport building and crossed to the small car park.

"Wise of you to wear a raincoat," he continued in the same tone of voice. "It's sunny today, but tomorrow it could rain for months. That's Galway weather for you. We've better get moving; I've hired this car."

He stopped before a small Nissan, then taking her bag he put it in the boot.

They set off driving through flat farmland with blue grey mountains in the background, taking the main road to Galway, a small, bustling town filled with American and German visitors, then onto the road for Oughterard.

Liane sat next to Brett in silence finding it difficult to be her usual cheerful self. He definitely had not given her a warm welcome. Had his feelings towards her changed? Had he regretted making her his co-writer, or had something happened in New York?

"You're quiet today Liane," Brett commented as they drove along winding lanes. "Not your usual talkative self. Worried about helping me to write the script?"

"A little. I'm hoping I come up to your expectations."

"Liane, on this script I'm sounding you out. Trying to see what you are capable of. Stop worrying. Changing the subject I've just been to the Aran Islands. There's an Iron Age fort there, built around 500 B.C. Nothing would have changed. There would have been the same love and hate, loyalty and treachery..."

Brett paused giving her a quick glance.

"I have the feeling I'm talking to myself." His voice was suddenly irritable. Ever since I met you at the airport you have been looking like a wet Monday. What is the matter?"

"Something is depressing you, and obviously you can't discuss it with me."

"I have got a problem, and I am not going to burden you with it. If you're thinking I didn't contact you when I was in the States you're mistaken. I did try to phone you. The person who answered the phone at the Priory said you had gone back to your hotel. I phoned your hotel and they said you weren't there. I phoned the next night; the same thing happened. After that I gave up."

"I'm sorry Brett. After I finished work I used to go for a walk along the banks of the Liffey." She paused and looked at Brett. There was a guarded look on his face. She continued, "I would like to discuss Tavanomore."

"What about Tavanomore?"

"You are going to sell Tavanomore and you didn't even bother to discuss the matter with me."

"There is nothing to discuss." He sounded puzzled.

Of course there was nothing to discuss, thought Liane ruefully looking away feeling suddenly embarrassed. She was acting in a childish manner. She hadn't been named in the will, she had no legal claim, and Brett had not proposed marriage to her. He could do what he wanted with Tavanomore.

114

"Or is it you have the Irish knack of keeping old grievances alive?" he added bitterly.

Liane gave him a look of resignation. "Are you going to sell Tavanomore? I only want to know."

Brett ignored the question. "Before I went to Egypt," he continued, "I put the farm in the hands of an agent because I was curious to know the true valuation. The real value of a property is what someone is actually prepared to pay for it, not a figure written down on a slip of paper by a valuer."

There was a look of deep irritation on Brett's face as he spoke. Something had definitely happened, and recently.

"Are you still selling?"

He shook his head, and Liane could see his thoughts were bitter and unhappy.

"Why are you so miserable and irritable?" Liane flung at him. She was losing her patience.

"I have a very difficult problem."

"Well, let's discuss it."

"I am not discussing it." His voice was hard and final.

It was like being in a dark tunnel; Brett was shutting her out from his world. If he had a problem she wanted to share it. She turned looking at him beseechingly.

"Please Brett..."

"Save it honey," he replied sharply.

If Brett could not discuss his problem with her, there was no relationship. And what could his problem be? He was in financial trouble? Was it connected with an emotional problem? He'd met someone else? Someone in New York?

Suddenly he grasped her hand so hard it hurt.

"Yes, I saw Maria in New York but she means nothing to me."

Liane gave him a weak smile. "I know she doesn't. Did she land herself a part in a Broadway play?"

Brett nodded. "A walk on," he replied. "Two lines. She was satisfied. Papa was not."

They were now travelling through rock strewn moorland where men were cutting peat and stacking it by the roadside. In the distance were the blue mountains of Connemara.

"We're going to stay in the Maam Valley," Brett told her. "It's a small farmhouse. I've stayed there before, and there is a sitting room we can use as an office."

For the next hour the only living creatures they saw were two cows and a donkey grazing by the roadside.

The farmhouse that Brett had booked was a single storied modern building painted white, built at the foot of the mountain range.

The farmer's wife showed them their respective rooms, and the small sitting room they could use where peat burnt a slow fire in the grate. They appeared to be the only guests.

"Let's write a few pages before dinner," suggested Brett as Liane put her typewriter on the table.

Then suddenly he lifted her hair and kissed the back of her neck. Liane felt a shiver run through her. Brett could generate anger and frustration, but the old magic was still there. He pulled up a chair and sat down opposite her.

"Let's see what kind of a writing partnership we have." There was a soft look in his eyes. "At this stage we are only doing master shots. I'll make a start on the opening scene."

Brett dictated and Liane typed. After a couple of pages he paused.

"What do you think? "

"I have an idea..."

"Go ahead."

She proceeded to relate it to him.

"I like it. Put it in."

Liane typed in her contribution to the scene. They continued in this manner for another two hours, then Brett looked at his watch.

Liane gave him an anxious look.

"What do you think?"

"Of the writing?" He gave her a reassuring smile. "I think you are going to be all right. Now there's one small problem, the lady here only does bed and breakfast, and you and I need an evening meal. I also want to phone Ian."

"I seem to remember a pub at the cross roads a mile back." Liane stood up putting the typed sheets into a folder and the cover back on

116

the typewriter. "Paddy's Bar I think it said. We might be able to get a meal, and there is sure to be a pay phone."

They set off on foot, the evening sun low in the sky. Paddy's Bar served meals, but unfortunately there was no Paddy behind the bar. In fact the pub was deserted except for an old man in the corner. They sat down to wait, sitting on high stools at the bar.

Liane didn't care how long they waited for Paddy. For all the problems that lay between them, it was heaven just to be with Brett. She looked at him and suddenly there was that far away look in his eyes, a far away unhappy look. If only she could bridge the gap that seemed to separate them.

He turned to her suddenly.

"Liane, you must trust me."

She touched his hand.

"I love you."

"Be patient honey."

"I'll try. But I don't understand..."

He placed his finger on her lips.

"Brett we have never discussed our future relationship."

"Liane, I can't make any plans for the future."

There was a hard look of determination in his face as he turned and looked away.

Liane sat there stunned. She couldn't believe it.

"You can't make any plans for the future?" she repeated, a tone of incredulity in her voice.

"That's what I said."

He leaned his elbows on the bar and seemed to be studying a row of whisky bottles.

"That changes everything," she said in a depressed voice.

Brett turned his head and looked at her, puzzled.

"It changes nothing."

"You are wrong." There was a lump in her throat, a tightness in her chest. "It means that - that night at Luxor was just, - just sexual gratification. You treated me like a common tart."

He spoke as if he was speaking to a silly child.

"You've got it all wrong. I love you."

117

"But not enough to ask me to marry you," she added in a bitter voice.

Brett didn't answer.

At that moment Paddy appeared full of apologies, and said he could only get them sandwiches. Someone had let him down. They ordered, then Liane glared at Brett, her mind full of anger.

Brett got off the stool.

"Will you excuse me Liane. I want to phone Ian."

Liane shrugged her shoulders wearily.

"Phone whoever you like."

Brett went to the pay phone in the little entrance hall.

He was the second man who had used her. Was there something about her that made her an easy target? Was she too friendly and opened with everyone? She should have done what her mother always told her. Play hard to get.

Ten minutes later Brett returned to the bar, as Paddy put the sandwiches in front of them.

They ate in silence for a few minutes.

"What did Ian have to say?" asked Liane, "Or can't you discuss it?" she added sardonically.

"I can discuss it," he replied, a hard tone in his voice. "The news is not good. The financial backer at the Priory may be cutting down on funds. Anyway, I'm not really worried. Ian can sort him out."

Liane was barely listening. She had been cheated. She felt hurt and angry and humiliated. Then a dreadful thought occurred to her. Perhaps he was already married! She was just trying to decide which day she was going to walk out on Brett when he suddenly turned to her:

"Oh by the way, a letter has arrived for you. Postmark is Istanbul. Ian has forwarded it to our Cleggan address. We'll be there to-morrow. It's a pleasant spot..."

"...I don't understand why there should be a letter for me from Istanbul," Liane interrupted. "I don't know anyone in Turkey."

"It's probably from a girlfriend," suggested Brett, then added in a morose tone. "Or that old flame of yours."

"If it is, it goes straight in the waste basket."

118

Brett looked pleased. When they had finished their modest supper, they returned to the farmhouse, the owners having thoughtfully left the door unlocked.

They stood in the small entrance hall.

"I know you're unhappy, but always remember I love you." Then he kissed her softly on the mouth.

How she hungered for him, ached for him.

"Brett, when will you be honest with me?"

"When the time is ripe. Good night Liane."

They went up a short staircase, Brett turning to the right at the top, and Liane to the left.

Liane lay in her lonely bed, her mind in a turmoil. What did he mean? When the time is ripe. As much as she loved him, she could not go on working with him under these circumstances. It would only prolong the agony.

In a couple of days they would be back in Dublin. She decided she would hand in her resignation and get another job. She thought of somewhere far away, perhaps Australia.

The next morning at breakfast a tired Liane looked across the table at Brett. She could eat very little. The farmer's wife had given them an Irish breakfast of such gigantic proportions under normal circumstances she would have had difficulty in eating it.

Neither of them spoke as they sat lingering over their coffee, gazing through the window at the blue grey mountains.

"I could stay here for the rest of my life," said Brett suddenly.

"Look Brett, I can't go on working for you. You'll have to get someone else."

Her eyes filled with tears.

He turned to her, grave concern in his eyes.

"If you knew the problems I face you would have sympathy for me," he replied quietly. "Just give me time, that's all I ask."

He gave her a gentle smile, his eyes warm and loving. She could feel herself relenting, just a little.

"All right. We'll finish the script, then I'll make a decision."

He gave her a look that was full of pain.

"Make the right decision Liane." Then he turned and looked

119

through the window frowning heavily.

"What's the matter?"

"We have a problem with the script. As you have no doubt realised it's about drug smuggling. There's a lot of it here on the west coast. There are dozens of islands with safe harbours."

"Does the entire story take place in the west of Ireland?" asked Liane.

"Only the opening. We do have a small problem," he continued, still frowning heavily. "The story moves to a foreign locale. Somewhere that invokes mystery and intrigue. Got any ideas?"

Liane shook her head.

"I'll think about it."

After saying goodbye to the farmer's wife they set off travelling through moorland and bogland, and always the blue grey mountains of Connemara towering above them, around them, always there.

In the early part of the afternoon they reached Clifden, a small market town. Then on to the road to Cleggan, through moorland covered in gorse and heather. The road eventually leading them to an attractive one storied house a hundred yards from the shore.

In the entrance hall the landlady handed Liane a letter.

"Arrived by yesterday's post," she told her.

Over tea and cake in the sitting room Liane opened the letter. There was a look of astonishment on her face.

"Who's it from?" asked Brett curiously.

"I can't believe it," she turned to him. "It's from our infamous friend Ahmed Shawki."

"He's got a nerve. What does he say?"

"'I am sorry my brother Hassan caused you distress.'" Liane read. "'I now have the painting and if you come to Istanbul we can do a deal. If you notify the police you will never see your painting again.

Send your reply to me, care of Ali Shawki, The Hera Palas Hotel, Istanbul. We can arrange a meeting at this hotel which will be of mutual benefit. Please come as quickly as possible. It is the only way.

With sincerity,

Ahmed Shawki."

Liane handed the letter to Brett.

"I'd forgotten about the painting. I thought I would never see it again."

"We can do a deal!"' Brett exploded. "I seem to remember hearing those words before. 'A meeting of mutual benefit'. It will be of benefit to Ahmed Shawki. Who the hell is Ali Shawki?"

"A cousin I suppose. Probably works there."

"What are you going to do?" asked Brett handing her the letter.

"I don't know," said Liane slowly. "I don't trust that viper as far as I can see him."

"The picture is worth half a million bucks," Brett reminded her. "Let's go for a walk and think about it."

They walked along the deserted strand leaving footprints in the wet sand. Overhead dark clouds loomed.

"It's going to rain," observed Brett, "And as I said, when it rains in County Galway, there is no let up. Let's go back. I want to dictate about ten pages. I want to get the Connemara sequence finished."

"I thought we were going to discuss Ahmed and the painting".

"Forget it Liane. That man and his brother are compulsive liars. I don't believe one word of it."

They returned to the house and Brett and Liane worked in Brett's room. At seven thirty they were in the dining room, taking a seat by the window, looking out onto the great grey expanse of the bay. A gentle rain had started and a mist was gathering over the sea.

"Brett, I'm concerned about Ahmed's letter. What do you think has happened?"

"This is what I think." Brett leaned forward. "Ahmed and Hassan are a couple of amateurs. They don't know the drill; art thieves always work in conjunction with receivers. So, they don't know where the receivers hang out.

I can just see it, our two thieves get across somehow to Istanbul and walk into the largest art dealer they can find, to be told that the painting they have is on the stolen property list. Looks as though Interpol have done a good job. Then they panic and wonder what to do next."

"Did you notice there is no mention of his brother."

"He may be with him, he may not." Brett's mind was on other

matters. "This roast lamb is superb."

"Brett, I don't know what to do. There is a chance of acquiring, say, a quarter of a million dollars, if he wants a fifty fifty deal."

"Forget it Liane. The whole thing could be a trick, and I don't want you to get hurt."

That night it took Liane a long time to sleep. The truth was, she wanted to go to Istanbul. She felt there was a chance that Ahmed was telling the truth.

Despite the fact that her relationship with Brett was in a dismal state, she knew that if Brett was with her difficult situations that could easily arise would be alleviated by his presence. There was still the memory of the marriage proposal. At breakfast the next morning, Liane sat opposite Brett, sleepy eyed, and yawning.

"Sorry Brett, I didn't sleep well last night."

Brett gave her a soft look. "You would have slept well if I had been with you."

Liane gave him a wry look, and ignored the comment.

"Decided where the rest of our story takes place?" she asked pouring the coffee.

"No," replied Brett promptly. "But I'm working on it."

"Brett, despite what you say, I really want to go to Istanbul and talk to Ahmed. As I said yesterday I could make say, a quarter of a million. Do you know how much money I have in my London bank account right now? I daren't tell you. When Dad died I took over the mortgage on the apartment. You don't know the struggle I have every month."

"Look Liane, I'm really sorry you have a hard time, but don't go to Istanbul."

"Since when do you make my decisions for me?"

Liane gazed through the window with a melancholy look on her face. A gentle rain was still falling, a mist was still over the sea.

"Liane, if you feel so strongly about it, go to Istanbul." His voice was brusque. "But there is one small point. I can't let you go until you have met your contractual obligations and worked with me on this script until the completion."

"How long will that be?"

Brett shrugged his shoulders.

"Can't say."

Liane sat deep in thought for a few moments.

"Move the story to Istanbul, then we're both satisfied."

Brett gave her a slow look. "Not a bad idea. Turkey is a drug smuggling centre, and through the centuries Istanbul has always been a city of mystery and intrigue. I'll think about it."

CHAPTER 13

It was dusk when Liane and Brett arrived at Istanbul and walked out of the small airport building into the warm scented air.

It had been such a rush. Liane had had to make a quick dash back to London, pack a bag with fresh clothes, phone her mother that her proposed visit would have to be postponed and she would see her at Islington on her return from Istanbul.

As Liane glanced at Brett's strong profile in the darkening taxi, her feelings were mixed. She was glad he was with her, but still disappointed and sad their personal relationship was poor.

In the fading light the Blue Mosque and its six minarets were black silhouettes against the silvery evening sky. Brett leaned back and turned to her:

"Well, let's hope this venture with Ahmed Shawki turns out for the best, but I have my doubts. Anyway, as far as the script is concerned, from what I have seen so far it should be a good decision. I think we can get some intriguing locales. When did you say you are meeting Ahmed?"

"Tomorrow morning, half past ten, in the Hera Palas Bar."

During the past few days Liane too had begun to have doubts about coming to Istanbul. Ahmed had proved he was untrustworthy, why should he suddenly change? Anyway, she still felt there was a chance, an extremely slim one, and she had to take it.

Her last bank statement confirmed she had an overdraft. She had been too ambitious when she had taken over her father's mortgage on the Islington apartment. She should have sold the apartment and moved into a smaller one. This she decided to do at the first opportunity.

They crossed the Galata Bridge, and down below ships lay at anchor in the Golden Horn, their lights twinkling in the darkness. Then making their way through the Beyoglu district the taxi stopped

124

outside the Hera Palas, a small nineteenth century hotel.

"Still one of the best places to stay in Istanbul," Brett told her as they got out of the taxi and paid the driver.

They entered the hotel, the interior richly elegant with marble pillars, crystal chandeliers, the architecture Arab influenced. Turkish carpets lay on the polished wooden floor.

A porter took them up to their rooms in a lift like a wrought iron cage, creaking and groaning, almost unchanged from its installation a hundred years ago, the lift attendant giving them a welcoming smile.

Liane found her large room contained two double beds, each covered in a superb gold and dark blue quilt. The same material covered two armchairs and a circular table. The furniture was nineteenth century, mahogany and elegant.

She unpacked and placed her modest cotton nightdress on the pillow. It looked poverty stricken. If everything went according to plan with Ahmed, which she prayed it would, besides paying her debts she would be able to indulge in the first luxury of her life and buy say, a nightdress from Harrods. She rather fancied pale turquoise satin trimmed with yards of lace. She smiled to herself at her foolish daydreaming, but such daydreaming, as Liane had discovered, made the harsh realities of life easier to bear.

There was a knock at the door; Liane went to open it. It was Brett. He walked in and surveyed the room.

"Pleased?" he asked Liane.

"Thrilled!"

"You know Liane, between the two of us we have four double beds. It's ridiculous."

His arms went around her, gently, tenderly, drawing her close.

"Look at the money we could save the Priory," he whispered in her ear.

"Brett, you're making me feel I'm a mean and selfish woman."

"You are."

He kissed her lingeringly on the mouth. When his mouth touched her neck, so lightly, so delicately, his hands touched her breasts; she ached with frustration. Pulling away from him; a playful smile on her lips, she summed up the situation.

125

"You're very cunning Brett. You think if you try hard enough there is a possibility of winning. You are wrong."

"We'll see about that. Come on. Let's go down and have a meal." Then added with a mischievous smile: "I might have better luck later on."

They went down in the wrought iron cage, the polite lift attendant smiling at them, and asking if it was their first visit to Turkey.

In the dining room a man was playing the piano, melodies from 'South Pacific'. Overhead two large chandeliers glittered. Liane had changed into a simple black dress.

Tomorrow she would do a deal with Ahmed, receive a large sum of money from the sale of the painting, and her financial problems would end. After that her life was in the lap of the gods.

What was Brett's problem, and why couldn't he make plans for the future? How she wished he would confide in her. She looked across at him wistfully. Was he a married man? The thought made her feel both sad and frustrated.

Brett looked up from his menu.

"Have you decided what you would like?"

"Anatolian soup, followed by Circassian chicken," she replied with a smile.

"And what about a bottle of wine?"

Brett ordered a Kavaklidere champagne.

"When I was in Dublin just before I left, I had a phone call from an old friend," he suddenly announced looking at Liane over his wine glass, watching her closely.

"Male or female?" she asked teasingly.

"Female," replied Brett a serious look on his face.

Liane felt a nerve tighten in her stomach. "You say she is an old friend." She tried to smile but only succeeded in looking tense.

"Yes. We were at college together," Brett replied. "She married my friend Curtis, and I thought, as everyone else did, it was an ideal marriage. They seemed to get on so well together."

What's the problem?"

"Haven't a clue, but she's left him. They had just started a European tour, which I gather was to try to improve the marriage, but

126

unfortunately when they got to London they had this almighty row. Charlene walked out on him. Curtis went back to the States."

"But where do you fit in?"

"If Charlene is in trouble she always turns to me."

"Always?"

Brett nodded. "I'm a father figure in her life."

"I've heard that before."

Brett ignored Liane's cynicism.

"She was so distressed I told her to join us here. I thought the change of scenery might do her good, help her to forget."

"And when is she arriving?" asked Liane suspiciously.

"Sometime in the next few days," he replied in a vague tone. "Now let's think about tomorrow. After the meeting with Ahmed, let's go wandering around, location hunting. Do that for say three hours then back here and work. Got plenty of paper?"

"I sure have."

A middle aged grey haired man approached their table.

"Excuse me. Are you Karmi Hussein? We have an appointment."

"I'm afraid you are mistaken. I am not Karmi Hussein," Brett told him.

The man apologised and left them.

"I must have a double," laughed Brett.

They left the dining room and wandered into the corridor that led to the lift, and the hotel foyer. Brett had never mentioned anyone called Charlene before. She felt puzzled and suspicious. She couldn't understand why he had invited her to Istanbul at all. They had a great deal of work to do in a very short space of time.

At the side of the lift was a wide staircase of white marble covered with a crimson carpet. An attractive young woman elegantly dressed in tight fitting black trousers and a black top covered in gold sequins was walking slowly down the stairs. She looked like a Vogue model. Even the pouting expression.

Her hair was long and black and lustrous, and her eyes were green, which suddenly lit up as she saw Brett. Letting out a cry of recognition she ran down the remaining steps, flung her arms around him and kissed him on the cheek. Liane's heart sank.

"Brett, darling, I'm so glad to see you. I had a horrible feeling you might have changed your plans, and I'd be stuck here all on my own. Anyway, the receptionist told me you had checked in."

"I thought you wouldn't be here for a couple of days," Brett replied, then turned to Liane, a small look of embarrassment in his eyes. "Oh Liane, may I introduce Charlene."

Charlene looked at Liane with a slight smile on her lips.

"I take it you're Brett's secretary," she spoke in a patronising voice.

"Liane is my co-writer," Brett informed her.

They wandered through a long ornate sitting room, walking on the soft Turkish carpet, past giant size Chinese vases to the bar. How could Brett do it thought Liane. Arrange to meet someone and not tell her. There had been plenty of time on the plane.

"Remember I told you Curtis and I were doing a European tour. Well, I managed to make a switch with the hotel bookings," Charlene continued, directing her conversation to Brett. "Never thought I would. I can't tell you what a comfort it is to see you again."

They sat down at a small table. Liane started to feel an intruder on a happy twosome. She was definitely on unsteady ground.

"Like to have a drink Charlene?"

Charlene gave him an eager smile. "I sure would, and you know what I like to drink."

There was an intimate tone in her voice.

"Martini, very dry," Brett told the waiter. "And I'll have a beer. And you Liane?"

"I'll have a gin and tonic," said Liane. Then she turned to Charlene. "You are an old friend of Brett's?"

Charlene nodded with a smile. "An old friend from way back."

"How interesting," Liane replied, giving Brett a hard look. "And where did you meet Brett?"

"Harvard of course. Where else? Best marriage bureau in the U.S.A. Except I married the wrong guy."

Charlene was looking at Brett. She had stopped smiling, and there was a sad look in her eyes.

What was she trying to say? She should have married Brett? Was she Brett's problem and the reason why he couldn't make any plans for the future?

Liane glanced at the young woman across the table. Charlene was everything she wasn't. A graduate of a famous university. Extremely beautiful, and from the look of her clothes, very prosperous.

But why hadn't Brett mentioned her? He had something to hide? He wanted to know all about her past, but not a word had been said about his. Then she remembered he had hinted at a sad love affair and that he felt he had been used. Was this the girl? And if so, why had he invited her to Istanbul?

Liane looked at Brett with suspicion.

"I have to explain," said Brett, a beseeching look in his eyes as he turned to Liane, "I feel rather guilty. You see I introduced Charlene to Curtis."

Charlene took a sip of her drink, then looked in a depressed manner across the room.

"Worse day of my life."

"It's all my fault," said Brett. "But how was I to know you were going to fall for the guy."

There was a look in Brett's eyes Liane failed to interpret. Charlene's eyes filled with tears.

"Come on Charlene," Brett spoke in a firm tone. "You and Curtis have got to stop behaving in this childish manner," he reprimanded her. "Marriage is for keeps, not until you have your first disagreement."

"Don't you start! It's bad enough with my mother. You see, you don't understand. It's more than just a disagreement." She spoke in a low voice, looking down into her lap. "He's found someone he likes better. I had felt for some time the marriage was getting stale. I think he got bored with me. So I suggested this European trip. I thought it would put some vitality back into our relationship."

"And it didn't?" queried Brett.

"At first I thought it had, but when we got to London things didn't go so well. First we had to pay hundreds of dollars a night for some crummy little room in South Kensington. Then one night he told me he was still seeing this other woman. I went mad."

"I'm not surprised. What happened?" asked Brett, looking at her closely.

"I didn't wait for an explanation. I just packed my bags and left. Then I had the idea of phoning you, and by luck you were going to Istanbul, which was on the itinerary, and all I had to do was switch the countries around."

Charlene burst into tears.

"He doesn't love me. What am I going to do?"

"I think a good night's sleep is the answer, and decide tomorrow what to do," suggested Liane. "Sleep on a problem."

Charlene rose to her feet.

"Good idea."

"Have you eaten?" asked Brett solicitously.

Charlene shook her head.

"I couldn't eat a thing."

They accompanied her to her room on the floor below theirs, with a promise to phone in the morning and collect her for breakfast.

"It's great having a wonderful friend like you," she told Brett tearfully at her door. "Without you I don't know what I would have done."

Liane and Brett continued to the next floor by the staircase.

"Why on earth didn't you tell rne you had arranged to meet her in Istanbul?" Liane demanded. "Got something to hide?"

"For God's sake, Liane~" exclaimed Brett heatedly. "You are not my keeper. The truth is I completely forgot."

"Forgot!" exclaimed Liane disbelievingly. "Am I right in thinking you and Charlene were pretty close at one time?"

Brett ignored the question. "I'm worried about you and that Egyptian crook."

They had now reach Liane's door.

"Stop giving evasive replies. I asked were you and Charlene close at one time?"

Brett looked at her, a serious expression in his eyes.

"The answer is yes, but it was all over years ago."

"Good night Brett," said Liane softly, her hand on his arm.

He kissed her quickly, and started to move away.

"Oh Brett."

He stopped and turned. There was a weary expression on his face. "What is it Liane?"

"Where did Charlene phone you?"

"Priory Theatre of course. Where else?"

"But how did she know you were there?" asked Liane.

"For God's sake Liane. I wrote and told her I was working for the Priory."

"And what is Curtis going to think when he hears you have teamed up with Charlene in Istanbul."

"I have not teamed up with Charlene."

"It looks to me as though you have."

"For Christ's sake Liane! I'm going to explode! Show a little compassion. When she spoke to me on the phone I thought she was going to take an overdose."

And with that Brett continued down the corridor to his room.

As Liane lay alone in her king size bed that night she felt troubled. Brett had told her he had had a love affair with Charlene before she had switched her affections to Curtis. But did Brett still love her? Did a spark still remain?

He had not taken the trouble to remember to tell her about Charlene. A guilty conscience? And she didn't like the way Charlene looked at Brett.

Liane had a very strong feeling if she didn't work fast she could lose Brett altogether. She had a feeling Charlene was up to something and Brett knew it.

Next morning Liane awoke with a headache. It was not surprising. She now had three problems on her mind, - Brett, Charlene and Ahmed.

It was already hot. She put on her best cotton skirt. It was long and full, a design of red roses against a dark green background. With it she teamed a simple white blouse she had bought at a Laura Ashley sale. That was the only kind of shopping she ever did. Always bargain hunting.

Brett knocked at her door at approximately eight o'clock.

He was wearing the light beige tropical suit he had worn in Egypt.

He looked well rested and ready to tackle the day's problems. They went down the wide staircase to the floor below.

"Be very tactful Liane?" he warned her. "Charlene is in a delicate state. To be quite frank, I don't know what to do with her." He spoke with an air of desperation.

Liane gave him a sharp look, wondering whether to believe him or not. Charlene opened her door in answer to their knock. She looked red eyed from weeping.

"Now come on Charlene," said Brett cheerfully. "Nothing is as bad as it seems."

They all went down in the lift to the dining room. It was a buffet style breakfast, and after they had helped themselves and settled at a nearby table, Brett kept up a cheerful banter of trivia, mainly about the trials and tribulations of the Priory Theatre, and the problems Ian had with an American television company. Liane sat listening, trying hard not to think about Ahmed Shawki and their forthcoming meeting.

When the meal had finished Charlene said she would be returning to her room because she had a headache. They left Charlene at the lift.

"You go on to the bar," Brett told her. "I want to go to the foyer to buy a copy of the Turkish Daily News. The local paper always helps me to get the atmosphere of the place. See you later."

Liane went to the bar room. At that time of day there were few customers, a couple of men leaning against the bar and a man and blonde woman seated at a table at the far end of the room.

There was no sign of Ahmed.

She stood a few minutes wondering what to do, then there was a step behind her. It was Ahmed. He was wearing a white cotton suit, his lustrous black hair brushed back from his forehead, and in his dark eyes there was the old flirtatious look.

"Hello Liane. I am pleased to see you." He grasped her hands. "Come with me. We cannot talk here. You are alone?" he added hopefully as they walked through to the long sitting room adjacent to the bar room.

"No, I am with Brett."

He looked disappointed.

"My heart still bleeds for you." They sat down.

"Ahmed, you'll find someone else."

He shrugged his shoulders. "Perhaps. In the meantime I would like to show you Istanbul," he said eagerly. "I could take you to the best nightclub in the city, where they have the best belly dancers in the whole of Turkey."

"Thank you but that won't be possible."

His eyes clouded. "Always you say it is not possible."

At that moment Brett entered the room, much to Liane's relief, gave Ahmed a brief nod of recognition and sat down opposite him.

"You were so long," commented Liane playfully, "I wondered if someone else had mistaken you for Karmi Hussein? He might be a big time financier," she continued, "or an international industrialist."

"He might be a big time drug agent," said Brett dryly, looking at Ahmed.

There was no reaction from Ahmed.

"Now let us discuss the painting you and your brother have in your possession." Brett's voice was hard. "Is he here by the way?"

Brett looked around the large room.

"No, he is not in this country," replied Ahmed.

"What have you done with him?" Brett gave Ahmed a fierce stare. "Left him in a psychiatric hospital in Luxor?"

"He is in Luxor and I have no interest in what he does."

"I assume you stole the painting from him," put in Liane, "and got across to Istanbul. Here you have cousin Ali to help you. I presume he is your cousin?"

Ahmed shook his head. "He is my uncle."

"What is he? A waiter?"

Ahmed nodded.

"I take it you have found it impossible to sell the Gorregiani, being on the stolen property list at all the art dealers in Istanbul," continued Liane.

"That is true. So what can I do?"

He shrugged his shoulders, his expression naive and innocent.

"I know what I'd like to do," said Brett menacingly. "Where is the painting now?"

Ahmed's face was expressionless.

"I cannot tell you," he replied in a low voice. "But it is in a safe place. Now Liane, I think the best thing is for you to take the painting yourself into the art dealer. I will of course accompany you. The gallery is called 'Marmara'. It is in the Istiklal Caddesi.

This street is the best street in Istanbul, and this art dealer is the best. He has many rich customers who live in grand houses on the Bosphorus. They will be very happy to buy your Gorregiani."

"What sort of deal have you in mind?" asked Brett, a hard look in his eyes.

"Fifty - fifty. I think that is fair."

"Fair!" exploded Brett, then lowering his voice added in a contemptuous undertone, "That painting is the rightful property of Liane. I've a good mind to get the police right now."

"If you do my friend, you will be sorry. Because you will never see the painting again. I would destroy it rather than hand it over to the police."

"We'll do the deal," said Liane anxiously. "Let's get it over and done with Brett. Then we can get on with our lives."

Ahmed gave her a smug look.

"You are wise Liane. Now have you proof that you own the painting? Evidence that the priest really gave it to you?"

Liane thought for a moment. There had been no correspondence between herself and Father O'Brien.

She shook her head. "I'm afraid not. How foolish of me not to have thought of it."

"Phone Father straight away," Brett told her. "Ask him to send you a letter stating you are the lawful owner."

Ahmed smiled, everything was going well.

"So we meet again on Saturday, here in this room, at the same time. You bring the letter with you. It is a pleasure doing business with you."

Then turning he walked quickly from the room.

"Come back to my room and make the call from there," Brett told her. "Have you got his number?"

Liane shook her head.

"You'll have to get Cairo Directory Inquiries."

They went up in the lift. The lift attendant turned to Liane from time to time, giving her a constant worried look. When they reached their floor as they were about to leave the man spoke.

"Excuse me madame, but the man you were speaking to ..."

"You mean Ahmed Shawki?" asked Liane. "Do you know him?"

The lift attendant nodded gravely. "I must warn you madame, it is not wise to be in his company."

CHAPTER 14

"What do you know about Ahmed Shawki?" asked Liane, surprised at the lift attendant's remark. The man looked away, an embarrassed expression on his face, and did not reply.

Liane gave Brett a puzzled look as they stepped out of the lift. Brett shrugged his shoulders, there was little else he could do under the circumstances.

They walked quickly along the corridor.

"So Ahmed has a bad reputation in Istanbul," commented Brett cynically as he opened his door. "Well, it didn't take him long. He's only been here a couple of weeks. Even the lift attendant knows about him."

"I think the lift attendant knows everything," Liane commented as she walked across to Brett's phone. "Last night I heard him telling someone that the French Ambassador had just arrived."

Brett flung himself into the armchair.

"You know I was never happy about this venture," he told her in a firm voice. "I had a gut feeling right from the beginning about this whole wretched business. You don't know where the painting is. Ahmed asks you to meet him with Father O'Brien's letter. You will notice he did not say he would meet us with the painting. I don't like it," he added, frowning heavily.

"If it turns out to be a disaster, at least we'll get a good script out of it. Anyway, thanks for coming."

Brett held out his hand and Liane grasped it.

"I'd do anything for you, you know that."

Anything, thought Liane, than the one thing I want.

She withdrew her hand and lifted the receiver. "I'll try to get Father O'Brien's number."

After a long delay Liane eventually got the number and dialled. The number rang for a long time, then Liane put the receiver down.

"No reply," she told Brett. "I'll try again this evening. Did you say you want to go out location hunting?"

They went out, Liane with a camera. First to the main street of the Bayoglu district, Istiklal Caddesi, a street of expensive shops. About half way down they saw the art gallery 'Marmara', and paused a moment to glance in the window. It was quite a large gallery. There were paintings by some well known European artists adorning the walls.

Liane and Brett exchanged glances.

"We'll see," said Brett as they moved on. "Personally, I forecast a disaster."

"Brett, try to be more positive about the whole business," Liane admonished him as they made their way through a labyrinth of steep streets that sloped down to the Golden Horn waterway.

There was the street of the drapers, the street of light fittings, the street of musical instruments. On the still hot air came the sound of the muezzin from a nearby mosque calling the faithful to noonday prayers, and everywhere there were areas of broken pavements, holes in roads, and litter.

They walked down a narrow street which seemed to be entirely residential. The houses looked French style, nineteenth century with shutters at all the windows. They had an air of long term neglect, with paint peeling from doors and windows. Sometimes a door stood open revealing a dark depressing passage.

At each end of this street there was a set of large wrought iron gates.

"I think we could do a scene in a street like this," observed Brett. "Take a few photos Liane for reference, and get the iron gates in."

Liane took several photos from various angles, and as she took a shot of a particularly depressing looking house a man and woman appeared in the doorway.

The man looked in his mid forties, heavily built, with black hair, moustache, and wearing a brown leather jacket. The woman was about the same age, very attractive with blonde hair. Liane then hurried away down the street to catch up with Brett.

But just before she left the street Liane turned and took a final shot

137

with the wrought iron gates in the background. The man and woman she had just photographed standing in their house doorway were now standing in the middle of the street.

Liane thought they seemed vaguely familiar, then she remembered they had been in the Hera Palas bar sitting at the far end of the room when she had met Ahmed. It must be a local meeting place.

"Let's cross the Galata Bridge and go into Old Istanbul," suggested Brett.

They crossed the bridge, beseiged by shoe cleaning boys, and gnarled old women with their begging bowls. The latter filled Liane with pity and she gave a coin to each one. At the mosque just beyond the bridge, they found Muslim men busy washing themselves at the outside fountains prior to entering the mosque.

"Let's go in," suggested Brett, then added with a smile, "Follow the rules and you'll come to no harm."

To the attendant at the entrance they handed him their shoes. He surveyed the length of Liane's skirt and decided it was suitable, then covering her head with a scarf like the other Muslim women, they entered the dimly lit grey stone interior.

The floor of the mosque was crowded with Muslim men on their knees, their foreheads on the ground, deep in prayer. The voice of the chanting muezzin was deafening.

"There is only one God and Mohammed is the prophet of God."

Liane had to sit behind a screen with the Muslim women. After a few minutes observation Brett beckoned her, and with relief she followed him out into the bright sunshine.

"I did resent having to go behind that screen because I am female."

They went and sat on a stone wall.

"There are the devout Fundamentalists who wear a black gown," pronounced Liane as she gave Brett a piece of chocolate. "And a black head veil that completely covers their face except of course for their eyes. Then there is the modern woman who wears western clothes and has a career. What are they called?"

"Sunnis," Brett replied promptly. "The stewardesses on the plane were Sunnis."

"Interesting," replied Liane, "I'm glad I'm a western woman."

Liane munched her chocolate thoughtfully for a moment. "Brett, changing the subject, is Charlene your problem?"

"No. Charlene is not my problem."

"Were you in love with her?"

"I suppose I was. Then she met Curtis and that was the end of me."

"Were you sorry?"

Brett laughed. "For a while. Then I got over it. Like you get over flu." He shrugged his shoulders, then looked at Liane intently. "For God's sake, don't do anything stupid like get jealous. There is nothing to be jealous about."

"I believe you, thousands wouldn't." She gave him a wry sort of smile.

"I think it is time we made our way back to the Hera Palas and do some work." Brett jumped off the wall, and helped Liane down. "I get the feeling you are looking for trouble."

"Sorry Brett. I was just wondering..."

"Well stop wondering. Every day we have to work. Every night Ian wants a phone call on our progress. And I have got to be back in New York within the next two weeks."

They started walking back, crossing the busy Galata Bridge, then climbing the steep streets they soon found themselves back in the Beyoglu district.

When they reached the hotel there was a man standing on the opposite side of the street, leaning against the wall, watching the hotel entrance. He was the man she had photographed in the street of the iron gates. The man in the brown leather jacket. Then she looked again, but he had gone.

In his room Brett took from the refrigerator two cans of coke and handed Liane one with a glass.

Liane sank into an armchair and drank the cool, refreshing drink.

"That will keep you going until dinner time," observed Brett as she handed him the empty glass. "We're behind schedule today. As before, we need a top and two copies."

Liane opened her typewriter, and threaded in the paper.

"Got any ideas for the opening scene in Istanbul?" asked Brett.

139

Liane made suggestions, Brett developed them. It was amazing how well they worked. They were on the same wavelength, at least as far as the script was concerned. Liane typed page after page. Four hours later they decided to stop.

Brett gathered his notes together, then sat down in the armchair by the window. He looked tired and stressed. Liane put the typewritten sheets into a file, then put the cover on the typewriter.

"Brett, we can't go on like this. When are you going to talk to me?"

"Why don't you try to get through to Father O'Brien and sort out your own problems?"

Liane decided it was best to leave him alone. She went across to the phone and dialled the number. She could hear it ringing, then a familiar voice answered.

"Father..." Liane began hesitantly.

"Liane. What a nice surprise to hear from you."

"I'm sorry to be a nuisance Father, but I'm phoning from Istanbul. I would be pleased if you could sent me a letter stating that I am the rightful owner of the painting you gave to me."

"Of course. What are you doing in Istanbul?"

"There is a chance of getting the painting back, a slim chance I have to admit. It is a complicated story Father, but if I do get it back, I want you to profit from it as well. That is only fair.

Right now I need to have this letter. Will you please send it to me. I am staying at the Hera Palas Hotel, Istanbul, Turkey. It's terribly urgent Father."

"I will write the letter immediately Liane, and it will be in the post tonight. I don't know how long it will take to reach you. I should think you would have it four days from now. I will remember you in my prayers."

"Thank you Father, and when it's all over I'll write and explain to you all the peculiar things that have been happening. Good bye Father."

Liane put the phone down.

"I'll say they're peculiar," Brett told her, a bitter smile on his lips. "Damn peculiar. Perhaps bizarre would be a better word."

Liane ignored his comments.

"Father said I should have his letter in about four days time. That will be Friday, and we have arranged to meet Ahmed on Saturday."

"I don't know what you're so pleased about. You're not going to get anything out of this. I reckon you'll be the loser."

"For goodness sake Brett, I've told you. Let's have a more positive outlook."

Liane walked across to the balcony and looked down onto a vista of pantiled roofs covering two storied dwellings. There was the sound of a baby crying. If only Brett knew how hard it was to keep her spirits up, thought Liane dismally, he wouldn't talk the way he does.

"Ahmed will cheat you out of whatever he apportions to you," he told her, joining her on the balcony. "He can't help himself. He's a born thief."

"Let's not jump the gun!'' replied Liane. Brett's pessimism was beginning to irritate. "Give him a chance. He wants to make money just the same as I do."

"Liane, where have you been all your life? Can't you see, the world isn't full of good honest folk. There a whole lot of evil bastards out there..."

"Brett," Liane cut in, moving back into the room."Isn't it nearly time for dinner? I wonder what sort of day Charlene has had?"

"Poor girl. We ought to go and see how she is getting on."

Brett glanced quickly at his watch.

"It's almost time to go down. Let's pick her up on the way."

On the floor below they knocked at Charlene's door. There was no reply. They knocked again. This time she answered, coming to the door with a woebegone look, her eyes red from crying.

"Come in," she said in a depressed voice.

They followed her into the room. She was dressed in an old pair of shorts, and tee shirt. On the dressing table were the pages of a long unfinished letter.

"I've been alone all day, and you never gave one thought to me." She looked accusingly at Brett. "I think you are selfish and inconsiderate. I thought you were a friend."

"Charlene, I'm terribly sorry about this, but we're here to work. I have a deadline to meet on a script."

"Of course, your work is more important than anything. I don't count."

"It's not like that at all. I don't get the work done, I'm in trouble. So is Liane. Come down and have some dinner. It will make you feel better."

"Yes, come down with us Charlene," added Liane, giving her an encouraging smile. She suddenly felt sorry for the girl.

"All right," Charlene agreed reluctantly. "Give me a few minutes to change. I'll see you in the dining room."

Liane and Brett went down in the lift. At the ground floor they made their way along the corridor to the dining room. The head waiter approached.

"Table for three," Brett told him.

He showed them to a table by the dance floor. The pianist was already installed at his grand piano, playing more nostalgia. This time it was George Gershwin melodies.

Brett picked up the menu. "Now what would you like tonight? More Turkish food?"

"Of course. I think I'll repeat the Anatolian soup," said Liane looking at the menu. "Followed by the lamb kebab and I hope the pianist plays songs from "Porgy and Bess," and that will make it a perfect evening."

At that moment Charlene entered the room. She had transformed herself. She looked stunning in a red velvet dress, low cut revealing her white shoulders and a shapely breast line. She sauntered slowly between the tables, male eyes upon her.

She looked stunning.

And as she seated herself between Brett and Liane, she made Liane feel positively dowdy. Liane knew then she was not going to enjoy the evening, or the rest of the stay in Istanbul. How could you compete dressed in a Marks & Spencer's outfit? She looked across at Brett. He was smiling at Charlene admiringly, and Liane felt a sharp pang of jealousy.

"Like it? Yves Saint Laurent. Bought it in Sloane Street when I was in London."

"It's very lovely," Liane murmured.

"I only buy designer clothes," Charlene continued. "I'd really like to be a dress designer."

"Why don't you go to art college and study it," suggested Brett. Charlene gave a sigh. "Good idea. I've got to do something with my life. I've spent all day writing pages and pages to Curtis, but I know our marriage is finished...."

Her voice trailed off and she looked down into her lap.

"Have a glass of Anatolian wine," suggested Brett.

He poured her a glass and she took a sip.

Dance music started on the loudspeaker system. Charlene's spirits seemed to suddenly rise.

"It's a big world," she said. "And there are plenty of pebbles on the beach."

A few couples moved onto the dance floor.

"Too true," said Brett. "Like to dance Charlene?" he added politely.

"Of course Brett. You know how much I love dancing."

They started dancing, whilst Liane watched. Brett was a good dancer, so was Charlene. They made a good dancing couple.

Twenty minutes later Charlene asked Brett to dance.

"It's the samba," she exclaimed. "You know how much I love south American dances."

Liane had the feeling if she had gone up to her room they wouldn't have noticed.

And as she watched Brett and Charlene dancing the sensuous rhythm she wondered again if Charlene was his problem and he was still in love with her.

When the dance finished they returned to the table. Charlene had to go and powder her nose.

Liane was starting to feel just a little bit irritated.

"I would like to be asked to dance," she hissed at Brett. "And I would like just a little thought and consideration. It isn't nice being a back number."

"Liane. I am very sorry. But I had got a guilty conscious about Charlene. I had completely forgotten about her today. Come on, let's

143

dance."

They moved onto the dance floor.

"I don't understand what you are getting worried about. I only danced with her a couple of times."

"It's the way she looks at you. And you are encouraging her. I understand she needs comforting, but there are limits."

"Look Liane, stop being jealous about poor Charlene."

"Stop being jealous! I think you're in love with Charlene," Liane flung at him. "She is your problem. You're in love with your friend's wife."

Brett gave her a stern look.

"You are being ridiculous."

"Prove me I'm wrong," Liane replied defiantly. "And for a start give me a satisfactory explanation why you invited her to come out to Istanbul."

The dance ended and they walked back to their table. Charlene was talking to a woman at the entrance to the dining room.

Brett frowned leaning his elbows on the table.

"I had been hoping to solve this problem of mine without troubling you about it."

Liane looked across at Brett. He looked so worried she started to feel sympathetic towards him.

"Tell me all," she said gently.

"It's financial..." he began.

Liane almost felt relieved. "Give me the details, no matter how bad it is."

"You see, I owe the bank £150,000."

"£150,000!" Liane repeated, shocked. "Why did you need such a great deal of money?"

"I can't go into that right now. Some other time. The point is two weeks ago I received a letter from the bank. They have given me three months to repay. Unfortunately due to circumstances beyond my control I have reneged on the terms of the contract. In other words I have been unable to meet the monthly repayments. I never thought they would treat me in such a harsh manner. It's been a terrible shock."

144

"What circumstances beyond your control caused you to renege?"

"An American film company owed me a lot of money. Before I could get my hands on it they went bust. Learnt about it during my last trip to the States."

Then Brett gave her a thoughtful smile. "But I have a plan. First I get Charlene here, then Curtis is going to join us. I am certain it is just a stupid misunderstanding. They love each other. And I am sure that within a short space of time they will have made it up and think how ridiculous they have been."

"Brett, I'm not following the plot. How can they help you with your problem at the bank?"

" I am going to put a business proposition to Curtis. Offer him a partnership if he invests £150,000 in my company."

"Is he a wealthy man?"

"I'll say. He's a multi millionaire. His family own a chain of hotels across the States."

"You could try. But why should he do you a favour?"

"I know Curtis very well. He's an old friend. And I know he's crazy about Charlene. Now if I'm responsible for bringing them together he may be more inclined to accept my proposition."

Liane shrugged her shoulders. She didn't know Curtis.

She didn't know details of Brett's company. "What's your next move?"

"Making a phone call to Curtis. I shall do it tonight. Tell him where Charlene is, and ask him to come over. Hi Charlene."

Charlene joined them at the table.

"I've been talking to a very interesting woman" she told them. "She's a journalist; just been to Kurdistan."

"Charlene," said Brett, looking pointedly at her. "You and Curtis must talk. You can't spend the rest of your life running away from your problems."

"I am not talking to him, and that is final, and please do not bring the subject up again. Now if you folks will excuse me, but it's bedtime for me."

"It's our bedtime too," said Brett.

The three of them stood up and started moving towards the door of

145

the dining room.

"Sorry I'm such dismal company," Charlene apologised to them both.

The three of them went up in the lift.

Charlene got out at her floor after giving Brett a peck on the cheek.

Brett and Liane continued to the next floor, then walked along the corridor to their rooms. They stopped before Liane's door.

"Brett, if I get some money from the deal with Ahmed. Would that help you?"

"It would help me enormously, but it is not going to happen. I only agreed to come to Istanbul to pacify you, not because I felt you were going to come into a fortune."

"Brett, be careful with Charlene. I feel she is a very cunning woman."

"Stop worrying about Charlene."

"Changing the subject, this afternoon when you asked me to photograph the street of the iron gates, there was a man and woman standing in the doorway of one of the houses. I took a picture of them, quite by accident, as they opened the door and stepped into the street.

Well, later in the afternoon when we returned to the hotel, I noticed this same man was standing on the pavement opposite the hotel. I got the impression he was checking who went in."

"What's your problem?" asked Brett, not following her line of thought.

"Nothing. Just commenting. Actually I thought him rather odd. I thought he had a furtive look about him."

"Liane, the man has every right to stand in front of the hotel. I think he was waiting for another woman and he doesn't want his wife to find out. That's why he had the furtive look, or in other words a guilty conscience."

"I know I'm being silly. Brett, I wonder where Ahmed lives? How does he pass the time? Does he have a job? He puzzles me."

"I don't know where he lives, what he does, and I don't even care. Liane," Brett lowered his voice as his arms encircled her waist, drawing her closer to him. There was a look of smouldering desire in his eyes. "I want to sleep with you, now. When I get my financial problems resolved we are going to get married."

Liane gave him a cynical smile. "And if you don't get your financial problems resolved we don't get married."

"Give me a break Liane," he whispered softly.

Liane leaned her head against his shoulder. "I accept your conditional proposal of marriage, which I think is the most unromantic proposal a girl could ever receive."

"I'm sorry about that."

"But regarding the request for sex tonight..." She hesitated a moment, then made up her mind. "The answer is no."

He kissed her, but it was a harsh, aggressive kiss, full of anger and frustration.

"Good night Liane," he said huskily and moved away down the corridor to his room.

Liane opened her door and entered the room; then switching on the bedside light she drew the heavy curtains across the window. The room seemed empty and depressing. She was suddenly filled with doubt.

Had she been wrong in refusing him? She had behaved indiscreetly at Luxor, letting her heart rule her head. She had done that before with Conal, and lost.

Now she wanted to be in control of the situation. She wanted marriage to Brett, that above all. The problem was, how far did she go in coping with Brett's sexual demands?

She got undressed, and got into bed. She wanted Brett's love more than anything in the world, and didn't want to do anything to lose him.

A warning voice told her if she was not careful she could lose him. He could turn to someone else. And that could easily be Charlene.

She decided the best plan was to speak to Brett tomorrow. Surely they could fix a definite date for their wedding, financial problems or not.

They would be married by special licence and it must be a church wedding, a long white gown, bridesmaids and confetti. Her mother would be so thrilled. She'd like to get married at Carrickballyduff, and as for Brett's financial problems, she felt confident they would be solved.

She fell into a contented sleep, her mind drifting to the church at Carrickballyduff. The organ was playing and she was walking down the aisle on Brett's arm.

Suddenly she awoke. She could hear a curious sound. It seemed to be coming from the direction of the door, a scraping metallic sound. Was someone trying to force the lock and get into her room?

She felt suddenly cold with fear, her heart pounding as she switched on the bedside light. The door was securely locked, with the key still inserted in the lock. Surely she was quite safe from any would-be intruder?

The scraping sound ceased. Whoever it was had decided to go away. She switched off the bedside light, and turned onto her back, staring into the darkness, thinking of Brett alone in the room next door.

Had she made the right decision to resist his demands? Now she wasn't sure. A frustrated man could go elsewhere to be comforted. She lay there wondering if he too was lying awake in his bed right now, filled with unhappy thoughts. Perhaps he saw her as a selfish, unfeeling woman?

Suddenly the noise started again. Whoever it was had decided to try again. She gave a shiver. It was a distinctly unpleasant experience. Who could want to break into her room?

The only money she possessed was in her handbag, and the only valuable item she had brought was her camera. It was a Pentax, second hand, the only luxury she had ever permitted herself. She had bought it the day before she flew to Turkey.

She switched on the bedside light, got out of bed, picked up her handbag and camera from the dressing table, and hid them under her pillow.

The noise continued for a few more minutes. Suddenly she felt angry. How dare some unknown person try to break into her room and steal the few precious possessions she had!

"If you don't go away," Liane called out, "I shall phone for the manager."

The noise stopped. She made the decision to phone Brett. Leaning across she dialled his number, and waited. She would ask Brett to come to her room.

She needed his protection, this person may decide to return. And if Brett decided to spend the remainder of the night in her bed, she no longer cared.

Brett was not answering his phone. Perhaps she had dialled the wrong number? She replaced the receiver and tried again. She could hear it ringing. She held on, waiting. Perhaps he was asleep? She held on for a long time, until it became obvious that Brett was not in his room.

She looked at her watch.

It was two thirty

CHAPTER 15

Liane replaced the receiver and switched off the light, then lay staring into the sombre darkness of the room. Where would Brett go in the small hours of the morning? A gambling casino? Istanbul was full of them. But Brett had never shown an interest in gambling. A nightclub? Surely he would have asked her to accompany him?

Then she thought of Charlene, and felt that there lay the answer. She mustn't think, she must blank out her mind, as she turned over in bed to settle for sleep, if it would ever come, with a hot feeling of jealousy surging through her at the possibility of Brett in Charlene's room.

Maybe she was being unfair and in the morning Brett would have some reasonable explanation as to why he was not in his room at 2.30am.

She must trust Brett, but it was so easy to think the worst. Had he been telling the truth when he had denied being in love with Charlene?

The scraping noise at the door did not return, and somehow she fell into a light slumber, awakening at dawn when the muezzin's plaintive chant sounded in the early morning air.

For a few sleepy moments she felt a deep sense of contentment, as she drowsily thought of Brett, loving him, working with him, and the future that lay ahead could become a golden reality. Curtis would enter into a business proposition with Brett and the debt at the bank would be repaid. Her dream would come true.

Then suddenly she remembered last night and the endless ringing of the phone and the sense of emptiness and anger it had evoked.

After that it was impossible to sleep. She thought of Brett attempting to bring two warring partners together. He was going to get bruised.

She got up at seven and showered, selected her red cotton dress, the back was scooped out and even though it was covered with a criss cross of narrow bands of material, there were large areas of her bare skin visible.

Not really suitable for an Muslim country, but Liane had reached a point when she didn't care anymore. Anyway, her red dress always cheered her up.

She went down to breakfast in a defiant, aggressive mood, ready for battle. She had almost finished the meal when Brett appeared, alone, a haggard look on his face. He sat down opposite her in silence. Liane glared at him as he drank his coffee.

"You look tired this morning," she said in a cold voice.

"I feel tired," he replied, "But two cups of coffee and a brisk walk down to the Galata Bridge and I'll be fine. Ready for today's work?"

"I am."

She poured him a cup of coffee and herself a second cup.

"Well, aren't you going to say something?" she enquired in a hard tone. "When circumstances permit we are planning to get married. Last night I was beginning to wonder."

"Will you kindly explain."

"I phoned your room at approximately 2.30am and there was no reply. I needed help. I had reason to believe someone was trying to force the lock on my door, but I had left the key in the lock, so it never happened."

Brett looked puzzled.

"I'm sorry about that. Who on earth would try to get into your room? Some thief I suppose who specialises in hotels. There will be little or no security here. The staff, I am sure are very carefully selected."

"They employ Ahmed's uncle," Liane reminded him. "We'll never know," she added wearily. "But I will have to report it to the management. The point is, where were you last night?"

Liane looked at him, deep suspicion in her eyes.

"I was with Charlene."

"Charlene! At that hour!"

"Let me explain."

"You need to do a lot of explaining," she continued, an angry note in her voice. "She is a friend from way back. You have admitted you

151

were once in love with her."

Brett grabbed her hand across the table. "When she went off with Curtis, whatever I felt for her, died. Believe me." Brett tightened his grip on her hand. "You're the only woman I love."

Liane gave a weak smile. "I know Brett. But why did you go to her room in the middle of the night?"

"I phoned her about eleven and told her I had spoken to Curtis and he's coming to Istanbul straight away. I felt I had to tell her immediately, give her time to think about it. He'll be here Thursday to sort things out with her. I can tell you she was not at all pleased."

Brett paused and looked deeply into Liane's eyes. "I guarantee by the weekend they will be totally reconciled."

"I think you are on dangerous ground, interfering with a friend's marital problems."

"I know, but it's a risk I have to take. I am in a desperate situation."

"You still haven't explained why you were absent from your room in the small hours."

Brett gave Liane a sheepish look.

"She phoned me about twoish. She was ill. Got this terrible headache and couldn't sleep. Did I have anything for a headache? I told her I had some aspirins and went round to give them to her."

"What happened?"

"I gave her the aspirins, then she started crying. She wouldn't stop. She kept repeating she doesn't want Curtis to come. She will never trust him again. You know the sort of thing."

"You are on dangerous ground..."

"Give me a break Liane," Brett interrupted wearily.

"So you stayed to comfort her?" Liane continued, staring at him disbelievingly.

"Of course I did," Brett retorted. "I couldn't just walk out and leave her."

"Of course you couldn't," Liane's voice was now distinctly sarcastic. "Perhaps her father could give you a low interest loan, and you couldn't do anything to jeopardize that possible opportunity. Anyway you haven't told me what the money has been spent on?"

"Setting up a company to finance my latest play in America. That way I'll be producer, director, and writer. Liane, I've told you what happens. I hand over a script to a director and he just does what he wants with it, - changes the dialogue, moves scenes around, cuts out a character.

It's been agony for me. I got to a state when I felt so frustrated I had to do something."

"And has it occurred to you, you may not get the loan from Curtis. He may not be interested in the proposition you are going to put before him."

"That has occurred to me."

"Very soon I will have quite a lot of money when I've sold the Gorregiani."

"Damn that painting," exclaimed Brett angrily. "You'll never get a cent."

"I will," replied Liane defiantly. "By the way where is Charlene?"

"Charlene gets up late. Are you ready? I want to get a lot done today. And stop worrying. It's all in your head. Charlene means nothing to me, except being an old friend who needs help."

As they left their table a middle aged waiter came up to Liane.

"Miss O'Neill?" he enquired politely. "I have a message for you from Ahmed Shawki. He would like to see you here in the hotel on Wednesday at five o'clock. He will meet you in the foyer if that is convenient to you."

"Certainly," Liane replied, somewhat puzzled at this new development.

"Thank you madame," said the waiter giving a slight bow, before hurrying away. Liane and Brett left the dining room, and walked towards the lift.

"Ahmed wants to see you?" queried Brett. "What on earth for? And who is the guy who carried the message?"

"That will be Ali Shawki," replied Liane. "An uncle I believe."

"This morning I want to go to Santa Sophia and make notes," Brett continued, "Bring your camera, and I don't think your wearing apparel this morning is really suitable. Beautiful, I must admit, but could cause temperatures to rise in local Muslims. They are not used to seeing the bare backs of females."

153

"My back isn't bare," Liane protested with a smile. "Well, only half of it, and I'm not changing."

Brett shrugged his shoulders. "Please yourself, but remember I did warn you."

Liane went up to her room to collect her camera, and in the lift coming down at the next floor Charlene stepped in, beautifully attired in a pair of close fitting lime green trousers with a loose cream satin blouse, buttoned close to the neck and sleeves three quarter length.

"Hi!" she greeted Liane with a eager smile. She looked well rested and ready to start the day.

"How's your headache?" enquired Liane sceptically.

"Headache?" she looked puzzled for a moment. "Oh, it's gone. Brett gave me these marvellous tablets and it went just like that. He was always great whenever I didn't feel well."

"How nice for you," said Liane quietly.

" What are you and Brett doing this morning?"

"We're going to the Santa Sophia Mosque. Brett wants to make notes and I'll be taking photos."

"Santa Sophia Mosque?" she exclaimed with a pleasant smile on her crimson lips. "Sounds a contradiction in terms. I haven't a clue about Turkish history. Would you mind if I came with you. It gets so boring being on my own. There's no one to talk to in the hotel except Germans and I don't speak a word of German."

"You'd better ask Brett."

Liane looked Charlene up and down. The trousers were much too tight, especially around the buttocks, and the cream satin blouse set off her jet black hair to perfection. She knew exactly what she was doing, demanding Brett's personal attention in the night, because she was ill. She looked an extremely healthy young woman.

In the foyer Brett was waiting for Liane. As soon as he saw Charlene, Liane detected the merest suggestion of embarrassment.

"Feeling better this morning Charlene?" he enquired solicitously.

"Very well thank you,".she gave him a big smile. "I say Brett, I'd love to come with you and Liane this morning. I promise you I'll be as good as gold and won't interfere with whatever you are doing."

154

Dance Amongst Thorns

Charlene insisted they went by taxi, too much walking in the hot sun made her tired, and she sat between Liane and Brett, completely at her ease, controlling the conversation which she directed mainly at Brett.

"Why does everywhere look so neglected?" she asked, looking out of the taxi window.

"Income tax is only 10%," replied Brett, "So you won't get much city maintenance for that."

Sometimes Liane looked through the rear window to get another view of something Brett had pointed out to Charlene. The second time Liane did this she noticed it was the same taxi behind them.

Their taxi sped over the Galata Bridge then made its way through a labyrinth of small streets, all the buildings two storied and shabby. And as usual, there were the broken pavements, holes in the road, everywhere litter lining the streets.

"Tell me some more about Istanbul," Charlene begged Brett.

"It's the only city in the world built on two continents," He told her.

Charlene smiled back at him, a secret sort of smile.

"You're the best guide I could ever wish for."

The taxi deposited them outside the Santa Sophia, a large mediaeval building with a grey domed roof and four minarets.

They entered the vast interior of the mosque. Brett making copious notes, Liane photographing. Then suddenly she saw the man, with his dark hair, and moustache, in a brown leather jacket. He was walking across to the mosaic of the Virgin and Child. How strange he should also have decided to visit the Santa Sophia mosque the same day and time as themselves, thought Liane as Brett walked across.

"This mosque has been turned into a museum," Brett told her. "You will have noticed that there is no one kneeling in prayer. That is the reason why you got in wearing that outfit. What's the matter Liane? Something is worrying you."

Liane turned and smiled affably at him. "It's nothing. It's just that I'm puzzled. The man from the iron gates street has also decided to come here today. He's over there." Liane indicated the man looking up at the mosaic.

"Never seen him before in my life," observed Brett in a bored voice.

"It's just a coincidence I suppose," she continued, "You see I felt someone was staring at me a moment ago and I turned round to see that man. Then he started walking away."

"It's that dress. The semi bare back sends these Muslim guys crazy. I told you not to wear it. I saw the Muslim attendant giving you a look..."

Charlene strolled across to them.

"Brett, you know such a lot about history, could you tell me something?"

Brett smiled at her. "Just ask."

Charlene gave him one of her flirtatious smiles.

"Overhead there is a mosaic of the Virgin Mary holding the Infant Jesus," Charlene pointed to the high dome over their heads. "Is this building Christian or Muslim?"

Brett smiled. "It's been both in its time. Santa Sophia started off as a Christian church built in the sixth century." The way Brett looked at Charlene, he liked her, liked her a lot. "When Istanbul was captured by the Ottomans in the fifteenth century, this building and all other Christian churches became mosques, and the citizens became Muslims, literally overnight."

Charlene was listening in rapt attention, her eyes gazing adoringly at Brett.

"You mean whether they liked it or not?"

"Certainly. If you didn't obey the sultan, that was a treasonable offence punishable by death."

Charlene shuddered and lowered her eye lids in a provocative manner. What Brett required above all else, thought Liane, was money, and that's just what Charlene had, if you could buy designer clothes in Sloane Street.

"Liane, will you go up to the balcony and take a couple of shots up there. If we want to do a scene here, we'll have to build a set in the studio. I can't see the authorities allowing film making in here."

Liane went up the steep narrow steps to the balcony.

There was no one up there except two German women. Liane took a number of shots at various angles and as she turned to go she saw the man again. He was walking towards her from the far end of the balcony. It was the way he looked at her with his dark staring eyes.

Suddenly a strange illogical fear pricked her skin, giving her goose pimples.

As she turned and hurried down the narrow steps to the ground floor, she wondered why she was reacting in this strange manner. She was being totally unreasonable, she told herself. Always she prided herself on reacting to peculiar situations in a calm manner. Why so different today?

The man had every right to be in Santa Sophia or to stand outside their hotel. She had now reached the ground floor, but where was Brett? He was not in the mosque. What had happened to him?

She walked quickly across the bare stone floor. Suddenly she saw him in the entrance. The relief was enormous.

"What's the matter?" he asked. "You look as though you've seen a ghost."

"I wish he was a ghost."

"What are you talking about?" Brett asked in an exasperated manner.

"It's that man. He was up in the balcony."

Brett gave her a patient smile.

"I've told you. It's that semi bare back and your extraordinary beauty that is doing it."

"Stop it Brett. I want you to be serious."

"Liane, Istanbul is a comparatively small town. If we were here long enough, we would probably be meeting the same people all the time."

"I know. I know I'm being unreasonable. Where is Charlene by the way?"

"Buying a picture postcard to send home."

They walked out of the mosque into the hot sun.

"So we have Charlene's delightful company until Thursday when Curtis arrives."

"Liane, try to have a bit of compassion for her. Try to be a little kinder to her."

"I have not been unkind to her. Brett I have bigger worries on my mind than Charlene. Who was trying to get into my room last night and what did he want?"

Brett frowned. "Your money? What time did you say this happened?"

"About two thirty."

"I went into Charlene's room sometime just before that. I went back to my room shortly after. I didn't see anyone."

"Thank goodness I left the key in the lock. That must have stopped him getting the door open. I'm beginning to wonder if it will happen again."

"Muslim laws on assaulting women are very severe," said Brett thoughtfully. "In some Muslim countries rape is a hanging offence and thieves have their hands chopped off. I must admit it puzzles me. Perhaps he was trying to get into the wrong room - mistook your room for someone elses."

"I don't know what to think. Brett, will he come back?"

"Perhaps. We'll have to work out a plan." Brett gave her a sly smile. "I think it time we went back to the hotel. What time does Ahmed want to see you tomorrow?"

"Five o'clock."

"I wonder what he's up to?" he said thoughtfully as Charlene joined them. They walked around old Istanbul for a while before hailing a taxi.

Liane was quiet in the taxi. Up to now Istanbul had seemed a friendly city. Now, she was not so sure. She was sat between Brett and Charlene.

"How many shots have you got left on that roll?" asked Brett suddenly.

Liane looked at the indicator.

"I've used up the roll."

"Let's drop it off at that twenty four hour shop near the hotel."

Liane took the roll of film out of the camera, then asked the taxi driver to stop at the photographic shop. And as Liane sat in the back of the taxi with Charlene awaiting Brett's return, suddenly to her surprise she saw the man.

He was standing on the opposite side of the road talking to Ahmed

Shawki. It seemed to be an angry exchange, both men waving their arms. Brett returned from the shop and the taxi continued on its short journey to the hotel.

Brett gave Liane a new film for her camera.

"I've just seen the man talking to Ahmed Shawki," Liane told Brett as she opened her camera and fitted the new film.

"Ahmed Shawki can talk to who ever he likes," Brett told her. "Really Liane. You're getting obsessed about this guy."

Brett was right thought Liane feeling a little foolish. She resolved not to mention the man again. When they arrived at the Hera Palas the three of them went straight to the dining room.

"Just a light snack for me. Bowl of soup," Charlene told the waiter.

"Make that two bowls of soup," added Liane.

"You might as well make it three," said Brett. Then he turned to Charlene.

"This afternoon Liane and I have to work on the script.

This is a working trip."

"O.K." laughed Charlene. "I've got the message. I shall go for a walk along the Istiklal Caddesi and I may do some shopping."

Liane went up to her room, depositing her handbag and camera on the dressing table. The hot afternoon was making her feel sleepy, so going into the bathroom she splashed cold water on her face, and brushed her hair vigorously. It always worked. Then going down the corridor to Brett's room, the work began.

She was so pleased Brett liked her ideas, her character development, her dialogue. When they finally finished, it was almost dinner time. Liane sorted out the sheets, put them away in their files, unplugged and put the lid on her typewriter. Brett was lying full length on the bed, his shoes off, his head cushioned by a couple of pillows.

"We're making headway Liane. I'll phone Ian in a few minutes. How I wish you had never got mixed up with that Egyptian crook. I don't trust him one iota."

"Neither do I," Liane agreed with him. "But I desperately want that painting. I need the money. I have financial problems too you know."

Brett gave her an amused smile. "How much is your overdraft?"

"About three hundred."

Brett's face creased into a big grin. "That, my dear Liane, is chicken feed."

"To you it is, not me."

"One day I hope I will be able to help you."

"Thank you Brett. You are very kind."

"When Curtis arrives here Thursday, I am hoping our problems will be solved. He had a successful gamble in a Broadway show a couple of years ago, so it looks hopeful."

"Plus the fact you are going to help him with his matrimonial affairs," added Liane. "Look Brett, that won't work."

"Let me be the judge of that," said Brett sharply. "Changing the subject I am most concerned about someone trying to get into your room. You can't sleep in that room again."

He got off the bed and walked to her. Liane stood up.

"Where do I sleep then?"

Brett's hands closed over hers in an iron like grip. Suddenly her heart was beating too fast, as his eyes stared into hers.

"You sleep here," he said in a low voice. "You'll be safer."

"You're right. I'll just go to my room to collect a couple of items."

Liane didn't care anymore, whatever the consequences of her action, she needed the protection of Brett. The person trying to get into her room could be just a common thief, or he could be a rapist, or a murderer!

Liane walked quickly down the corridor feeling she had made the right decision. She unlocked her door and entered. From beneath her pillow she withdrew her blue cotton nightdress. Next she went into the bathroom and picked up her toilet bag. It was when she returned to the bedroom that she noticed that only her handbag was on the dressing table.

Someone had stolen her camera!

CHAPTER 16

Liane stood by the dressing table perplexed. Was her memory at fault and she had actually placed the camera elsewhere? Swiftly she looked around the room.

There was no camera on the bedside table, the table by the refrigerator, the two chairs, the beds. No it had definitely been stolen.

But who would want to steal her camera? Even though it was a Pentax and took good pictures, it was not an expensive model and the casing was a little battered. The resale price could not be great. The money in her handbag was more than the camera was worth.

A sudden fear clutched her. Quickly she opened her bag and counted the money. It was untouched. Why take a shabby looking camera and not take the money?

"My camera has been stolen," she told Brett the moment she entered his room. "Thank goodness we took the film out this afternoon. But who could prefer that battered Pentax to the cash, British passport, and bank credit card in my bag?"

"Very peculiar," said Brett thoughtfully. "I wonder if it's the same person who tried to get in last night?"

"Perhaps. We don't know. But I'm definitely not sleeping in that room again."

"Let's go down to dinner, and collect Charlene on the way. And," Brett looked questioningly at Liane, "I'm thinking of telling Charlene tonight about the proposition I am going to put to Curtis when he arrives on Thursday."

"Brett, what is the security against the loan?" Liane suddenly asked, as they walked down the corridor.

He gave her an enigmatic smile. "I'll tell you tonight in my room."

They had now reached Charlene's door and Brett gave a firm knock.

Charlene was back from shopping. She came to the door dressed in the afternoon's purchase wearing a black chiffon blouse, and a pair

161

of blue silk trousers.

"I would never have thought I could buy Uphoff clothes in Istanbul. But there was this shop in the Istiklal Caddesi and I just couldn't resist them."

In the dining room the waiter who had given Liane the message from Ahmed took their order. He gave no sign of recognition. Brett ordered a bottle of Altin Kopuk, a Turkish champagne.

"I adore champagne," Charlene told them. "Remember the summer balls at Harvard?" She looked across at Brett. "They were always open air, coloured lanterns hanging in the trees, always a moon. Let's drink to the memory of those romantic evenings."

They raised their glasses. Liane felt a kind of desperation. Would this woman never stop?

And all this fraternising with Charlene could be for nothing. Curtis could quite easily arrive, and there would be no patching up of the frail marriage, nor interest in Brett's business proposition. Backing a play was a real gamble. You could make a fortune, you could lose it.

Then she thought of the night that lay ahead and the way Brett had looked at her when he had said she must sleep in his room. It was all a question of trust. Suddenly Charlene's angry voice interrupted her thoughts.

"My God, I can't bear it," she heatedly exclaimed. "The thought of Curtis arriving on Thursday! Brett you should never have done it. I know you did it for the best, but it isn't the best for me. Please phone him and tell him not to come. The marriage is finished, I can't put it any plainer."

"Charlene I can't," protested Brett. "First I phone to say come, then I phone to say don't come. He'll want to know what the hell is going on. Besides I have a very attractive business proposition to put to him."

Charlene gave a hard laugh. "Curtis won't be able to help you. All the family money is tied up. Anyway it would take a board meeting with all the family in agreement."

Brett looked dejected.

"Brett, you're in trouble," said Charlene, grave concern in her voice. "You must tell me what it is all about."

"I desperately need £150,000," said Brett in a low, almost inaudible voice.

"What do you need it for?"

Brett outlined the plans for the company he had recently formed. Charlene listened attentively. At length she spoke.

"I'll lend you £150,000 Brett, on the understanding you make me a partner," adding with a smile, "I am a business woman. Anyway, I have faith in you and your plays. I know I'm backing a winner."

"That is very kind of you Charlene. I'll think about it."

"It is fortunate that Curtis and I always kept our money separate," she continued. "That was the one wise thing I did. Brett, I'm tired of Istanbul. Come back to New York with me Thursday and we'll go to my lawyer and get it all signed up."

"But Curtis is arriving Thursday."

"You'll just have to tell him not to come."

There was a look of hesitancy in Brett's face.

"The sooner the better, catch him before he leaves," Charlene urged. "Personally, I find him so difficult to talk to. He will not see my point of view. He's got the most rigid mind I've ever come across.

Anyway, I've made up my mind I'm filing for a divorce, so there is no point in him coming here. And by the way Brett, if you don't come to New York with me Thursday, the deal's off."

Brett left the dining room. He did not look a happy man. Charlene made small talk until his return. It was mainly about clothes and skiing holidays in Switzerland. Liane felt doomed.

If Brett accepted Charlene's offer, lending him the money he so desperately needed placed him firmly in Charlene's control. And what were her plans after the divorce Liane thought gloomily. Brett? It was possible.

Brett returned to the dining room and resumed his seat.

He looked weary.

"Did you get him?" asked Charlene.

"There was no reply," came Brett's answer.

"You'll just have to keep trying, that's all."

Suddenly the lights dimmed, and hypnotic Turkish music began. A young Turkish dancer clacked her castanets and gyrated her hips.

Liane glanced at Charlene. Charlene was looking at Brett, and as she gazed at him across the table there was a look of covetous greed.

It made Liane shudder.

The belly dancing finished, and the lights came up.

Western dance music started.

"I'd just love to dance," said Charlene looking at Brett. Brett obliged, and as they smooched around the dance floor Charlene clung to Brett, her arm around his neck.

I might as well not be here thought Liane feeling angry. Had Brett spoken to her this evening? Barely.

The dance finished, Charlene and Brett returned to the table and to Liane's surprise Charlene said she was tired and going to bed, and as she walked out of the room Liane turned to Brett. She had to rid herself of some of her pent up anger.

"Tired my foot. There's nothing wrong with her. She's probably meeting someone in the bar.

"Liane, don't talk like that about Charlene. And remember she has made me a generous offer and the only stipulation is I make her a partner."

"Are you sure that is all she wants?" asked Liane menacingly.

Brett did not reply, and Liane continued: "You did a good job tonight trying to make her happy. Recalling all those happy memories." Her voice was icy.

Brett stood up. "Instead of being pleased Charlene has offered to help me, you are showing a childish jealousy. Let's go up to bed."

He looked at Liane with an air of exasperation, then turning he left the room. Liane followed. She was the one at fault.

When they reached his room, Brett flung himself in an armchair and picked up a copy of the Turkish Daily News. Liane walked into the bathroom and started cleaning her teeth furiously.

Brett had upset her. As usual Charlene had received all his attention. True she had offered to help him solve his financial problems, but she, Liane, had been merely background, and it hurt. It hurt like hell.

She came out of the bathroom and sat on the far bed her spirits heavy.

"You had better phone Curtis again."

Brett got up from the armchair and flung himself down on the other bed, staring at the ceiling.

"I'm not in the mood."

"But you've got to. It's not fair to him. The poor man will arrive here..."

"You do it," Brett told her sharply.

"All right. What's the number?"

She leaned across and picked up the phone whilst Brett dictated the number.

She could hear it ringing in Curtis's New York apartment. After an interminable length of time he answered it.

"Is that Curtis?" asked Liane.

"Sure is," came a hard masculine voice.

"My name is Liane O'Neill. I'm phoning on behalf of Brett McMahon. The message is..."

"Here, give me the phone," and Brett took it from her hand.

"Hi Curtis. Got some bad news. Don't come. Charlene is off to New York Thursday so it will be a wasted journey. Sorry about that, I wanted to see you about another matter. Am I going with her? Haven't made up my mind. Sure I'll phone you . "

He put the phone down and looked across at Liane.

"He's not coming."

Liane gave him a stern look.

"Brett, if you accept Charlene's offer, you'll be her lapdog. Well,I'm going to get that Gorregiani if it is the last thing I do. I will sell it, and give all the money to you so you won't need Charlene's money."

"Thanks Liane," Brett got off the bed and walked across to her and drew her to her feet, then put his arms around her.

"You know I love you. I only came to Istanbul to pleased you."

Suddenly he grabbed her and kissed her hard on the mouth.

Liane struggled to get away.

"Now that Charlene is not here," she told him angrily, "I get all the attention. Brett I am not in a happy mood tonight. Tonight I had a walk on part and I did not like it one bit."

165

"You're just being supersensitive. What do you want me to do? Ignore her?"

"I think it's time you told me the security you gave the bank against your loan."

He went and lay on the far bed.

"Tavanomore is the security," he said quietly.

Liane stared at him, her eyes blazing.

"Tavanomore!" she repeated, incredulity in her voice. "How could you do it?" she stormed.

"I had no alternative," he replied sternly. "I was desperate. A desperate situation requires desperate measures."

Liane walked across to the window and drawing back the curtain looked at the night sky.

"I remember staying there as a child sleeping on the third floor beneath the sloping ceiling," she said softly. "And as I lay in bed I could see a large beautiful star in the sky, and it seemed to be resting on top of a tall tree in the garden. And I remember a feeling of utter contentment.

I remember through my childhood and teenage years the conversations with Dad were invariably about Tavanomore. 'It is your home Liane,' he would say. 'One day you'll live there.' Now it will never happen," she ended sadly.

Slipping off her shoes and unzipping her skirt, Liane lay down under the cover of the far bed, staring at the wall, her thoughts far away. There was silence for a few minutes before Brett spoke.

"If I accept Charlene's offer there would be no question of losing Tavanomore. Why do you think you will never live there?"

"Because I feel I am slipping from the picture."

"Don't be silly, of course you are not."

"I presume you set up your company soon after inheriting."

"Correct. Liane, it is going to be the realisation of a dream. Don't you know what it means to me? To have my own company?"

"Of course I know, but until this evening you were quite happy to risk losing Tavanomore in order to achieve your objective," Liane pronounced, a bitter tone in her voice, then added wearily, "I suppose you think me an utterly self centred woman..."

166

"I don't, because I know what the farm means to you," he retorted. "How could I be happy about the possible sale of Tavanomore? I've been desperately unhappy about it.

"Brett, I've lost you."

"Don't talk nonsense."

"Can't you see what's going to happen? You'll end up accepting Charlene's offer. She becomes your partner. That makes for a nice, cosy relationship. And where do I fit in? I don't. Charlene would see to that."

There was silence for a moment. "What a negative outlook you have on life," came Brett's quiet voice.

"Negative! I'm being realistic. You're the one at fault. You're the dreamer."

"Maybe life is a dream," came his sleepy reply.

"In the morning I shall change my room."

"Come across and have a cuddle."

"No." She turned and faced the wall, feeling angry and depressed. A few minutes later, she heard the sound of gentle breathing. Brett was asleep.

Liane switched off the bedside light, trying to relax and sleep, but her mind would not be still. When she grew tired of worrying about Brett and Charlene her mind drifted onto other matters.

Who had taken her ancient Pentax and not touched the money in her handbag? Could it have been Ahmed Shawki's uncle? He was a member of the hotel staff and could gain access to the room. But why the camera and not the money in her handbag? Finally unable to solve the problem she fell asleep.

The following morning she was the first to awake. She looked across at Brett still asleep in the other bed. The lines of strain had gone, and in its place there was a youthful boyish look. Whatever happened she would always love him, and unselfishly prayed everything would go right for him.

She got out of bed and walked across to the bathroom. She undressed and switched on the shower, wishing life was simple, that a few prayers could solve everything. After she had dried herself and dressed she stood before the mirror brushing her hair.

167

The door opened and Brett stood there, in his briefs, his hair tousled, stifling a yawn.

"I borrowed one of your towels," she said almost sheepishly looking at him through the mirror. "I hope you don't mind."

Brett smiled sleepily at her. "You can borrow anything."

"I'm sorry about last night," she continued, her voice now contrite, turning to face him. "I want you to know that despite my annoyance, I wish you luck."

"Thanks," he replied walking to the wash basin and picking up his razor.

"Where does the research take us today?"

"A trip up the Bosphorus. Liane?"

"Yes?"

"Bear with me just a little longer. Now will you let a guy shave in peace?"

Twenty minutes later Brett was ready and they went down in the lift. She thought the lift attendant gave her a curious sort of smile. When they reached the ground floor Liane turned to Brett.

"I'm going to reception to change my room."

He placed his hand on her arm momentarily restraining her. "You know you don't have to," he said quietly.

"It's no good Brett. I've made up my mind."

Brett gave a sigh. "I'll see you in the dining room."

Liane walked through to the foyer, spoke to the receptionist, then went up to her room, packed, and moved into her new room. She joined Brett in the dining room.

"I'm now in Room 510."

"I hope you'll be happy," he told her with a certain bitterness in his voice. "And I hope no one tries to get in. I think you are making a mistake." Then he gave her a cold look.

"What do you think I am, some macho rapist? Or is it some kind of punishment?"

Liane decided to ignore the questioning.

"Charlene coming with us this morning?"

"If you don't mind."

"But I do mind, but my opinion is not important."

Brett gave her an angry glare.

"I want to think about today's work. There is a lot to do." He took a quick glance at his watch. "We have to leave in half an hour."

They met Charlene in the foyer, then the three of them took a taxi down to the docks at Karakoy, boarding a shabby rusty looking vessel.

It was a delightful trip up the Bosphorus, though tinged with the sad thought that today might be her last day with Brett if he accepts Charlene's offer and returns with her to America.

On the return journey Liane's thoughts turned to the strange things that had happened since their arrival in Istanbul.

There was the man in the brown leather jacket from the iron gate street for a start. There was the stolen camera. Then she remembered on the first day in Istanbul Brett had been mistaken for someone called Karmi Hussein. Who was Karmi Hussein? A middle east crook? A drug dealer? Was there a connection between him and the man in the brown leather jacket?

The boat docked at Karakoy, and Brett, Liane and Charlene with the rest of the passengers disembarked, then walked through the narrow uphill streets back to the hotel.

Liane had now decided the man was a weirdo obsessed about European blondes and she would pay no further attention to him. Anyway, he hadn't been on the boat, they hadn't seen him at all that day, it was possible that he had lost interest in the pursuit.

"That boat trip was invaluable. We now have a new subplot," Brett told her as they entered the hotel.

"I'm going up to my room to make a few calls," Charlene announced. "Call me when you go down to dinner."

Brett and Liane went up to his room. Brett called room service for sandwiches and coffee, Liane plugged in her typewriter and the work began.

Just before five o'clock she remembered the appointment with Ahmed.

"I'm coming with you," said Brett. "In case he tries anything."

Ahmed was in the foyer standing by a bronze candelabra, a tired, strained look on his face as he greeted them. Liane glanced quickly around the crowded area. Suddenly she tensed. A man was standing in profile by the newsstand and appeared to be reading a newspaper.

It was the man in the brown leather jacket. There was no mistaking him.

"What's the problem Ahmed?" asked Brett in a sharp voice.

"There is no problem." He gave them a weak smile. " I just want to be sure you have written to the priest to send the letter. It is very important."

"I did it immediately," Liane replied. "I should have the letter Friday or Saturday."

"I am pleased." Ahmed gave her the full impact of his smile.

"When we meet on Saturday, will you bring the painting with you?" asked Brett.

"Of course. I will not cheat you."

"We cannot be sure of that. You have done it once, why not again."

"I give my word."

Brett gave him a look of contempt, and Ahmed looked furtively from side to side, and lowered his voice.

"On Saturday I do not think it wise to meet here."

"Where do you suggest?" asked Liane.

"The Pudding Shop at eleven o'clock. It is a favourite restaurant for the English and Americans. It is near the Blue Mosque. You will have no difficulty in finding it. You tell no one of this meeting."

Liane looked across to the newsstand. The man had gone.

"Ahmed, a few moments ago there was a man in a brown leather jacket standing by the newsstand reading a paper. I saw you talking to him yesterday in the street, not far from the hotel. Who is he?"

"Yesterday I do not speak to anyone in the street."

"But I saw you," persisted Liane. "You were arguing."

"I did not speak to anyone," repeated Ahmed. Now his voice had taken on a sharp, angry tone.

"You are lying to me Ahmed."

In his eyes was a sheepish crestfallen look.

"I bid you goodbye until Saturday."

Then he gave a short bow and hurriedly left the hotel.

CHAPTER 17

"Let's get back and finish the work." There was an impatient tone in Brett's voice as he moved towards the lift.

"What a waste of time," he continued, "Arranging a meeting just to see if you have contacted the priest. Then changing the venue for the next one. I'm getting the impression Ahmed is going neurotic."

They stepped into the waiting lift. "What's the matter Liane? You look worried."

"It's nothing."

If she told him she had just seen the man in the brown leather jacket she knew Brett would not take it seriously. There would be some joking remark that would only irritate. She couldn't explain it, but she had the strangest feeling the man was keeping a check on her, for what purpose she couldn't think.

He must be confusing her with someone else. Or was it Brett? Was it Brett he was trailing? Did he think Brett was Karmi Hussein, whoever that mysterious man was.

"Don't you think it strange that Ahmed denied he spoke to the man yesterday?" she asked Brett as they got into the lift.

"Everything Ahmed Shawki does is strange. Are you sure it was Ahmed talking to him?"

"Positive. I'd know Ahmed anywhere."

"I should forget it."

"Brett, I'll be glad to leave Istanbul.

"Leaving the lift they walked the corridor to his room. Once there, Brett's mind switched to work, and the writing continued. Liane was glad of the work, glad to have something to keep her mind occupied.

She had a creepy sort of feeling it was more than a coincidence she had seen the man three times in three days. Was it an obsession about blonde European women, or was it something more, something sinister?

"Liane, I havea feeling your mind is not on your work. What is

171

wrong?"

"I'm sorry Brett. I'm feeling a little tired today. I didn't sleep too well last night."

At half past seven, they finished for the day. Liane wearily sorted out the pages and pushed them into the appropriate files.

"The script is coming along fine," Brett told her, a satisfied look on his face. "I'm lucky to have you as a co-writer."

He gave her a soft smile.

Last night she had ruined what could have been a memorable romantic night with the man she loved. They would have made love, then slept together in each other's arms. Now she regretted it. Every single moment with Brett was precious.

"I'll make a call to Ian, and join you in the restaurant. Perhaps you'd like to collect Charlene."

Charlene had changed for dinner and was now wearing a black dress low cut showing a great deal of her ample bosom.

They went down in silence in the lift, the waiter showing them to their usual table. On the small stage the pianist was playing more melodies by Gershwin.

"Brett will be down in a few minutes," Liane told Charlene as she picked up the menu. "He has to make a daily call to Dublin notifying progress, or lack of it. Actually we are doing very well. We've almost finished the script."

"How nice," Charlene replied playing with the gold bracelet on her wrist. "I wish I had a career. I need something to occupy my mind. What a relief I'm not meeting Curtis tomorrow. I don't think I could have coped with him." Then she looked thoughtfully across the room. "It's a great comfort to have Brett around."

Liane looked across at the pianist. He was now playing Rhapsody in Blue. She had to tell Charlene.

"When Brett has sorted out his financial problems, we are getting married."

There was a tense silence for a few moments, then Charlene turned to her, her eyes furious pools of green.

"Is that so?" she said in an arched voice. "How long have you known each other?"

"A couple of months."

At that moment Brett entered the dining room and made his way towards their table.

"Sorry I've been so long. Took ages to get through to Ian." Brett turned to Liane. "Anyway, he's pleased with our progress."

"Now Brett," said Charlene, giving him one of her best smiles. "I want to talk about tomorrow. My plane takes off at 5.00pm. I thought I'd get a taxi to the airport around 3.30pm. I hate being in a rush."

Brett listened carefully, a serious look on his face.

"Liane and I will be out in the morning doing a little research," he told her. "But we should be back in the hotel around 2.00pm."

"Don't forget," warned Charlene, a hard look in her eyes. "If you're not here, and I have to go to New York alone, the deal's off."

Brett gave her a careful look. "That's fair enough."

The waiter approached to take their order.

"Now will you excuse me, I have just remembered a few calls I have to make." Charlene rose to her feet and looked at the waiter. "I'll have something in my room."

And with that she walked swiftly from the dining room. Brett watched her exit with an anxious look on his face.

"What's the matter with Charlene?" he asked, after they had placed their order with the waiter. There was a worried tone in his voice.

Liane shrugged her shoulders. "Who knows?"

It was a subdued sort of evening. Liane ate without enthusiasm. All she could think of was tomorrow. Tomorrow they might part. And all their problems were about money, she thought disconsolately. And as for Charlene she had to be told about their future plans.

She looked across at Brett as if memorising his face. She looked at his firm mouth, his firm jaw. She looked at his eyes. Sometimes they were full of love for her, tonight they were dull with worry.

And when she thought of the painting, deep in her heart she knew Brett was right. Ahmed was not to be trusted and there was a good chance that nothing would come from the Saturday meeting. But she couldn't give up, she would remain hopeful to the end.

There was no dancing that night, so when they had finished coffee, they rose from the table and left the dining room. The lift was empty and waiting, and when they reached Liane's floor, Brett gave her a smile.

"I'll see you in the morning," he said. "I've got a pile of letters to write. Sleep well."

He gave her the briefest peck on the cheek. The lift attendant closed the doors, and the lift sped up to the next floor.

Liane walked along the corridor to her room. All he cares about is Charlene and her money she thought angrily.

The following morning, Charlene did not make an appearance at the breakfast table. Liane and Brett ate breakfast in silence. Brett looked depressingly preoccupied.

It was going to be another hot day, and a difficult one, and it was going to take all Liane's self control from preventing a big, blazing row breaking out between them.

"We forgot to collect the photographs," Liane reminded him as they left the hotel.

They walked to the end of the street and collected the photographs from the shop on the corner. Brett pushed the envelope containing the photographs and negatives into his pocket, then crossing the road they went down the steep narrow street of electric light fittings.

"I thought we'd go to the Blue Mosque," Brett told her, "And then that is the finish."

It was when they were crossing the Galata Bridge they paused a moment to look down on the ships passing beneath the bridge, a thoughtful look came into Brett's eyes.

"I want to be rich Liane."

Liane gave him a sad look.

"I've thought that all my life," he continued, "I never told you the hard time I had at Harvard. I got there on a scholarship, but with insufficient money to live on. So I had to work part time at the docks at Boston. It was a hard life, but I got through.

I have had plays produced on Broadway, but I was never in the big money, didn't have the name. Working for Ian at the Dublin Priory has status but there is little money in it.

Then I wrote a script for an American film company, - the biggest fee I have ever been offered, you know the rest."

174

They continued across the bridge. The usual salesmen pestering them to buy carpets.

When they reached the Blue Mosque they handed their shoes to the attendant, then entered the vast interior. Great marble pillars supported the dome, the predominating colour blue. Liane leaned against the cool stone, as she watched Brett walking up and down making notes. There was no dark haired man in a brown leather jacket. He had obviously lost interest in her, and now it all seemed unimportant. She smiled to herself remembering. Now she had far greater worries on her mind.

Would Brett leave with Charlene this afternoon? If he did she would feel bereaved. Would she and Brett ever meet again? She felt a lump rise in her throat as she looked across at his tall manly figure busy writing in his notebook.

"I've finished here. Let's go."

They left the Blue Mosque, walking through a small garden and crossed the road. They were now standing at the modest entrance to the underground Roman Cistern.

"Like to go in?"

"What exactly is it?" Liane asked as they walked down the dimly lit steps.

"Underground water storage in case the city was beseiged. Built in the sixth century."

Suddenly they had walked into an underground cathedral of gracious stone arches with raised platforms over vast areas of water. Music was playing, one of Beethoven's symphonies, a great powerful sound. And the darkness was pinpointed by a number of small lights.

Liane wandered off along the raised platforms over the water, turning to the left, turning to the right, lost in a world of sixth century Roman conquerors.

The symphony ended and the vast underground cistern was filled with a deep silence. Suddenly she heard footsteps behind her in the dark. She turned. She could see no one in the dark shadows, then the footsteps ceased, and there was silence.

She continued walking, and after a couple of minutes paused in an area of light to look down into the water. Again she heard footsteps behind her and again turned to find there was no one there, and the sound of the footsteps ceased.

When this had happened for the third time the place began to take on a claustrophobic atmosphere. She had to get out of the place. All the magical romance woven by the music, the water, the gracious cathedral-like arches had gone.

Suddenly she thought of Brett. What had happened to him?

"Brett!" she called, but there was no answer.

Then the music started again, a loud, passionate sound. She must get out of this place. She could feel goose pimples running along her arms. She longed for the open air, the sunlight, the milling crowds outside.

"Brett!" she called again as she hurried towards the exit. But it was not the exit she was hurrying to, but more platforms over more water. Her sense of direction was never good at the best of times, and hopeless in this murky darkness. Then by luck she bumped into an old lady in the dark.

"I'm terribly sorry," she exclaimed, trying to sound casual, "Which way to the exit?"

"That way," the old lady pointed, in a strong German accent.

Liane hurried in the direction the old lady had pointed, thankful to see daylight again, and the hot blue sky as she climbed the steps. Brett was standing at the top waiting for her.

"Brett, am I glad to see you."

"What happened?" He gave her a knowing smile. "Am I right in thinking someone has been following you?"

She gave him a defiant smile. "Of course not."

He put his arm around her. "I don't think we are telling the truth."

"Well, for a few minutes I did wonder... Brett, it was a very unpleasant experience."

"Get your flight booked as soon as possible. I think you can forget your date with Ahmed on Saturday." He gave her a derisory smile.

"I'm beginning to think I will."

They walked to the main road and stood by the kerb.

"Which is the quickest way back to the hotel?" mused Brett.

Liane brought the map from her bag and handed it to him.

"You decide," she told him. "Let me have a look at the photographs."

Brett handed Liane the package containing the photographs and negatives, whilst he endeavoured to study the map.

"On the way back to the hotel, what about a quick look at the Grand Bazaar?" he asked without looking up. "It's only half past eleven."

Liane could stand it no longer.

"Brett, what have you decided to do..."

"May I help you?"

Liane looked round to see a woman standing before her. She was dressed in western clothes, - white trousers, a black cotton shirt, secured at the waist with a wide gold belt. Her head was completely covered in a headscarf, not white as was the custom with Muslim women, but of a vivid floral design. She wore large sunglasses. She looked prosperous and European.

"I think you are lost." The woman gave them a pleasant smile. Liane liked the look of the woman, and returned her smile.

"We are trying to find the best way of getting to the Grand Bazaar," she told her.

"You are a long way from the Grand Bazaar," the woman replied. Then giving them an enquiring smile continued. "You are American?"

"I am English," Liane told her. "And Brett is American."

"I am so happy to meet you. I love to speak English with English and American people. How long have you been in Istanbul?"

"We arrived Sunday," Brett promptly answered her.

"And when do you leave?"

"It may be today, it may be tomorrow."

"That is a very short visit to this interesting city. Before you go you ought to visit our National Art Gallery."

"You are interested in art?" asked Liane, looking curiously at the woman.

The woman nodded happily. "I am an artist, and I am also a collector."

"Who do you collect?" Liane asked smiling. The woman intrigued her.

"At the moment it is sixteenth century Italian."

Liane looked at Brett. His face was a blank.

"I'm very interested in sixteenth century Italian art."

The woman gave her a big smile.

"In that case you must come to my apartment and look at my collection. It is small, but I am very proud of it."

"Like to go?" asked Brett. Liane nodded happily.

"Good, that is settled. And afterwards I take you to the Grand Bazaar. Come my car is parked nearby."

The car was an unfamiliar Turkish vehicle, new and quite comfortable. Liane and Brett got into the back and they set off, crossing the Galata Bridge, then following the road bordering the Bosphorus.

"Do you live far?" asked Liane.

"No, not far at all," she replied. "The apartment is on the outskirts of the city. When you go to the Grand Bazaar, is there anything in particular you wish to purchase?"

"I'd like to look at leather jackets," said Brett, giving Liane an amused look.

A long conversation ensued about the merits and demerits of leather jackets. This was followed by a discussion between Brett and the woman about leather goods in general. Liane brought the photographs from her handbag and started to look through them. They were good quality pictures and she felt pleased with them.

Then she came to the photograph she had taken in the street of the iron gates, and the one of the man and woman at the door of their house.

The man who had been following her was definitely the man in the photograph. Then it suddenly occurred to her, had he been following her because she had taken his photograph? And if so, why? Was he a man on the run?

She returned the photographs to the envelope and pushed them into her handbag feeling puzzled, wishing she knew the answer. Then she caught sight of the woman looking at her through the driving mirror.

"You live a long way from Istanbul?" ventured Liane, trying to think of something to say.

Actually when they had first got into the car Liane recalled that the woman had said she lived only a short distance from the city. They had been in the car now half an hour.

"We are almost there."

She pointed to a small block of modern apartments ahead of them on the right. Turning into the drive, she stopped near the front entrance.

"It is a pleasant spot," she told them as they walked in through the main door.

The foyer of the building was filled with flowering shrubs and on the right a receptionist sat at a desk. She gave the woman her key and they stepped into the lift.

"It is very kind of you to come with me," the woman told them, as the lift sped upwards, stopping at the fourth floor. They walked down a softly carpeted corridor, the woman stopped at one of the doors and inserted the key.

"Now you are going to have a cup of real Turkish coffee."

She smiled at them as they entered an attractive apartment furnished with modern Turkish furniture in the form of two long low divans before a low coffee table.

"Make yourselves at home," the woman smiled, "Whilst I go in the kitchen and make the coffee."

She left the room, still not having removed her hair scarf and sun glasses. There was something vaguely familiar about her thought Liane as she and Brett walked across to the window.

About a quarter of a mile away flowed the blue Bosphorus, and between the apartment block and the Bosphorus was a landing strip, and on the landing strip was a helicopter.

Brett and Liane looked at each other.

"I like the helicopter," said Brett.

"You can move around quicker," smiled Liane.

"The lady is taking a long time making the coffee," commented Brett in a low voice.

Then suddenly it happened. The door opened and the man standing there was the man in the brown leather jacket.

CHAPTER 18

They had walked into a trap; kidnapped in broad daylight! The woman probably couldn't believe her luck. And had all this happened because she had taken a photograph of their house in the Beyoglu district, and the man and his wife had appeared in the doorway at the precise moment she had clicked the camera. Liane could think of no other explanation.

"Sit down," the man spoke in a commanding tone.

Liane looked at him carefully as she sat down next to Brett on one of the divans. The tell tale sign was an occasional nervous switch in his right eye.

They had to get out of this apartment and quickly. Liane stood up, glanced swiftly at her watch desperate for an excuse. Pretend everything is normal she told herself. Pretend you don't recognise him.

"We've come to look at your wife's art collection." Brett spoke in a breezy manner.

The man did not answer.

"Actually we can't stay long." Liane spoke in a hurried manner. "Brett is..."

"Sit down," the man barked.

Liane sat down, glancing at Brett. He appeared to be very calm. Didn't he realise who the man was?

"Who owns the helicopter?" he asked in a cheerful voice.

The man remained silent, regarding them with his dark staring eyes.

"I've always wanted to learn to fly one," continued Brett in a light hearted tone. "Perhaps I will one day."

"Whilst my wife is making the coffee I would like to ask you a few questions."

Liane tried to give Brett another warning look, and still did not succeed.

"Fire away!" he smiled.

"Why are you in Istanbul? I think you are not tourists."

The man looked at them, his eyes narrowing with dark suspicion.

"We certainly are not," replied Brett, leaning back on the divan; he appeared to be enjoying it. "Actually we are here to write a screen play."

There was no reaction. The man's face was a mask.

"Why did you meet Ahmed Shawki twice in the last few days?"

Brett gave a slow smile. "I'm surprised you know such a devious character. Anyway, that is Liane's department."

She gave Brett a quick look then turned to the man.

"Before I answer your question, I would like to know why you have been following us."

"Respectable people do not have meetings with Ahmed Shawki," he replied smoothly, his dark eyes staring hard at her.

She had to defend herself.

"He stole a painting from me, a Gorregiani, and asked me to come to Istanbul so that we could do a deal."

A surprised look lit up the man's face.

"So you are the owner of the painting!"

Liane nodded, puzzled. "Of course I am the owner. Why, did Ahmed tell you he owned it?"

The man pursed his lips.

"You would have done better to have gone to the police," he replied. "Where is the painting now?"

"Ahmed has it."

"And where does Ahmed live?"

"I don't know."

"You do know," he replied accusingly, a toughness in his face.

Liane looked at Brett.

"We genuinely have no idea where the man lives," Brett told him in a firm voice. "We always meet him in the Hera Palas."

"Did he ever discuss me?" The man looked at both of them, watching them carefully.

"Never," Brett replied. "Why, are you a friend of his?"

"Not a friend," he replied, an unpleasant smile on his face. "I am a business acquaintance, shall we say."

181

"On the two occasions when we met Ahmed Shawki," Brett continued, "The conversation was entirely about the painting. Actually I have no faith in the man and I am only here to please Liane. Personally I think we should never have come."

"And when do you meet him again?" continued the man.

Liane's annoyance was increasing. What right had this strange man to ask such pertinent questions.

"Why should I answer your questions? And why are you so interested in what we do?" she asked, a sharp tone in her voice. "And you still haven't answered my question. Why have you been following us around Istanbul for the last few days?"

"Because I think you are working for Ahmed, both of you."

"You are talking nonsense," exploded Brett. "Why on earth should we be working for him? I can't stand the man."

"You are lying. Why did you take a photograph of my wife and myself?"

"I don't know what you are talking about," said Brett. "I asked Liane to take photographs for reference purposes. We may have to build a set at the studios in Dublin."

The man shook his head. "You are a clever man, but I am more clever than you. This morning you collected the photographs from the shop. Give them to me." He looked at Liane menacingly.

"Let him see the photographs," said Brett in a weary voice.

Liane brought out the envelope and handed it to the man. Hastily he flicked through them until he came to the ones taken of himself and his wife. He studied them carefully, then taking the negatives, he held them up to the light, looking at each one in turn. Finally he replaced them all in the envelope and put it in his pocket.

"Excuse me," said Brett, holding out his hand. "Those photographs and negatives are my property."

The man shook his head. "Now they are mine. I do not take chances.

"What's the matter with you?" asked Brett in an angry voice. "I don't understand what you are talking about. I need those photographs, particularly those of the iron gate street."

"You and Ahmed Shawki were planning to blackmail me," said the

182

man in a low menacing voice.

"Blackmail?" repeated Liane in an incredulous voice. "Why on earth should we want to do that?"

"Ahmed has certain connections," the man replied with an enigmatic air.

"I'm not surprised Ahmed Shawki has dubious connections," Brett told him. "But you can phone the Priory Theatre Dublin. Ian Stratton will vouch for us. We are law abiding citizens in this country solely to write a screenplay. I never heard such nonsense in my life."

"We met Ahmed in Egypt," Liane told the man, "We know very little about him. He did tell us he had been to Sicily buying church art treasures."

The man laughed. It was a distinctly unpleasant laugh.

"You mean stealing church art treasures," the man corrected her.

Liane looked at Brett.

"We can't disagree on that."

"He knows Gantini," the man continued, watching closely for their reaction. There was now a sense of suppressed violence about him that made Liane inched closer to Brett on the divan.

"Who's Gantini?" Brett stood up, he was losing his patience with the man.

"Come on Liane, we've wasted enough time here. We have to get back to Istanbul.

Liane stood up. Suddenly the man brought out a small revolver from his jacket pocket and pointed it at them.

"You're not going anywhere. Sit down or you will get hurt."

Brett sat down. Liane felt a nerve twist in her stomach, as she sat down next to him. A pain started in her head. It can't be true, she kept saying to herself. This is unreal. Brett was speaking to the man.

"By taking possession of those photographs you have caused me the extra work of going round and taking them all over again."

It's a nightmare thought Liane desperately, and any moment she was going to wake up.

The man shrugged his shoulders. "That is your problem."

"Who are you?" asked Brett angrily, staring down the barrel of the gun. "Who are you? How did you get to know Ahmed Shawki? Up to a few weeks ago he was in Egypt."

The man declined to answer.

Brett had a sudden thought. "Am I right in thinking you were in the art dealer's when Ahmed tried to sell the Gorregiani?" he asked suddenly.

From the look on the man's face the answer was in the affirmative.

"Hearing it was stolen you thought you could do a smart deal with him."

There was a barely suspectible nod of the man's head.

Liane moved closer to Brett on the divan.

"Ahmed was going to double cross," the man said, "I decided he was not going to ruin my life. Now tell me where the Gorregiani is."

"I don't know," replied Liane.

The man aimed the gun at Liane. There was total silence in the room save for the quiet ticking of a clock.

"I ask you once more. Where is the Gorregiani?"

Her mouth was dry, her voice strained. "I don't know," she repeated.

"If you don't tell me, I will shoot both of you, the woman first."

There was a pulse beating in her head, her heart was thumping like a sledge hammer. She heard the man click the safety catch. For a brief moment the room seemed to be slowly revolving, she was going to die, and Brett was going to die. She ought to be praying, but no prayer would come, then suddenly her brain swung into action.

"Don't shoot. I will tell you where the Gorregiani painting is."

The man kept the revolver on Liane, his eyes fixed on her.

"I am listening."

"It's at... it's at..." She paused recalling that a few evenings ago she had been reading a guide book on Turkey and the story that the Virgin Mary had lived at Ephesus after the crucifixion of Jesus had made a great impression on her.

"It's at Ephesus. The house next to the church of the Virgin Mary."

"Interesting," the man said slowly, his eyes never leaving Liane's face. "Continue."

She felt she was standing on the edge of a precipice, one false move and both she and Brett would topple to their deaths.

She felt Brett grasp her hand.

184

"Ahmed felt it best to store the painting at Ephesus, a long way from Istanbul."

"Why should it be safer at Ephesus?" queried the man.

For a moment Liane could not think of an answer.

"It is obvious," she replied. "Why Ephesus is safer. The town is a long way from Istanbul. In Istanbul Interpol are looking for the painting. They have notified all the art dealers. Anyway, it was impossible for Ahmed to sell without my help, and that would take time." Liane never paused, speaking in a quick, nervous manner.

"When Ahmed first contacted me I was working in Ireland. I had to finish my work there then travel to Turkey. Now I am waiting for the letter from the priest who gave me the painting. The letter will state that I am the lawful owner of the painting, and you can do nothing without me and the letter," she added in a firm voice.

"That is true," said the man slowly.

The door behind the man opened and the woman appeared carrying a tray bearing four small cups of coffee. She had now removed her headscarf and sun glasses. She was undoubtedly the woman in the photograph.

"I am sorry Mario I have been such a long time," she apologised.

The man motioned her to hand round the coffee.

Liane took a sip of the strong, black liquid. She shuddered. It had a peculiar bitter taste.

"Like some sugar?" asked the woman.

She handed them a bowl of sugar, and they each took a spoonful. It certainly made the drink more palatable.

The man never moved, the gun trained on them.

"When do you expect to receive this letter?" he asked in a quiet voice.

"Tomorrow, or Saturday at the latest."

"Interesting," murmured the man.

"The painting is very valuable," Liane continued, now she could not stop, she was talking to save her life and Brett's. "At least half a million American dollars. Could be a lot more. I'm meeting Ahmed on Saturday, and he will bring the painting with him, and we will go to the biggest art dealer in Istanbul. Ahmed is probably in Ephesus

185

right now..."

The man gave a wry sort of smile. "He is not in Ephesus, and you will not be meeting him on Saturday. I have dealt with him."

Liane felt a sudden shiver run through her. She lowered her eyes. She could not look at Mario, for suddenly he was the most evil human being she had ever encountered. Brett touched her hand.

Mario's wife left the room.

"So, the painting is in Ephesus," the man spoke in a slow deliberate manner. Liane could not look at Brett, for she knew his troubled eyes would tell her she was getting into deep waters, she was getting herself into a situation from which she may not be able to extricate herself.

"Tell me," said the man, "Who lives in the house next to the christian church in Ephesus?"

"Ahmed's old uncle," she replied quickly.

"What is his name?"

"His name? Abdul... Abdul Shawki."

"And how did you acquire such a valuable painting?" the man continued.

Liane told him about the christian priest at Luxor, and her father's lifelong friendship with him.

The woman returned to the room, picked up their empty coffee cups, put them on the tray and left. Mario was still staring at them.

She was starting to feel sleepy, must be the heat of the afternoon she thought as she laid her head on the back of the divan. Brett was doing the same.

" My wife and I must leave you," said Mario. "We are going to Ephesus and will return here as soon as possible with the painting." As the man continued his voice was getting fainter and fainter.

"Tomorrow I will go with you first to collect your letter from the priest, and second to the art dealer to sell the painting. Do not try to be clever, my gun will be in my pocket and I would not hesitate to use it."

"You must ask for cash, then I will bring you back here. After that I will decide what I will do with you..."

Her eyes were now closed. It was impossible to keep them open.

She was leaning on the gate of Tavanomore looking at the house. The place was filled with a deep silence, even the birds were not singing. She could see a man in the stableyard. His back was towards her, and when he turned she could not see his face.

Liane had the sensation of swimming under water and coming up for air. She opened her eyes. She was lying full length on the divan and Brett was still asleep, lying curled up on the floor by the coffee table.

How strange they had fallen asleep, and now the first pale light of dawn was stealing into the room. Her head was aching, her eyes were aching.

She sat up and brushed her hair from her face. It was the coffee that had done it. It had been drugged. What fools they had been! At the first sip she recalled, it had had a strange, peculiar taste.

There was total silence in the apartment. Were they really alone? Where were the man and woman? Then her sluggish brain started to work. Of course, they had gone to Ephesus to search for the painting.

She stood up and went across to the window. What madness had made her say the painting was at Ephesus? Well, he had demanded to know, and she had said the first thing that had entered her head.

She drew back the curtains. The helicopter had gone. They had to get out of this apartment, for when Mario and his wife discovered the painting was not at Ephesus, they would surely come back and kill them.

Liane went across to Brett and kneeling touched him gently on the shoulder.

"Brett," she said in a soft voice.

Brett smiled. "You saved our lives. I didn't know you were such a good liar."

"I didn't know myself."

"Give me a kiss."

"Stop it Brett, we've got to get out of here and fast." Liane scrambled to her feet. "How we do that I haven't the faintest idea. They could be back any minute."

Brett stood up.

"Has the helicopter gone?"

187

Liane nodded. "Because it's not there, doesn't necessarily mean they went in it. They could have gone by car."

"I could do with a cup of coffee, but not from that kitchen. First I suggest we examine the front door. I noticed yesterday there isn't a balcony."

They went into a small hall and examined the door. It had the kind of lock opened by a key inserted either at the front of the door or the back.

It was locked and the key was missing. They walked back into the sitting room and looked through the window. They were four floors up. It looked a long way to jump.

"We could knot a few sheets together," suggested Brett.

They went into the two bedrooms where each contained a set of twin beds. There were eight sheets available.

Next they examined the windows. All of them were divided into small panes of glass, and none of them opened.

In the kitchen they found Liane's Pentax camera on a shelf. She put it into her bag.

"Brett, if none of the windows open how do you get a breath of cool air?"

"You switch on the air conditioning," Brett told her as they walked back to the sitting room, a heavy air of depression settling over them.

"I'm really puzzled," Liane sat down on one of the divans. "The man and woman own, lease, or rent a house in iron gate street. What are they doing here?"

"I would say this is a block of holiday apartments. You can rent for three months, you can rent for twenty four hours." Brett spoke in a weary tone sitting down next to her. "More convenient to get us here, four floors up and extremely difficult to escape."

Brett put his arm around her shoulder.

"Well Liane, the sheet idea is no good. Got any other ideas?"

For Liane tears were near. "We're trapped Brett. Like a couple of flies in a spider's web. He'll come back and kill us. What are we going to do?"

They sat in silence for a moment. Liane rested her head on Brett's shoulder.

"It's all my fault. When we came out of the Roman Cistern the woman looked so friendly."

"It's pointless crucifying yourself," said Brett softly. "Let's think hard. There must be a way."

"A telephone," Liane suddenly exclaimed. "We could telephone the police."

They rose quickly with renewed hearts and searched every room in the apartment, - the kitchen, the sitting room, the hall, the bathroom, the two bedrooms. There was no telephone.

They returned to the divan.

"We could smash the glass in one of the windows," suggested Brett. "And when someone walks in the garden below shout for help."

Suddenly they heard the sound of a key scraping in a lock. Liane froze, looking at Brett with fear in her heart.

"They're back," she whispered. "Oh Brett, what are we going to do?"

Brett took her hand in his. "We're in this together, to the bitter end."

There was a deadly silence for a few long, excruciating minutes, then suddenly to their astonishment they heard the sound of a vacuum cleaner in the hall.

"I don't believe this," Brett exclaimed.

Rising to their feet, they walked with trepidation across the room and opened the door. A Muslim woman in her white head scarf and long flowing ankle length skirt was busy vacuuming the hall. She saw them immediately, and switched the machine off.

"I am sorry, I did not know you were here, but I must clean this apartment every morning before nine. I am so sorry. I will come back if you so wish."

"Don't worry about us," Brett told her as he opened the front door. "We were just going anyway."

CHAPTER 19

They were free! Liane couldn't believe it as she and Brett walked swiftly down the carpeted corridor. Any moment she expected to see Mario and the woman to suddenly appear. She wanted to break into a run so intense was her desire to leave that building, and it was with difficulty she restrained herself from doing so. Brett had a grim expression on his face.

"Am I dreaming this?" she asked Brett as he pressed the button for the lift.

"We're not out of the building yet," he reminded her in a tense voice.

In the lift Brett started to relax.

"They forgot about the cleaner," he said with an amused smile on his lips. "She does all the apartments like a chamber maid in a hotel."

"That was a bit of luck. Let's hope it holds out until we get back to England."

When the lift reached the ground floor they crossed the plant filled foyer and walked out through the main entrance. As they did so a taxi arrived. The door opened and a woman with a child stepped out, smiling at them as she entered the building.

"Could you take us to Istanbul?" Brett asked the taxi driver, a casual tone in his voice, a relaxed smile on his lips

"Which part?" asked the man.

"Anywhere near the Istiklal Caddesi," Brett replied as they sat down. "Taksim Square would be good enough."

The taxi set off, down the short drive to the main road turning left towards Istanbul.

It was going to be another hot day. Brett's hand closed over Liane's, a smile of reassurance on his lips. It was like waking up from a bad dream.

"I can take you to the Blue Mosque, Santa Sophia..." said the taxi driver looking at them through the driving mirror. "Very cheap."

"Thanks, but we've been."

The route took them along a dusty road through villages where even at this early hour men had already gathered at the pavement cafes, playing draughts as they drank their coffee.

Liane sat at Brett's side, utterly relaxed, the relief enormous to be out of that dreadful apartment. Never again would she take a stranger at their word.

At length they were in the outskirts of Istanbul, and soon after that, they were at Taksim Square, bustling with crowds and traffic.

The taxi stopped by the Monument to the Republic. The Istiklal Caddesi branched off from the square. Liane and Brett started walking down the crowded street filled with early morning shoppers and people on their way to work. The occasional tram clanged past, and Liane had the feeling good fortune was now on their side for good.

"I wonder what has happened to Charlene?" she asked Brett as they turned into a narrow street that would lead them to their hotel.

"She'll be in New York now ," he replied unsmilingly. "And the deal with be off."

"How do you feel?" asked Liane giving him a close look.

"I never intended going to America with her."

They walked the remainder of the street in silence. When they reached the hotel Liane went to the receptionist's desk.

"Any mail for me? Liane O'Neill. Room 510."

The girl handed her a letter with an Egyptian stamp on it.

"There is also a letter for Mr McMahon."

She handed Brett an unstamped letter. They went into the long sitting room adjacent to the bar and ordered coffee.

Liane opened her letter. It was, as she had expected, from Father O'Brien, stating as she had requested, that she was the lawful owner of the painting. The letter ended with his prayers for her future well being. She felt in his debt.

"Who's the letter from? The priest at Luxor?" asked Brett idly.

Liane nodded, with a happy smile on her lips. "What I have been waiting for," she exclaimed joyfully to Brett. "Proof at last that I own the painting."

"Good," murmured Brett in a disinterested voice. "This letter is

191

from Charlene. Wrote it just before she left yesterday afternoon."

Brett shrugged his shoulders. "As I expected she states the loan is off as she now has to depart for New York alone."

"Isn't it strange," mused Liane. "I never wanted you to go to New York with Charlene."

Brett gave Liane a sour look. "And what do I do now? You tell me."

They took the lift to Liane's room, where Brett stood, a tense figure by the window.

"Everything is going wrong!" he exploded. "On Charlene's instructions we tell Curtis not to come. Then Charlene clears off. We get kidnapped and threatened. There's no hope of getting that picture. The guy told you, you won't be seeing Ahmed, he's 'dealt with him".

Liane, get packed straight away. We're getting out of this damn city, fast. While you're doing that I'll make a call to Ian. We've got problems with the script. You know I'm not happy with the last sequence. I want something startling to happen. Got any ideas?"

"I'll think about it."

Brett dialled the number, then leaned back on the bed and waited. Liane sat hesitantly in the armchair.

The last thing she wanted to do was pack up and leave. The fact she now had the letter from Father O'Brien had changed everything. She had to make one last effort.

"Brett..."

Brett waved her to stop speaking.

"Hello Ian. Sorry I didn't phone you last night, but Liane and I were unable to get to a phone. It's a long troublesome story which you will find hard to believe. What was that? Everything happens to Liane and me? You're dead right. Anyway we'll have a long talk when we meet. How's everything?"

There was a long pause whilst Brett listened to Ian's news. His face took on a depressed expression.

"I'm extremely sorry to hear your bad news. I'll catch the first available flight to Dublin."

Brett put down the phone, a sad look in his eyes.

"The backer of the Priory Theatre has withdrawn his financial support. He's been threatening to do it for a long time. Now it has happened."

"But why?" asked Liane. "The Priory Theatre puts on first class productions in the theatre section and in the films division..."

"Nothing to do with that." Brett's voice took on a sad note. "The gentleman in question has big financial problems in the States. I gather he's been gambling on the commodities market and lost."

"What's going to happen now?" asked Liane, a worried look on her face.

"We're going to be fired, unless a new backer is found. Not easy in the present economic climate."

"And all this work we have done in Connemara and Istanbul was for nothing?"

"Looks like it.

"Anything else on the horizon?"

"I was hoping my new play would open in Boston, Massachusetts in the fall. If it was any good, it would be transferred to Broadway. Anyway, I can forget that," he added dismally, "it was tied up with the bank loan. What are your immediate plans Liane?"

"The usual I suppose," she replied in a depressed voice. "Temping until another film job comes my way."

"You are going to marry me."

Brett pulled her to her feet and held her close. "You are not going to do any temping. I'm not exactly poverty stricken."

"How long has the bank given you to repay the loan?" asked Liane suddenly.

"It's now approximately ten weeks."

What did she have? The apartment at Islington with the large size mortgage. An overdraft at the bank. Liane's spirits dropped. She had got to do something.

"You haven't started packing," Brett reminded her. "And I'd better phone the airport and get us booked on the first available flight to London."

"Hold it Brett," said Liane, an idea germinating. "I own a painting valued at half a million dollars, and it's somewhere in this city. What are we going back to? No job and soon no Tavanomore. How can I leave without making some effort to find that painting?"

"You're forgetting something," Brett reminded her. "The guy told you he has 'dealt with Ahmed'. You know what that means, and Ahmed had the painting."

"It could mean anything," Liane replied, grasping at straws. "They had a big quarrel. They had a fight..."

"You know what it means..." interrupted Brett. "You are leaving with me and that is final." His voice was firm as he rose to his feet. "I have had enough. I came here to write a film script, and what happens? We are held at gun point in that wretched apartment. We're lucky to be still alive..."

"But for my quick thinking."

"I acknowledge that. And when those two get back from Ephesus we're got to be out of this country. Can't you realise our lives are in danger?"

"I know everything you say is true, but at the same time I can't leave. I've got to do something to try to get that painting back, what I'm not sure."

"Ahmed won't be at the Pudding Shop tomorrow, that's for sure."

"Maybe Mario was bluffing," suggested Liane hopefully.

"Bluffing my foot. Who are you kidding? Look Liane, I am fed up with that bloody painting. It's brought us nothing but trouble."

"Brett, Ahmed lived somewhere in this city. Perhaps a rented room in a private house? A cheap hotel? He must have hidden that painting somewhere."

"And how are you going to find it?"

"I don't know," Liane replied in a dispirited voice.

"Forget it Liane. You are coming back with me. We'll go straight to Ian and have a long talk with him. Poor guy, he's devastated. Everything cancelled. It could take months to get another backer, and if he doesn't get one, the Priory is up for sale."

"I'm not going back with you."

"Stop this nonsense, you are."

"I'm serious. I am not."

"Get those clothes in your bag. I'll phone the airport. Things are in such a mess in Dublin we've got to get there as quickly as possible."

Brett dialled the number.

"I want to book two seats on the first available flight to London. Right, I'll hold on."

"I've told you Brett..."

"Shut up Liane!" Brett raised his voice. "You are now making me angry. I'm sorry, what was that? The plane leaves at four o'clock, check in at three. The name is McMahon and O'Neill. Thanks."

He replaced the receiver and turned to Liane.

"Whether you like it or not you are on the four o'clock flight out of Ataturk Airport."

"I am not."

"I'm going to my room to pack. Be ready when I get back."

He left the room slamming the door behind him.

Liane slumped down in an armchair. If she decided to go with Brett, what were they going back to? No job. No Tavanomore. The future was bleak. No, she could not go. She had to stay here and make one last desperate effort to try to recover the painting.

There was a knock at the door.

"Liane!"

It was Brett. "Are you ready?"

She walked slowly to the door and opened it.

"I've told you I'm not coming."

Brett walked past her into the room, scowling heavily.

"You must be mad," he shouted. "If Mario and the woman find you they'll kill you. They're violent people. Can't you understand that? You are putting your life in danger. You will never find that painting."

"I will do my best," Liane replied defiantly.

"I beg you..."

"I'm not coming," Liane replied, her face now white and strained. Brett tightened his mouth in a hard line.

"You stay here and that's the end of you," he fumed. "Do you understand?

Liane stared wide eyed, into his tired, tense face. He moved towards the door.

"How many times do I have to tell you I'm not coming," said Liane in a quiet voice. Couldn't he see she had to stay. She had to do her utmost to try to recover that painting. It was her one chance to acquire money, the one commodity that would solve all their problems.

"Brett, you don't seemed to understand that I have to stay. I have to try. I can't give up now. I can't bear failure."

"All right." There was a note of finality in Brett's voice. "If that's the way you want it go ahead. I'll leave a message for you at the Priory. My future plans are uncertain."

Then without kissing her goodbye he picked up his bag and left the room closing the door firmly behind him. Liane sank onto the bed, her spirits couldn't have been lower.

She lay there a long time, her hands behind her head, staring at the ceiling thinking of Brett, and how stubborn and pig headed he was. His future plans were uncertain she thought with a sudden sense of panic. What was he trying to tell her? That the marriage was off? She felt rejected, cast off.

She wanted to cry but no tears would come.

She walked to the window and opened it, walking onto the balcony feeling more lonely and isolated than she had ever felt in her life, looking down on the broken pantiled roofs of nearby houses.

There was a woman hanging washing over a balcony. A baby cried and she hurried into the house, returning a few minutes later nursing the child lovingly in her arms, singing a soothing lullaby.

Had she made a terrible mistake? In her desire for money to solve their problems had she lost the one thing she prized above all else - Brett's love?

That was so depressing she had to switch her thoughts to something else. She thought of the painting, the reason why she was here.

There was Ahmed's uncle, Ali Shawki. She was surprised he hadn't got his nephew a job as a waiter in the dining room. Surely Uncle Ali would know where his nephew lived, and what had happened to him. It was a chance. New confidence surged through her.

She went down to the dining room crowded with lunchtime diners, and asked the head waiter if she could speak to Mr Shawki for a few moments.

The head waiter shook his head. "I am sorry madame, but Mr

196

Shawki does not come on duty until five. I will tell him you wish to speak with him."

Realising she had not eaten since yesterday Liane ordered lunch. And as she did so, a man had entered the dining room. He was of medium height, muscular build, black hair, and dressed in a brown leather jacket. He was speaking to the head waiter.

She felt her blood run cold, and suddenly all her confidence and bravado was seeping away leaving her lonely and vulnerable and wondering what on earth had possessed her to behave in the way she had.

Then the man turned and looked in her direction. He was not Mario.

It was now two o'clock and she had to wait three hours to speak to Mr Shawki. When she had finished her light lunch she went up in the lift to her room.

When Mario returned to Istanbul he could come immediately to the Hera Palas looking for her. She decided to stay in her room until five o'clock, locking the door. That way she felt safe.

It was now a question of passing the time. She had a guide book on Turkey and when she was tired of reading about the Ottoman Empire and the great reformer Ataturk, she switched on the television and watched CNN from America.

Anything to stop her thinking about Brett. Whenever she thought about him she felt a chill feeling around her heart. She longed for him, ached for him.

And what must he think of her? The foolish woman who was searching for the pot of gold at the end of the rainbow.

At half past five Liane decided she had to go down to the dining room to find Ahmed's uncle. At that time of day the waiters were busy changing the table cloths, setting out the cutlery, and changing the flowers in the vases in preparation for the main meal of the day.

She saw Ahmed's uncle straight away and walked across to him.

"Excuse me, Mr Shawki, but could you tell me where your nephew Ahmed lives. I have to speak to him very urgently."

The man's face was a blank. "I do not know where Ahmed lives." He shrugged his shoulders. "I know it is somewhere near the hotel. I am sorry I cannot help you."

197

"I'm sorry too," said Liane with feeling giving him a sad smile.

Then the man seemed to visibly relax. "I am worried about Ahmed. I have not seen him for many days. Sometimes I have seen him with people who are not good people. You understand?"

Liane nodded.

"I'm sorry I cannot help you."

Then the man continued setting the cutlery on the table. Liane left the dining room and walked through to the foyer of the hotel. A porter was selling copies of the Turkish Evening News. On a sudden impulse she bought a copy.

It was a column tucked at the bottom of the front page and suddenly her eyes were riveted to the small headline:

'MAN'S BODY FOUND IN BOSPHORUS.

This morning fishermen found the body of an unknown man washed up on the shores of the Bosphorus near Besiktas. He had been strangled. There were no identification papers on him.'

Could it be Ahmed thought Liane? Much as she disliked the man, she never wished him any harm. And if so, was it the work of Mario?

Brett had been right all along. The best thing was to get out of Istanbul as fast as possible. It was too dangerous, and nothing would come of her staying behind.

As she turned towards the short flight of steps that would lead her to the lift, her attention was suddenly distracted by the sight of a Muslim woman, her hair covered in a white scarf, her long skirt swishing about her ankles as she paused in the hotel foyer wondering what to do.

She was an uncommon sight for all the hotel residents without exception were American, English, or German, and any Turkish nationals who stayed there from time to time, were invariably in Western style clothes.

Liane watched the woman with interest as she walked nervously to the hotel reception desk.

"I want to speak to a waiter in the dining room. His name is Mr Shawki."

"He is very busy at the moment and you will have to wait," replied the receptionist in a superior tone.

198

"I must speak to him now. It is very urgent." The woman raised her voice. "It is about his nephew Ahmed. He rent a room from me and he has not paid any money. I am only a poor widow. Who pay for the room?" she demanded.

Liane walked up to the woman.

"Perhaps I could help? I - I am a friend of Mr Ahmed Shawki. Perhaps we could talk outside."

Liane led the woman out of the hotel. The woman was now weeping, holding her hands together in a beseeching manner.

"I am a poor widow. What will become of me?"

"I will pay the money owed by Mr Shawki."

"Thank you madame. He owe me 7,000 lira."

Ahmed was hard up. He would have been better off working as a waiter in the Hera Palas dining room.

Liane opened her bag. "I will pay you, if I may be allowed to visit the room."

"But of course," said the woman, smiling for the first time.

Liane counted the lira and handed the money to the woman, who pushed the rolled up notes gratefully into her pocket.

"We go now."

"Mr Shawki has something belonging to me and never returned it." Liane told her as they crossed the road and entered an alleyway opposite the hotel. "It might be still in his room."

"Please, you come and look."

The narrow alleyway was a mixture of dingy looking shops and private houses, all with an air of neglect, paint peeling off the windows, some abandoned.

The woman entered an open doorway which led into a dimly lit corridor. Liane followed. They went up the stairs where plaster had fallen off the walls in many places. The woman opened a door on the first landing.

"Mr Shawki's room," she said. "I touch nothing. I am an honest woman."

Liane walked past her and into the room. It was poorly furnished with an iron bedstead against the far wall, a large wardrobe against the opposite wall, and a broken chair by the window.

The woman left her and Liane heard her footsteps clattering down the uncarpeted wooden stairs. First she knelt down and looked underneath the bed. There was nothing there.

Then she walked across the room and opened the door of the wardrobe. Hanging on coathangers was a black leather jacket, a pair of trousers and a couple of shirts. Carefully she removed the clothes. Now she could see a small flat object leaning against the back of the wardrobe covered in a piece of canvas.

With beating heart Liane lifted it from the wardrobe, laid it on the bed, and removed the canvas covering.

It was the Gorregiani,- Virgin and Child! Unmarked and still in good condition. Whatever had happened to it since Liane had last seen it on the Nile cruise boat it had been well looked after.

She must work fast. First she covered the painting with the canvas and leaned it against the bed. Then returning the clothes to the wardrobe, closed the door, picked up the painting and left the room.

Liane hurried down the dimly lit stairs. She met no one, the woman seemed to have disappeared, then along the corridor and she was out into the alleyway.

The alleyway was deserted. At the end of the alleyway Liane crossed the road and entered the hotel. Such a sense of triumph, of victory. At last the painting was in her possession! It was hard to believe! She now had to get out of the country as quickly as possible.

At the reception desk she asked the young woman if she would phone the airport and book her on the first available flight to London.

The young woman spoke for a few minutes on the phone then turned to her with a smile.

"You are on the morning flight, Turkish Airlines. The flight leaves at eight o'clock, check in at seven. Your bill has been paid by Mr McMahon."

"Thank you . "

Nice of Brett to remember, thought Liane with a smile, considering how difficult and stubborn she had been.

Picking up the painting, Liane walked across and climbed the few steps leading to the lift, then idly turned her head in the direction of the sitting room.

Beneath the chandeliers, enjoying a pre-dinner drink, sat Mario and his wife.

CHAPTER 20

Liane quickened her pace, her heart beating fast, and stepped into the waiting lift praying that Mario and his wife had not noticed her. The lift attendant gave her a friendly smile, closed the door and the lift began its ascent. She was the only passenger.

"Been shopping?" he asked, looking at the canvas covered painting with mild curiosity. He was the friendly one who usually made some mild comment.

"Yes," she replied. "Nice to have a souvenir."

When they reached the fifth floor giving the attendant a brief smile she stepped out of the lift, and carrying the painting in both hands, walked along the corridor to her room. Once inside she firmly locked the door behind her. Then leaning against it for a few moments she reflected on the relief to be in comparative safety.

Mario and his wife could be out for an innocent evening at the Hera Palas. Or were they planning to attack like a couple of piranhas, stealing the painting of course, and the letter from Father O'Brien?

Liane decided she was letting her imagination run riot. The Hera Palas was a popular meeting place. Mario and his wife had dashed down to Ephesus, failed to find the painting, returned this morning to find Liane and Brett had gone, entirely through their own negligence, and feeling depressed had decided to have an evening out.

She propped the painting up on the dressing table and withdrew the canvas cover, gazing at it for a few moments. It was incredible that the painting was once again in her possession, and by sheer good fortune, by being in the foyer at the precise moment when Ahmed's landlady had entered. Now this painting would solve all her financial problems and Brett's, but what of their emotional ones?

He had been very angry earlier in the day, in fact she had never seen him so angry. Was it all over between them? If it wasn't, their relationship had been severely damaged, by her obstinacy, by refusing to see his point of view. But wouldn't he forgive, now that she had the precious Gorregiani?

She lay on the bed propping the pillows behind her head, wishing he was here beside her, kissing and making up, running her hands through his hair. Thinking about him only made her feel more lonely and sad.

She had achieved her objective, but by so doing had she lost Brett?

Then her thoughts turned to Mario and his wife sipping their drinks in the sitting room below, and that gave her a queezy feeling in the pit of her stomach.

I wish Brett was here, she thought again, and if he was everything would be so different. They would work out how to deal with Mario. She would feel happy she had the painting. She would be full of optimism and confidence for the future.

But it was a waste of time thinking such thoughts. Brett was not here she told herself firmly. At this moment he was probably at Heathrow waiting for a plane for Dublin, and she was alone in Istanbul with a half a million dollar painting that two people downstairs desperately wanted.

Liane decided the safest course of action was to stay in her room until six thirty tomorrow morning when she would hurry down in the lift, and get a taxi, the receptionist had assured her there were always plenty of waiting taxis outside the hotel. Then she would drive to the airport for the seven o'clock check in. Once in the airport she would feel safe.

Liane looked at her watch. It was seven thirty. She had eleven hours to endure. She packed all her belongings, phoned the receptionist to give her an early call at six a.m., she would have to forget breakfast in the dining room - she could take no risks.

She rose from the bed and walking across to the window looked down on the little street below. The woman had taken her washing off the balcony, and she could still hear the faint cry of the baby.

How she wished she was just an ordinary citizen in that little street, instead of being a prisoner in this room, because that was virtually what she was. By morning she would have grown to hate the room.

When she was tired of looking at the broken pantiled roofs of the nearby houses, she turned from the window and walked across to the refrigerator.

She took out a can of coca cola, and this together with a packet of salted peanuts temporarily satisfied her hunger.

With all her heart she longed for Brett. Her longing for him was almost unbearable. I wish he was here she kept thinking to herself as she contemplated watching Turkish television for the next hour or so. Anything to take away the immense feeling of vulnerability and isolation.

Suddenly there was a knock at the door.

She tensed herself, feeling suddenly cold with fear. Was it Mario? His wife? She remained silent waiting for the next knock.

"Liane! It's me! Open up!"

It was Brett! The one person she wanted to see! Heaven had answered her prayers!

Liane jumped off the bed and ran to the door, and literally fell into his arms.

"Oh Brett!" Her eyes filled with tears. "I've been lying here wishing..."

She kissed him on both cheeks then on the mouth.

He closed the door and locked it, then turned to Liane, a soft expression on his face, his eyes full of love.

"If I'd known I was going to get such a warm welcome I would have come sooner."

His arms tightened around her as he drew her closer to him. His cheek touched hers; he needed a shave.

"I thought you would have been in London by now."

"The plane was delayed, and I sat there thinking about you. And in the end I couldn't get on any plane. I had to come back to see you.

Liane, you and I have been obsessed about money. Money seemed to be ruining our lives. It was ruining the lives of your grandfather and my father."

"I don't understand..."

"Didn't your father ever tell you? Your grandfather borrowed large sums of money from my father."

Liane looked bewildered. "Why should he do that?"

"To finance business ventures, and they all failed."

"What sort of business ventures?"

"Buying dubious race horses at fabulous prices. They never won, and there was heavy betting."

"I remember Dad once told me grandfather was very fond of horses, but I had no idea... Was a lot of money involved?"

"An enormous amount. The next one is always going to be a winner, and it never is. You get on a kind of treadmill and you can't get off. So in the end the only way to settle the debt was by leaving my father the farm."

"Why didn't you tell me?"

Brett stroke Liane's head gently. "Tell you that your father lost Tavanomore through your grandfather's stupidity. Liane, you would have hated me."

"I could never hate you," said Liane softly, looking up into Brett's eyes.

He smiled gently at her. "Liane, forget money, it's being together that is important. And anyway, how could I leave you alone in this city, after what happened to us?"

Liane laid her head against his shoulder.

"Have you forgiven me for losing my temper?" Brett asked, his voice soft and tender. "I didn't mean a word I said..."

Liane looked up at him, smiling benevolently.

"Of course I have."

Suddenly Brett's eyes alighted on the Gorregiani.

"I don't believe it!" he exclaimed excitedly walking across to the dressing table and picking it up. "How did you get it?"

"Sheer good luck," Liane told him happily, "I just happened to be near the reception desk when a Muslim woman came in asking to see Ahmed's uncle. She was very distressed because Ahmed had been renting a room from her and owed her rent. I offered to pay the rent and went back with her."

"But how did you find it?"

"I told her Ahmed had something belonging to me and had not returned it and asked if I go in his room. I found the painting leaning against the back of the wardrobe behind his clothes."

"Clever girl."

"Lucky. Did you see the news item about a man's body found by fishermen in the Bosphorus?"

Brett nodded. "I did. What do you think? Ahmed? He was heading for trouble."

"I think it is possible it is Ahmed, and I think the same person who pulled a gun on us in that apartment could be responsible! Makes me feel ill thinking about it." Liane gave a shudder.

"Oh by the way," she continued as she covered the painting with the piece of canvas, "The man in question and his wife were in the hotel sitting room about two hours ago. They looked as though they were having pre-dinner drinks. I don't think they saw me. Well, nothing has happened; perhaps that is because I took the precaution of not leaving this room. Did you notice them when you came in?"

Brett looked thoughtful for a moment shaking his head. "I looked in the dining room, and the sitting room, and the bar before coming up here. Actually I was looking for you. No, I didn't see them."

"I don't want to take any risks," said Liane, slipping her arm through his. "I don't want to leave this room. I'm booked on the eight o'clock flight in the morning. And what about you?"

"I'll be on that flight if it's the last thing I do." He gave her a firm look as he drew Liane closer to him.

"I'm hungry," he said softly, his mouth near hers.

"Me too."

He started kissing her gently on the lips, and at the same time, his hands were gently, tenderly exploring her body. He was breathing rapidly; Liane was trembling.

She looked up into his eyes. They were dark with passion. She could feel her own need for him was reaching a crisis. Her whole body ached for him. Then the telephone rang.

"Will you be requiring breakfast in the morning?" came the easy voice of the receptionist. "Room service can bring it to you."

"Thank you, but I will be having breakfast at the airport." Then a sudden thought occurred to her. "Will you ask room service to bring dinner for two as soon as possible?"

"Certainly madame. I have the menu here." The receptionist read

206

the menu over the phone.

Liane looked across to Brett:

"How would you like chicken with aubergine and cheese, followed by cream pudding with pounded almonds?"

"That sounds fine with me."

She gave the order to the receptionist then put the phone down.

Brett's arm went around her waist.

"When I said I was hungry," he said, giving her an amused smile. "I wasn't thinking of food."

"I know."

Liane could feel Brett's arms tightening around her waist pressing her close to him. "I can't wait much longer Liane," he whispered, an urgency in his voice.

"Brett," Liane spoke in a gentle voice. "I think the waiter will be here very soon, and thinking ahead, in the morning we have to leave at six thirty. We have to make a quick start...

"Liane," Brett interrupted, "I don't think the waiter should see a valuable painting in this room. Hotel staff gossip. I think you ought to hide it."

Liane walked across to the dressing table, picked up the painting and pushed it under her bed, whilst Brett placed his bag next to Liane's near the door.

The waiter arrived soon after that, and the young man set out their feast on the table by the window.

The chicken was superb, the cream pudding and almonds excellent. By the time the meal ended Liane's worries had completely disappeared.

She looked across to the bed concealing the painting.

"Brett, do you realise what this means? We can now pay off the debt at the bank, and what about investing in the Priory Theatre?"

Brett nodded with a thoughtful smile. Then he glanced around the room. "Is the painting under the bed or under the mattress?" he asked with a whimsical smile.

"It is definitely under the bed," Liane told him firmly. "And you are going to sleep in that bed, and I will sleep in this one."

"We could move the two beds together, or do you still insist on playing hard to get my sweet?"

Brett took her by the hand and led her to the window. It was now dark, and a full moon was shining over the pantiled roofs of the Beyoglu district, a gentle breeze moving amongst the branches of a tree below.

"The moon shines bright," quoted Brett, "In such a night as this, When the sweet wind did gently kiss the trees..."

"And they did make no noise," quoted Liane happily, it was one of her favourite quotations. "...in such a night..."

"I love you Liane, and I want to marry you, but the problem now is people will think I am marrying you for your money."

"I'm only concerned with what you think. And you came back for me, and you thought at that time I was penniless. Remember, you told me it is being together that is important."

He gave her a slow look that set her blood tingling.

"Where would you like to get married?"

Liane thought for a moment."I'd like us to get married at Carrickballyduff, and our wedding night at Tavanomore."

"That it shall be."

Liane rested her head on his shoulder, feeling the softness of his shirt against her face.

"Oh Brett, I didn't think it possible to be so happy."

There was a knock at the door.

"That will be room service to take away the tray."

Liane walked across the room and opened the door. It was the waiter. He picked up the tray and left the room. Within two minutes there was another knock at the door.

"It must be the waiter," said Liane walking across the room again to open the door. "Perhaps he has forgotten something."

Liane opened the door and gave a cry.

Mario was standing there, his eyes dark and evil, and as she hastened to close the door he quickly rammed his foot in the opening, then in a flash he was in the room, locking the door behind him. Liane stood there speechless.

"Leave the room at once or I call the manager," said Brett from the window.

208

In reply Mario brought out a gun and motioned Liane to stand next to Brett. Liane moved across to Brett. Her heart thudding against her ribs, she felt sick.

The phone was a five tantalising feet away. If she edged towards it, very slowly, perhaps Mario might not notice. Slowly she started to move her right foot in the direction of the phone. But Mario was quicker than her.

"Keep away from that phone, or I'll shoot."

Then he walked slowly across to them, and positioned himself between them and the phone.

"Ephesus!" he gave a harsh laugh. "The house by the church of the Virgin Mary. There was no house by the church. No one in the town by the name of Shawki. You made a fool of me. No one makes a fool of Mario," he added menacingly. "Give me the painting."

He was looking at Liane.

"We haven't got it," Liane told him. Then she wondered if he was bluffing and the gun was empty.

"I said give me the painting," he shouted.

"You heard what Liane said. We haven't got it," Brett told him.

"You are lying. The lift attendant told me the girl has a painting. She brought it to this room a few hours ago."

Liane looked at Brett, panic was near. She must keep calm. Keep a clear head.

"It isn't here now," she said slowly.

Mario shook his head. "I do not believe you. If you do not tell me where it is I will kill you." His dark eyes narrowed.

"It - it's in the bathroom," she replied quickly. "Behind the shower curtain." She had to look away from those dark staring eyes. There was something hypnotic about them. Made her feel afraid.

Mario stepped back towards the bathroom door keeping the gun trained on them all the time. What must be the next move when he discovers there is no painting behind the shower curtain thought Liane desperately, touching Brett's hand. They didn't have long to live. There would be a blessing, they would die together.

Mario kicked opened the bathroom door, and stood in the entrance of the unlit room, his hand groping for the switch. Then he moved inside the room cursing.

"Where do you switch on the light?" he called from the bathroom.

"I'll switch it on for you," Brett called as he sprinted across the room.

He switched on the bathroom light, the switch being positioned outside the room near the bedroom door, then entered the bathroom. Liane tensed herself, waiting.

There was a quick scuffle, then the expected crash as someone fell to the floor. She shuddered, expecting the worst, then to her relief it was Brett who backed out of the bathroom holding the gun. Liane ran to him.

"Don't move," Brett warned Mario who was scrabbling to his feet holding his injured jaw in the centre of the bathroom.

Without taking his eyes off Mario Brett rasped out to Liane.

"Quick. Phone the police."

CHAPTER 21

Liane ran immediately to the bedside phone and picked up
the receiver. The receptionist answered.

"May I help you?" came the girl's polite voice.

"Get the police, fast." Liane's voice was swift and urgent. "There's
a thief in my room. We have taken the gun from him."

"Immediately madame."

Liane put the receiver down, her heart beating fast.

"What did she say?" Brett asked, his eyes never leaving Mario.

"She's getting them straight away."

Brett gave Mario a sardonic smile.

"Well, Mario, if that is your real name, the police will be here in a
few minutes. In the meantime I'd like to ask you a few questions.
You started following us around Istanbul because you thought we
were in league with Ahmed on a blackmailing racket. Why are earth
should Ahmed want to blackmail you?"

Mario shrugged his shoulders wearily and remained silent. He
looked ill.

"What have you done?" persisted Brett.

Again Mario declined to answer.

"I feel curious about you," Brett continued, "Where are you from?
Italy? You speak English with an Italian accent."

"Not Italy," Mario replied sullenly.

"Well, if it's not Italy, it's somewhere near. Sardinia? Sicily?"

Again Mario did not answer.

"Liane, open the door, so the police do not have the trouble of
knocking."

Liane went across and opened the door. There was no one in the
corridor.

"Ahmed was in Sicily earlier this year," Brett continued
thoughtfully. "My guess is you met him there, or you both have a

211

mutual Sicilian acquaintance. You mentioned the name Gantini. Are you by any chance a member of the Mafiosi?"

There was a nervous twitch in Mario's eye and he tightened his mouth.

"I think the answer is yes. And why were you hanging around a small type crook like Ahmed Shawki? I thought you Mafiosi men were in the big money selling drugs and protection rackets. What happened? Did you have to get out because you broke the rules?"

Mario glared silently at him.

"Where is your wife?" asked Brett suddenly.

In reply Mario's face grew red with anger. "Leave Sophia out of this," he shouted waving his arms in an excited manner. "She did not want me to come. She say stay away..."

"Keep still." Brett warned him. "Don't try anything or I will shoot. Now you met Ahmed in the art dealer's," Brett continued.

Mario nodded sullenly.

"The one in the Istiklal Caddesi. And when the dealer told him the painting was on the stolen property list you thought here is an opportunity to make some quick money."

Mario nodded. "I speak to him in the street. I think we can do business but he have other ideas. He cheated me."

"And I think Ahmed discovered you were on the run from the Mafiosi," continued Brett grimly. "So you decided to kill him. He knew too much."

"He deserve it," replied Mario sternly.

"And we were also on the hit list, until you realised you needed Liane's help."

At that moment there was a movement at the door and two police officers entered the room.

"We have heard everything," said one of them as he handcuffed Mario.

The other police officer took the gun from Brett.

"We all go to police headquarters," he told them. "There is a police car waiting outside the hotel."

They all went down in the lift; - a strange party, the two police officers, the handcuffed Mario and Brett and Liane. Hotel guests cast them curious glances as they walked quickly through the foyer and out to the waiting car. Then with sirens sounding they drove to police headquarters.

There, Mario was led away to a cell to await his trial, whilst Brett and Liane made statements in the presence of the police superintendent.

Soon after Liane and Brett were driven back to the hotel in one of the police cars. The police officer thanked them for their prompt action and wished them good night.

It was now half past midnight. Brett and Liane went up to her room. Exhausted and fully clothed she flung herself down on one of the beds.

Brett was standing by the dressing table, opening his brief case, his face creased into a smile.

"I've got an idea how the script should end. I want to make a few notes; I'll show them to you tomorrow. All right?"

There was no answer from Liane. She was asleep. An hour later she felt the warmth and pressure of Brett's body as he slid beneath the cover beside her, then she felt his arms encircle her as he held her tightly to him.

She could feel her lips parting as the tip of his tongue delicately touched hers. Then his mouth moved down to her breasts kissing each nipple in turn. She could not stop the excitement that swept through her as she lay there quivering in his arms.

"I thought you were playing hard to get," he murmured. She did not answer for her body was on fire. Then it was like Luxor all over again, but this time better, and in the Turkish moonlight soon Liane was soaring to the stars.

At six a.m. the phone rang to give them their early morning call, and as Liane looked at Brett's dark head on the pillow beside her from across the Galata Bridge came the faint dawn call of the muezzin calling the faithful to Allah.

Thirty minutes later Liane and Brett were in a taxi on their way to the airport driving through the deserted streets, the sun breaking through the early morning mist revealing the dark silhouettes of mosques and minarets.

"There is one thing for sure," Brett told her as they paid the taxi driver and walked into the small airport building, "I will never forget Istanbul."

Their plane took off on time, heading west for London. Brett had been lucky enough to secure a seat next to Liane, and the painting being too large and precious to go in the overhead shelf was leaning, securely covered by the canvas material, against Liane's knees.

Brett turned to her, a soft smile on his lips.

"How are you feeling?"

"I'm still sleepy," she replied, unfastening her safety belt. "And in a daze. I can't believe all this has happened. Normally nothing happens to me."

Brett was reading a copy of the Turkish Daily News he had bought just before boarding the aircraft.

"It's in the paper!" he suddenly exclaimed. "Gunman holds up couple in Hera Palas," he read, "Attempted to steal a sixteenth century painting by Gorregiani. Was foiled by the quick action of Brett McMahon and his wife."

Brett gave her a quick smile. "You'll have to marry me now, it's in the paper."

Liane smiled happily leaning against his shoulder as Brett continued reading a thoughtful expression on his face.

"Liane, I'm thinking about Mario and his wife, if she is his wife. Do you remember how angry he became when I mentioned her?"

Liane nodded. "What do you think it was about?"

"My theory is that he committed adultery with Sophia who is wife of, maybe, the boss man, or one of the men. The penalty for adultery within the Mafiosi is death. She is a very attractive woman.

So they were on the run and decided to start a new life in Istanbul. But when Mario met Ahmed and saw a chance to make a quick buck he couldn't resist it."

"And that was his downfall," added Liane. "It is possible Ahmed had discovered his background and was planning to blackmail him.

Actually I think the truth is that Ahmed knew nothing of his Mafia association; all he wanted to do was sell the painting at the best possible price. The unidentified body of a man found in the Bosphorus two days ago, - What do you think?"

"It is highly possible it is Ahmed."

"What do you think will happen to Sophia?" continued Liane.

"She'll survive. I have no doubt that she and Mario have a nice sum tucked away in a foreign bank account."

"Brett, when they hired the Bosphorus apartment I think they took it under a false name, planned to do the dirty deed then disappear. Easy."

"I think you're right."

"Who was Karmi Hussein?"

He shook his head. "We will never know."

"And who tried to get into my room?"

"That also we will never know."

"Regarding my camera, I think, somehow the wife got into my room and took it, not knowing the film in question had been deposited at the twenty four hour shop."

Brett turned and smiled at her.

"You're quite the detective."

"Brett, I've reached a point when this painting makes me positively nervous having it in my possession. I suggest that when we get to London we go straight to an auctioneer and arrange for the auction."

As soon as Liane and Brett landed at Heathrow, they took the underground to the west end of London and went straight to the offices of Darcy and Johnson, a company that had been established over a hundred years, auctioneers in fine art with an international reputation that was second to none.

Liane and Brett entered their premises in Albemarle Street, with a sense of relief and confidence. They were shown into the manager's office where a silver haired gentleman courteously dealt with them.

"You have the Gorregiani, Virgin and Child?" he looked surprised. "There was something about it on the radio this morning. An attempted theft in Istanbul. May I look at it, and of course your proof of ownership."

Liane showed the manager her letter from Father O'Brien.

He read it with care, then with a satisfied smile on his face, handed it back to her.

Next he took the painting from Liane, placed it on a stand, and withdrew the canvas covering. He stared at it for a long time, frowning and rubbing his chin. Liane gave Brett an anxious look. Then the man turned to them.

"This painting will of course have to be verified by our expert who specialises in sixteenth century Italian art," he told them, a serious expression on his face.

"Unfortunately he is away until Monday," he continued. "If he confirms that it is a Gorregiani it will be in our catalogue for the following Monday. Will that be all right with you? And remember, I can do nothing without his confirmation. Perhaps you will give me your telephone number."

Liane gave him her phone number, and the manager bid them good day.

Liane and Brett left the premises of Darcy and Johnson less confident than when they had entered it.

"On Monday when you get the manager's call, phone me immediately at the Priory," Brett told her.

At Piccadilly Underground they said goodbye. Then Brett took the train to Heathrow to catch a plane for Dublin and Liane travelled to Islington.

When she arrived at her apartment, she was glad her mother had already arrived. It was a difficult weekend. Never had Liane known time to pass so slowly.

On Sunday, to Liane's surprise, there was an item about the attempted theft in all the Sunday papers. Finally Monday arrived, and about the middle of the afternoon the expected call came.

"Miss O'Neill. This is Darcy and Johnson. I have pleasure in telling you that our expert has examined your painting and confirms what you told me. That it is a Gorregiani, the Virgin and Child. It will, as I have already told you, be included in next Monday's catalogue. The auction starts at ll.OOam."

Liane immediately phone the Priory Theatre and told Brett the news.

"I will be on the early plane Monday and will meet you at Darcy and Johnson's just before ll.OOam." Brett told her.

216

Liane and her mother spent the week painting the kitchen and cleaning the apartment. Liane decided it was best to be well occupied, - to be too busy and too tired to think and worry. So many dreadful things had happened in connection with the painting, now she couldn't bear it if anything went wrong. She knew she could not be contented until it was sold and the money in the bank.

Finally Monday morning arrived. A dismal day, chilly, and raining. Liane went alone to London arriving at Darcy and Johnson's just five minutes before eleven a.m.

Brett was already waiting for her at the entrance. She was so glad to see him. He kissed her, and they moved inside the building climbing the wide staircase to the auction room on the first floor.

"What's the news from Dublin?"

"Ian likes the script, but he's depressed about the future of the Priory."

The auction room was already crowded, but they managed to find two empty seats at the back. As they sat down, someone called their name. It was George and Frances, waving to them.

The auction began. For the first hour it was English nineteenth century painters, than at around twelve o'clock the auctioneer put Liane's painting on the stand.

"Ladies and gentlemen, we have here a little known Gorregiani, the Virgin and Child. It has been checked by our expert and therefore bears our seal of authenticity. It was bought in Italy some thirty years ago and has since hung in a church in Luxor.

It has recently been in the news." The auctioneer paused until the murmurs subsided. "And now is your chance to acquire it. Who will start me with £500,000?" The auctioneer looked around the room. There was evidently no bid. "£400,000... £300,000... £200,000... £100,000... Ladies and gentlemen," his tone was now one of deep exasperation. "This is a rare opportunity to acquire a Gorregiani."

Somebody please bid, prayed Liane clenching her hands together. There was not a sound in the auction room, then suddenly the auctioneer spoke.

"Thank you sir," he said looking at someone in the front row. "Now who will bid me £150,000?"

The bidding was slow and gradually reached £500,000.

Suddenly Liane felt she could relax. They could now pay off the debt at the bank and Tavanomore would be safe. Then to Liane's astonishment, the auctioneer continued:

"Who will bid me £550,000?" He looked at someone in the front row. "Thank you sir. £600,000?" He looked around the auction room and nodded to someone at the back. "£650,000?"

Liane couldn't believe her ears. A struggle to acquire the painting seemed to be developing between two men. Liane listened breathlessly, her heart pounding. At one million pounds the bidding ceased. The auctioneer brought down his hammer.

"The Gorregiani, Virgin and Child, sold for one million pounds."

Liane felt faint, Brett gave her a smile, and pressed her hand. George and Frances approached.

"This calls for a drink to celebrate," said George.

Later that day after they had said goodbye to George and Frances the first thing Liane did was to phone Father O'Brien and tell him the extraordinary events that had led to the recovery of the painting and the subsequent good news of the auction.

"We had a desperate financial situation," she told Father, "which forced us to sell the painting. I hope you will forgive us for selling your gift. After we have paid our debts the balance is yours."

At first Father wouldn't take a penny but by skillful arguing he reluctantly accepted half.

Liane and Brett were married a month later at the little church in Carrickballyduff. Father O'Shea officiated and the church was filled to capacity, - relations, friends and well wishers from the Priory Theatre.

Liane's mother was there, and Brett's uncle and cousins who had flown in from Boston, Massachusetts. George and Frances came. Charlene seemed to have disappeared. There was a rumour she was in South America. Curtis came alone and seemed quite happy. Ian Stratton was best man and Fay her bridesmaid.

After the nuptual mass and signing the register, Liane holding Brett's arm, walked down the aisle looking radiant in her Victorian crinoline gown. In her hand she carried a small posy of red roses.

The reception was held at the County Hotel and afterwards when all the toasts had been drunk and speeches made, at a convenient moment the bridal couple made their escape, driving in Brett's car through the main street of the little town, taking the road to Cavan, and there just a mile out of the town, on the right side of the road was Tavanomore.

Brett stopped the car and opened the five barred gate, then drove up the short tree lined drive to the house, the eighteenth century home of her ancestors, with its long windows spaced evenly on each side of the impressive front door, and the dormer windows in the roof. It was now really theirs, every brick, every tile, every acre of land.

It was like walking in a dream for Liane as she stepped

from the car and climbed the steps to the front door. The debt at the bank had been paid, Father O'Brien had received his cheque and had already made the first move in setting up his clinics, the play in Boston was in rehearsal and going well, and they had made a substantial investment in the Priory Theatre.

Brett opened the door and picking up Liane in the traditional manner carried her over the threshold, his eyes warm with love, said all she wanted to know.

"Happy?" asked Brett softly.

Liane placed a gentle kiss on his lips, her eyes shining with tears.

"The moon shines bright, in such a night as this...'"

Brett spoke softly as he took her by the hand and led her slowly up the stairs.

She had come home.

Dance Amongst Thorns

Maureen Stephenson was born in Manchester of Irish descent.
She started writing at an early age. She was fifty when she had her
first novel published. Since then she has been published world wide.
THE FLOWERS OF TOMORROW has been highly successful in the
U.S.A. and Germany. I'LL WAIT FOREVER has been equally
successful in Italy.

She now lives in Warwickshire, is married and has three children.

Dance Amongst Thorns

By the same author

Ride the Dark Moors

The Flowers of Tomorrow

Autumn of Deception

Roses have Thorns

The Enchanted Desert

I'll Wait Forever

Never Too Late

The Love Dance

Dance Amongst Thorns